# DROP BY DROP

By Morgan Llywelyn from Tom Doherty Associates

*After Rome*
*Bard: The Odyssey of the Irish*
*Brendán*
*Brian Boru*
*Drop by Drop*
*The Elementals*
*Etruscans* (with Michael Scott)
*Finn Mac Cool*
*Grania*
*The Horse Goddess*
*The Last Prince of Ireland*
*Lion of Ireland*
*Only the Stones Survive*
*Pride of Lions*
*Strongbow*
*The Wind from Hastings*

THE NOVELS OF THE IRISH CENTURY

*1916: A Novel of the Irish Rebellion*
*1921: The Great Novel of the Irish Civil War*
*1949: A Novel of the Irish Free State*
*1972: A Novel of Ireland's Unfinished Revolution*
*1999: A Novel of the Celtic Tiger and the Search for Peace*

MORGAN LLYWELYN

# DROP BY DROP

**TOR**

A TOM DOHERTY ASSOCIATES BOOK

NEW YORK

DROP BY DROP

Copyright © 2018 by Morgan Llywelyn

A Tor Book
Published by Tom Doherty Associates
175 Fifth Avenue
New York, NY 10010

www.tor-forge.com

Tor® is a registered trademark of Macmillan Publishing Group, LLC.

The Library of Congress Cataloging-in-Publication Data is available upon request.

ISBN 978-0-7653-8866-7 (hardcover)
ISBN 978-0-7653-8868-1 (ebook)

Our books may be purchased in bulk for promotional, educational, or business
use. Please contact your local bookseller or the Macmillan Corporate and
Premium Sales Department at 1-800-221-7945, extension 5442, or by email at
MacmillanSpecialMarkets@macmillan.com.

First Edition: June 2018

Printed in the United States of America

0  9  8  7  6  5  4  3  2  1

*In loving memory of Sonia Schorman*
*and as always*
*for Charlie*

# DROP BY DROP

# 1

He awoke with a start in the middle of the night. Night as black and featureless as ink. He lay still, taking a moment to orient himself. All he heard was the ticking of his travel clock on the nightstand and the slight rustle of Egyptian cotton sheets on his naked body when he turned onto his side. Instinct awakened him whenever he was expecting trouble, but this time he'd gone to bed with an easy mind. Another job done, his reward stashed in the false bottom of his suitcase. He should be snoring his head off by now.

Danger prickled his back and shoulders; the sudden flood of adrenaline he thrived on. His lips drew back in a humorless smile. He waited. Five minutes; ten. Nothing happened. He kicked away the covers, swung his long legs off the bed and stood up.

The open window framed a view of the desert beyond. An apron of parched grass separated his hotel from a low brick retaining wall. On the other side of the wall a succession of sand dunes rose in pale waves like a moonlit sea.

Whatever you're looking for isn't out there, he told himself. So what woke me?

The nearest dune appeared to move. A few grains of sand at

the top slid down, followed by more and then more until there was a miniature landslide, as if the dune were being shaken.

He rubbed his eyes.

Damned imagination's running away with me. They say if you're in the desert too long that can happen.

When he closed the window to shut out the cold of the desert night, the illusion of moving sand was replaced by his reflection in the glass. Rumpled black hair, a hawkish nose and clean cut jaw. A man not yet forty, but with weary eyes.

It's time to go home again, Jack.

Drop by drop, the Change came to Sycamore River. Slowly and quietly in the beginning, not enough to cause a ripple on the placid surface of the town. Few people noticed at first. Change can be like that.

Eleanor Bennett—known to her friends as Nell and to her husband, in private, as Cookie—was already opening her handbag as she approached the Sycamore and Staunton Mercantile Bank on a sweltering summer morning.

The headlines in the newspaper dispenser on the sidewalk reenforced her need for retail therapy.

**TERRORISM ON THE INCREASE**
**EXPERTS FORECAST RECORD HEAT**
**CONGRESS DEADLOCKED OVER MILITARY BUDGET**

Dear God, thought Nell, does nothing ever change?

The slender woman in the coral-colored sportsuit inserted her bank card in the cash machine, cued in her number and waited for the bills to whisper into the cash drawer. Meanwhile she mentally rehearsed her conversation with the hairdresser at Snips. She was going to ask for a Parisian cut and more highlights in her ash-blonde hair.

Only yesterday her daughter had said, "You look absolutely *ancient,* Mom. Nobody wears those short skirts anymore."

Jessamyn knew everything; she was sixteen.

Her brother, Colin, a year younger, had joined in with, "Fuck it, Jess, she *is* ancient. Her hormones've dried up."

Ancient. At thirty-six and a bit. That's what comes of marrying too young.

When Nell discovered she was pregnant with Jessamyn it had been Rob who insisted on marriage. He was ten years older than she was, dynamic and exciting, and his uncontrollable passion was thrilling. She had not anticipated how soon it would fade into indifference.

If they had just lived together it would have been easier to walk away.

There's one thing that changes, Nell told herself. People.

Except me. I'm too stubborn to admit failure.

She awakened from her reverie to realize she had not heard the click of her bank card emerging from the slot. She peered at the machine with its multicolored façade of options; like a slot machine in the arcade, only this one had to pay out.

She punched buttons. Waited a few seconds and punched more buttons. Neither card nor money was forthcoming. The cash machine began making weird noises.

What finally emerged was not a card.

She stared at it in disbelief, then turned to the boy and girl waiting in line behind her. Attractive teenagers wearing matching sweatshirts, concentrating intently on their AllComs. Each had the other on the screen of their personal communicator. The digital conversation between the pair was silent. They were indifferent to her problem and the world at large.


Mrs. Robert Bennett entered the bank lobby to the staccato accompaniment of high heels that added more pockmarks to those already scarring the imitation teak parquet. The columns supporting the high ceiling were not imitation anything. Solid red marble with acanthus leaf capitals in the Corinthian style, they had been installed about the time the trains first came to Sycamore River. The broad counters were solid oak, polished to a deep gleam by two centuries of transactions sliding across them. Bulletproof windows acknowledged the twenty-first-century need for security.

Cobwebs clung to the corners of the ceiling like lace draperies from a gentler time.

Air-conditioning chilled the lobby. Flower arrangements were strategically placed to brighten the atmosphere, but their perfume had to compete with the aroma of past generations. A faded memory of black broadcloth, celluloid collars and mustache wax; Evening in Paris cologne, cotton wash dresses and home permanents; drip-dry suits, pancake makeup and polyester slacks. Overlying these was the pervasive smell common to all banks, a faintly metallic whiff of concealed anxiety.

The town of Sycamore River considered itself progressive but preferred its largest bank to be traditional. Civic bedrock.

Eleanor Bennett headed for the row of tellers' cages. Gilded bronze and floridly baroque, they were art in their own right. The computer age had made them redundant, but one was still in use for those die-hard customers who insisted on personal attention. A gleaming brass plate below its window identified "Miss Beatrice Fontaine, Chief Teller."

Through the half-open door of the vice president's office Dwayne Nyeberger had observed Eleanor Bennett's arrival. "Married a war hero," he muttered to himself. "Sure she did; homecoming queens like Nell Richmond always marry heroes. Some bastards have all the luck."

Dwayne had a small potbelly and an overbite that should have been corrected in childhood, but his parents could not afford it. Nothing could correct his air of dissatisfaction with life in general. Every hunting season he went out with a supply of weapons, including a high-powered rifle and a formidable shotgun, and took out his ire on anything with fur or feathers.

His wife, Tricia, had been a cheerleader in high school, the plump, pug-nosed girl at the end of the line who couldn't jump as high as the others. She had one undeniable attraction. Patricia Penelope Staunton was the daughter of O. M. Staunton, president of the bank and fourth generation of the founding family. Marrying her had been a calculated move on Dwayne's part and his one big success. She had no brothers. He would be the logical choice to succeed her father in the bank. All he had to do was wait.

Tricia's weight had ballooned during the years she bore five unmanageable sons. So far the oldest Nyeberger boys—Sandy, Kirby and Buster—had avoided being hauled into juvenile court because of their grandfather. Their little brothers, twins Philip and Daniel, more usually referred to as Flub and Dub, showed every indication of following in their footsteps.

"A litter of born criminals," was how O. M. Staunton referred to his grandchildren.

When Nell reached the chief teller's window a man was there before her. The occupant of the cage was patiently enduring his complaints.

Bea Fontaine was a woman in her middle fifties with a full bosom and a ramrod spine. Dark eyebrows contrasted with a braided coronet of silvery hair. Her complexion was the envy of younger women. Although optical technology had made eyeglasses obsolete, she wore spectacles rimmed with gold wire which complemented the décor of the bank.

In her youth Bea had been called handsome. A number of

men thought she still was. Her lack of a permanent male partner was one of the town's enduring mysteries.

When Fred Mortenson lost the dispute over the bank statement from his dry cleaning business, he began teasing Bea about her cats. Fred was constitutionally unable to avoid teasing anyone who would allow it.

Bea refused to be ruffled. "Every town should have several town drunks and a lady who rescues cats," she told her would-be tormentor. "Since Ozzie Walsh and Mort Franklin died we just have one town drunk, but I'm still here."

"You and your hundred cats."

"Only seven."

"Only seven!" Fred mocked. "Betcha can't name 'em all."

The chief teller recited, "Apollo, Hector, Castor and Pollux—they're twins—Aphrodite, Polydamus—he's a polydactyl, of course—and Plato."

"What kinda names are those?"

Standing behind him, Nell fixed her eyes on his bald spot and chewed her lip. The incident with the bank card had shaken her.

"I'm sorry you lack a classical education, Mr. Mortenson," Bea said as if she meant it. "Now, if you'll excuse me? Mrs. Bennett is waiting." She politely waved him aside.

"Thank you, Miss Fontaine."

"Not at all, Mrs. Bennett. What can I do for you?"

When they met outside the bank they were Bea and Nell, in

spite of the twenty years' difference in their ages; their families had been friends for generations. But this was the Sycamore and Staunton. Proprieties must be observed.

Bea Fontaine was one of the bank's chief assets. She understood the proprieties and her air of calm authority was invaluable. As soon as she heard Nell's problem she rang the discreet bell that summoned the vice president.

Hurrying from his office, Dwayne Nyeberger sucked in his stomach and tried to arrange his sharp features into a combination of trustworthy officialdom and boyish charm. "Nell! What a nice surprise."

"Nothing to compare with the surprise I got when your ATM ate my bank card," she said, taking a step backward. She always did when Nyeberger insinuated himself into her personal space.

"What do you mean, it ate your card?"

"Just that. I put my bank card in the slot and it never came out. Nothing came out but sticky ooze!" She realized her voice was getting shrill. "I'm going shopping after I close my office this afternoon and I'll need my bank card. And some cash for the kids. Rob insists they be familiar with real money."

"Very wise of him," Nyeberger echoed on cue. "Wait till I get the keys to the machine and we'll have your problem sorted out in . . ."

His words stuck in his throat. He stared toward the windows at the front of the lobby. The bulletproof glass did not distort his view.

A woman with auburn hair brushing her shoulders was walking past the bank. She wore a pale blue toga-and-leggings outfit that concealed more than it revealed. He could not tell if she had high cheekbones and slightly slanted eyes, but he had no doubt those eyes were green. Her legs were every bit as long as he remembered. Her undulant walk was unique.

The unforgettable subject of a thousand wet dreams: Lila Ragland.

A decade earlier she had been notorious among a segment of Sycamore River's male population—until the night she disappeared, leaving rumor and wreckage behind.

The night Dwayne Nyeberger's rosy future came crashing down around him.

# 2

He staggered back until he encountered the reassuring reality of a desk. The color drained from his face.

"What's wrong, Mr. Nyeberger?" asked the chief teller.

"I saw . . . I mean . . ." He sank lower, resting his buttocks on the desk.

"Are you sick?" When he didn't respond to her question Bea snapped, "Dwayne!" Still no response.

She hurried from her cage. As she passed Nell Bennett she murmured, "Help me, will you?"

Nell swung into action. Bracketing Dwayne between them, the two women loosened his tie and fanned his face.

He was embarrassed. Having Nell observe him in a moment of weakness was bad, but not as bad as what he had just seen.

"It's her," he said hoarsely.

Bea leaned closer to him. "What are you talking about?"

He waved a hand in the direction of the front windows. "Lila. She's back." A large vein began throbbing in his temple.

"He's having a heart attack," Nell determined. Someone else's emergency was having a steadying effect on her own nerves.

Bank staff and customers gathered around the stricken man.

"Make him bend over and put his head between his knees," said a portly man wearing plaid golf trousers.

"No way," the woman with him contradicted. "With a heart attack they have to lie down."

A bank clerk added, "If he's having a fit, don't let him swallow his tongue."

"It's not a heart attack or a fit," said Bea. "He's just upset. Sit down, Dwayne, you'll be all right in a minute." She steered him to the nearest chair.

"I know what I saw!" He waved toward the windows again. Stabbed the air with his forefinger.

The others turned to look, but by then it was too late. Ordinary people were passing by, going about ordinary business.

Dwayne Nyeberger moaned like an animal in pain. "Lila Ragland's come back to ruin me!"

Nell patted his shoulder. "Ssshhh, it'll be all right."

He responded with an inarticulate croak and flung his arms around her hips.

While Nell was prying him off, two women entered the lobby, paused, looked at each other and left. "What d'you s'pose that's all about?" one asked when they were outside.

"Maybe she just paid off a gigantic mortgage," the other guessed.

Dwayne was taken to his office and given a glass of water. He dutifully drank while wishing for something stronger. Much stronger. In the bottom drawer of his desk was a practically full bottle of single malt, but he didn't want to take it out with Bea

Fontaine watching him. The chief teller had strict views on alcohol in the workplace.

What he really needed was . . .

No, that was what got him into trouble in the first place. When he was younger. And stupid.

What had Lila said? "It's fairy dust," she had told him, laughing. "Takes your troubles away."

It had for a while.

But sometimes when he least expected it the evil fairies came back.

Dwayne bent over and vomited into his lap.

Nell flinched away to avoid being splattered.

"Go on home," Bea whispered to her, "and we'll take care of him. This has happened before, it's only an hallucination." She squared her shoulders, raised her voice and became the chief teller again. "I'll see that your bank card is replaced, Mrs. Bennett—it'll come to you in the mail—and if you'll stop by the front desk on your way out, Janine will arrange for your cash. Just tell her how much."

When Nell left the bank the heat off the sidewalk hit her like a giant fist. She paused for a moment to catch her breath.

Lila Ragland? Wasn't she the one who . . .

Nell recalled the headline in *The Sycamore Seed*. Ten years ago, but not forgotten. The scandal had hit the quiet town like a thunderclap.

## LOCAL GIRL FEARED MURDERED

The story had run for weeks. The local newspaper had boosted its circulation dramatically by relating the lurid details of a drug-fueled party on the north side, with everything available from horse tranquilizers to Zee tablets. The police had staged a raid and arrested several men, including the mayor's brother-in-law, but the town's best-known party girl had disappeared under mysterious circumstances. The river was dragged for her body, but it was never found.

Dwayne Nyeberger had been among those questioned, to the embarrassment of his wife and the fury of her father.

Nell had good reason to remember that time. She and Rob had been planning a "second honeymoon" to make up for not taking one after their marriage. She had been too heavily pregnant with Jessamyn when she walked down the aisle. Except there was no aisle, just the registry office, with her mother looking embarrassed and her father assessing Rob's prospects. Two giggling bridesmaids, hastily recruited. A bouquet purchased at the last moment, comprised of lilies that shed pollen all over her not-white maternity outfit.

Three years later, with their two toddlers temporarily lodged with her parents, the locale of their long-delayed trip had become a source of contention. She had wanted to go to Europe— to Paris. For years she had dreamed of honeymooning in Paris.

Over breakfast Rob had announced they were going to Panama City.

Nell set down her coffee cup. "But what about Paris?"

"Paris is such a cliché, Cookie," he'd chided. Pushing his

plate aside, he had propped his new AllCom on the table and begun scrolling through the stock quotations. Earlier AllComs had employed several metal alloys for the sake of versatility, but now were considered too heavy. More recent models used plastics that imitated metal in everything but weight. Rob's, which was waterproof, functioned as a videophone and texter and provided full internet access as well as computing. The insatiable consumer market created by PCs and smartphones had morphed into a demand for total electronic connectivity. Microchips were embedded in every possible object. AllComs could even control security systems and household appliances from miles away.

Nell sought to get her husband's attention. "What's so romantic about Panama City, darling? I don't even know where it is."

His eyes had remained fixed on the small screen. "It's in Central America and there's a famous cathedral. You really must expand your horizons."

"*Paris* would be expanding my horizons. Please, Rob, I've been looking forward to this for ages."

They had gone to Panama City.

Rob had made business contacts in the Canal Zone and spent most of the time in meetings. Nell went shopping for clothes she would never wear again and souvenirs that would mean nothing to the people she bought them for. The semitropical heat caused sweat to pour from her scalp. Constant rain depressed her. When she retreated to the relative comfort of the hotel beauty salon, they insisted on brightening her hair with peroxide and ruined it.

I wonder if Lila Ragland dyed her hair, Nell thought now. Probably. Did Rob know the girl? Probably not.

In the years following their marriage the ferocious determination that had allowed a young Robert Bennett to destroy an enemy sniper nest single-handed had been channeled into his business. RobBenn had become his obsession, his one true love.

It would have been easier to compete with Lila Ragland.

Nell resolutely tucked her handbag under her arm and headed toward Mortenson's In-a-Minnit to pick up her dry cleaning. From there she would go to her office, two rooms on the first floor of the Liberty Life and Casualty Building. Tasteful black-and-gold lettering on the glass door identified "Eleanor Bennett, Real Estate."

When she reached the corner a sudden impulse made her glance back at the bank. Someone else was struggling with the ATM. Shay Mulligan, the red-haired veterinarian who took care of the Bennett dogs, pounded the machine with his fist and looked around in frustration.

At this moment Shay reminded Nell of a small boy—though he was a widower struggling to raise his son by himself. It couldn't be easy. Evan Mulligan was a few months older than Nell's daughter, Jessamyn, and horse crazy at an age when only girls were supposed to be horse crazy.

When he saw Nell looking in his direction Shay called out, "Damn thing's chewing up my card, Miz Bennett!" His easy drawl was as much a part of him as the forest of freckles he had never outgrown.

"Don't wait, go inside and ask Bea Fontaine to help you. Hurry up now, beat the rush!"

Shay nodded his thanks. The Bennetts were valuable customers. Their three dogs—two pedigreed Irish setters for Eleanor and the kids, and a massive Rottweiler for Robert Bennett—were given the best care money could buy.

You could tell a lot about people by their animals, Shay thought, as he passed through the security doors and entered the bank. The setters, Sheila and Shamrock—known as Rocky—were smarter than their breed's reputation would suggest and devoted to Nell and the children. The Rottweiler was a status dog, purchased to guard the house and grounds. On rare occasions Bennett walked the dog on a very short chain to impress his neighbors. Poor Satan—and what kind of man calls his dog Satan?—wouldn't have felt any attachment to Bennett. Mary Shaw, the housekeeper, fed him and let him into the garage on stormy days. She was his god in an apron.

Dogs, thought Shay. Dogs know who people really are.

The scene inside the bank caught his attention. The door of the vice president's office stood wide open. Dwayne Nyeberger could be seen inside, with his arms folded on his desk and his head resting on them. Other people were milling around the lobby, eagerly telling each other what had just happened.

Shay found Bea Fontaine at her window. The position enabled her to keep an eye on the vice president's office. "Yes, Mr. Mulligan?" She sounded distracted.

"It's about my bank card and the ATM . . ."

"You too, I suppose. How much cash did you want?"

"I . . . uh . . . enough for a good tip in a French restaurant. I'm taking Angela to the . . ."

For a moment he had Bea's full attention. "Are you still going out with the Watson girl? It's been three years that I know of; you should marry her and give Evan a mother." Bea slid a withdrawal slip toward him on the counter. "Here, sign this and we'll give you your cash."

Shay's ears reddened with embarrassment. Why did people keep pressuring him to marry? His son's feelings had to be considered; the boy loved his mother very much and had taken her death from cancer hard.

The vet fumbled with the counter pen in its black plastic receptacle, but he could not free it to sign the withdrawal slip. When another customer came up behind him, Shay gave the pen an impatient shake. It seemed to be permanently affixed to its plastic cup—which was not only chained to the counter, but stuck to it. He tugged harder.

Pen and cup stretched like bubble gum.

Bea leaned forward. "What happened? Oh. Uh, don't try to

force that, I'll give you another one." From a drawer below the counter she took a black ballpoint pen imprinted with the bank's logo.

The pen softened in her hand like melting chocolate and began to ooze down her wrist.

# 3

The staff door at the rear of the lobby opened and, to Bea's relief, O. M. Staunton entered. Whatever lunacy was afoot today she could dump in the Old Man's lap.

O. M. Staunton—the initials stood for Oliver Morse, a name he hated—was called the "Old Man" behind his back, but never to his face. Customers also knew better than to refer to his bank as "the S&S" within his hearing. As president of the leading bank in the area he held the financial reins of the Sycamore River Valley in his hands, and sought to retain the standards of an earlier time. A time before the national economy began its long downward slide.

For as long as anyone could remember Staunton had carried his two-sandwiches-and-an-apple lunch to the bank in a brown paper bag. In a card-dominated economy he paid his personal expenses in cash and asked for receipts, even for a single cup of coffee. A common saying around town was, "The Old Man has so much money he makes loans to God."

Gesturing to Shay to wait, Bea called, "Can we talk to you, Mr. Staunton?"

The Old Man had just glimpsed his son-in-law in a state of collapse in his office and was making his way toward him.

He stopped in increments as stiff joints received new instructions from his brain. With a curt nod, he turned toward Bea. In any contest between Staunton's chief teller and his daughter's worthless husband, Bea ranked first. When he reached her window she held up her hand so he could see the black stuff sliding down her arm.

"What the hell have you done to yourself, woman?"

"Tried to pick up a pen, that's all."

"Nonsense."

For the first time in his life Shay Mulligan addressed the legendary Old Man personally. "It's not nonsense, look at this." He attempted to hand the ruined counter pen to Staunton. A dark substance like gritty mud seeped between the vet's fingers and onto the countertop.

Drop by drop.

Staunton's mouth fell open. "What the hell is that? Some kind of stunt?"

"We don't know what it is," said Bea, "but our cash cards are dissolving too."

"Bea, that's crazy." A shrewd light crept into the Old Man's eyes. "Would my son-in-law have anything to do with this, by any chance?"

"I wouldn't think so."

"Then what's wrong with him?"

Bea hesitated. "Hallucinations again, I'm afraid."

"Damn 'im! I didn't want my girl to marry that young

nobody in the first place, but she was convinced no other man would ask her."

Which was true at the time. As they both knew, the drug bust on the north side had changed the balance of power in the Nyeberger marriage.

Staunton ordered the receptionist to contact his daughter. "Say her husband's had some kind of seizure and she needs to take him home. I'll be in my office if she wants to talk to me."

Dwayne Nyeberger had acquired a paranoid fear of leaving the bank building. He was afraid Lila Ragland was waiting. When Tricia Staunton arrived, complaining about being called away from her favorite game show on their interactive wallscreen, Dwayne refused to leave with her. He shouted at her to go clean the house. She turned on her heel and left the bank. "The dumb bastard can walk home," she announced on her way out.

In the privacy of the president's office, surrounded by portraits of previous bank presidents who all had the same craggy features, Staunton made a call of his own. Two burly male nurses were summoned from the Hilda Staunton Memorial Hospital to administer a strong sedative to the distraught man. As soon as it took effect they bundled him out of the bank and into a private hospital room without alerting the press.

A psychologist was summoned to examine him.

Meanwhile Staunton told the staff to tidy up the mess and dispose of the ruined bank cards. As they began work, a red plastic hair grip worn by one of the bank's customers dissolved and ran down her neck. The woman had hysterics.

Staunton ordered the "Closed" sign put on the front door.

"It's going to be a long day," predicted Bea Fontaine.

He was waiting for her when her car turned into the driveway; a tall, lean man in a white shirt and faded jeans, sitting with his feet propped on the porch railing. "You took your time about coming home, Aunt Bea," he said as he unfolded himself from the green wicker chair. "Was it car trouble? You should trade in that old heap; with an auto-drive you could sit back and enjoy the ride."

"Your car is older than mine, Jack," she said sharply. "Besides, I like to do my own driving."

"My Ford Mustang's a classic. Your VW's just transportation."

"That classic of yours practically lives in the repair shop, but Abraham never gives me any trouble."

Jack Reese smiled; a flash of white teeth in a deeply tanned face. The warmth did not always reach his pale gray eyes. Strangers found this unnerving. "Only you would call a Volkswagen 'Abraham,' Aunt Bea."

"Just think how furious that would make Adolf Hitler," she replied as she locked the car. With her AllCom in one hand and handbag in the other, she crossed the neatly mowed front yard. "I guess you'll want supper?"

"Some of your fried chicken would hit the spot about now. Shake it in a paper bag with flour and seasoned salt?" He spoke as if he had only been out for the afternoon and come home hungry, though he had been abroad for over two years. That was typical. Jack used Bea's home as a base when he was in town and came and went as he pleased. Their affection did not depend on propinquity.

As Bea climbed the steps to the front porch she said, "I'm fresh out of chicken, Jack. I didn't know you were coming."

"You must have some eggs, though; you always do. I could make an omelet for us."

Bea tilted her head back to look up into his face. "Have you added cooking to your list of accomplishments?"

He gave a nonchalant shrug. "Took a couple of courses in France, for a bachelor it's a matter of self-preservation. A pal of mine in Belgrade married a woman because she was a terrific cook and it turned out to be the biggest mistake of his life. And put your AllCom away, you don't have to unlock the front door. I already . . ."

"Went in through the back, I know."

"Which reminds me, I brought you a present. The latest AllCom with all the bells and whistles. It has the usual functions, but it also monitors your heartbeat and blood pressure and alerts the emergency services if you need help."

She glared at him. "*You're* raising my blood pressure; I'm not some old woman who's about to keel over." Then her smile surfaced like sunshine after a shower. "I really am glad to see you, though. And thanks for your offer to cook, it's been an awful day and I'm bone tired."

"Show me where you keep the spices, then. Any fresh herbs in the garden?"

As Jack prepared supper Bea watched from a kitchen chair, sipping a restorative cup of coffee. Letting the day's tension drain from her body. Enjoying the sight of Jack in the home of his boyhood. The old rubber tire he had used as a swing still hung in the backyard. A bold little boy, he had climbed every tree in the neighborhood and did not cry when he fell and broke his leg. All he said on the way to the hospital was, "Did you see me, Aunt Bea? Did you see how high I got?"

Jack's mother, Florence, had been Bea's older sister. When Florence and her husband were killed in a car crash Bea had taken their son to raise. Their home was the house she had inherited from her parents.

By the time Jack was grown Bea was middle-aged, but her nephew had no doubt there were men in her life. She obviously liked men and they liked her. For a long time Jack had suspected that one of those men was Oliver Staunton, but he was never sure. The image of the two of them together was not one he relished.

Aphrodite, a plump tabby cat of dubious morals who refused to acknowledge that Shay Mulligan had neutered her, rolled seductively on the floor to display her belly to Apollo, who ignored her. He had whiskers to clean.

Jack remarked, "I hope I never get like him."

"It would serve you right," said Bea.

She knew her nephew was a born adventurer. He spoke with firsthand knowledge of exotic places many people only knew from the pages of *National Geographic*. He went from country to country, job to job—and woman to woman—with effortless ease, never finding anyone or any place that could hold him for long. The only real stability in his life was her house.

Aside from her time in college Bea Fontaine had spent her entire life in Sycamore River. When asked if she ever got bored, her invariable answer was, "A town can be the whole world in microcosm."

The cat flap in the back door banged several times as the other members of Bea's feline family entered the room. They knew better than to beg for food; they would only be fed after she had eaten. They contented themselves with making figure eights around the ankles of the humans. Silent reminders of their presence.

Jack put the dinner plates in the oven to warm while he grated cheese for the omelets. "Tell me about this awful day of yours, Aunt Bea. Did they have the bank auditors in?"

"I wish it were that simple. Actually we had a couple of rather nasty incidents. This morning Dwayne Nyeberger suffered a nervous breakdown in the lobby; for a while it looked like he'd lost his mind. He had a hallucination that really scared him. Aren't those omelets ready? I'm starving."

They ate at the kitchen table. Bea sat with her back to the sink, Jack preferred to sit with his to the wall. The table was laid with a checked cotton tablecloth, as practical as it was plain. Over the years Jack had brought his aunt Belfast table linens and damask napkins from Belgium, but she never used them.

After one bite of her omelet Bea put down her fork and beamed at her nephew. "That's absolutely delicious! What on earth did you put in the eggs?"

"Bit of this and pinch of that. You should know, you watched me."

"Watched you work some sleight of hand, more like. You must have stirred in cream cheese when I wasn't looking. By the way, there's still coffee in the pot if you want any."

"I'd prefer some of that vodka you keep in the freezer."

"That's Stolichnaya from St. Petersburg, the genuine article! One of our best customers brought it to me."

"You have life by the short and curlies, don't you?" Jack teased. "Break out the Stoli and I'll replace it the next time I go to Russia, I promise." He sketched a cross over his heart. "You mentioned a couple of incidents at the bank, Aunt Bea. What was the other one?"

"What were you doing in Russia?" This was an old game between them. She tried to put together the patchwork quilt of his life from the bits and pieces he chose to reveal.

"Handling a little matter for North Atlantic Refineries."

"A refinery?" she said eagerly. "Do you know much about oil?"

"I've needed a basic knowledge of petrochemistry because of some of the work I do. And I have degrees in—"

"I know all about your degrees; you have a mind like a vac-
uum cleaner, but you've never used any of that education to get
a permanent job." It was an old sore point between them. Bea
pushed back her chair and stood up. "I have something to show
you; wait right here. And finish your supper before it gets cold."

She went into the living room and returned with her black
leather handbag. From its capacious depths she produced a
white handkerchief stained with a dark, partially clotted substance. She held the handkerchief toward Jack's face. "Sniff this.
What is it?"

# 4

Jack's nostrils flared at the acrid odor. He drew back and gave her a puzzled look. "That reeks of crude oil, Aunt Bea. And something else I can't identify. Why's it on your handkerchief?"

"This morning it was a counter pen in the bank."

"I don't understand."

"Neither do we. But our pens and their holders have turned into this stuff."

"Weren't they made of plastic?"

"They were this morning; this evening they're like the goo on my handkerchief. Our bank cards have dissolved too."

Jack raised a single eyebrow. It was a trick he had practiced for hours in front of a mirror when he was a teenager. "They did this while pigs were flying overhead?"

"No, really. They turned to sludge in a matter of seconds. I was hoping you could explain why, as you're a fund of useless knowledge."

Jack laughed—and this time the warmth reached his eyes. "No knowledge is useless if you need it." He enjoyed showing what he knew; he had what his aunt called "a lecturing voice."

"Let's start with the basics, Aunt Bea. Crude oil is liquid petroleum formed by the decomposition of organic matter."

"Even I know that," she said impatiently.

"Okay. Petroleum contains hydrocarbon compounds that can be extracted and used to create petrochemicals, which are a major component of fuels, explosives—and all the items we call plastic: meaning synthetic material cheap to manufacture and easy to mold into any shape you want. A lot of people pay good money for things they think are wood or metal but which are really plastic. It fattens the profit margins.

"As for your question—that's a tricky one. When plastic breaks down it usually disintegrates into tiny bits that are damned near indestructible. Marine biologists say there are more tons of plastic rubbish in the world's oceans than tons of fish. But some plastics will dissolve to a certain extent if they're broken up and boiled with oil. In poor countries the fumes are distilled and used as a substitute for gaso—"

"What about my handkerchief?"

"I can't identify the stuff on your handkerchief, Aunt Bea. But there's no doubt what its base is."

She lowered her spectacles and gave him what Jack called "the Aunt Bea Look." Without glasses her eyes were dark hazel, almost amber. She was the only person who could intimidate him. "I don't want a tutorial. All I want is to know is why our plastic's doing what it's doing."

"Beats hell out of me," said Jack Reece.

When they finished their meal Bea said, "You've used every dish and bowl I have. Help me clean up?"

"I'll load the dishwasher, but I want to catch the main news on the wallscreen."

"Then we'd better hurry," she said briskly.

When speaking of his aunt Jack often remarked, "She takes no prisoners."

By the time they entered the living room the network news had concluded. On the wallscreen a commentator in three dimensions was saying, ". . . due to the ongoing danger of cyber sabotage. Now for something lighter: We have a couple of stories that prove the Silly Season has arrived. In San Diego an amusement park owner has claimed that vandals are destroying the concessions. The little plastic ducks in the . . ."

Bea caught Jack by the arm. "Do you hear that?"

"Ducks in San Diego?"

"No, my dishwasher; it shouldn't be making those churning noises. We'll have to unload everything before it breaks my plates. I'll call the service man tomorrow."

Jack switched off the wallscreen. "Don't waste your money, I'll take a look at it right now. Sounds like a bearing's going, or maybe it just needs greasing. If it's not purring like one of your cats by morning I'll buy you a new one. In the meantime why don't you have a cool bath and tuck up in bed with a good thriller? I brought you a couple from the airport, real books with covers. They're on your bedside table."

Hours later, with the dishwasher performing normally and the kitchen littered with the contents of his aunt's household tool box, Jack realized he was tired too. His flight had been a long one and the taxi driver did not know he was a local, so had tried to bring him to Sycamore River the long way.

A mistake the man soon regretted.

The following morning Bea let Jack sleep late. When he returned from wherever he had been, doing whatever he did, he usually slept around the clock and awoke with his batteries fully charged. It was an ability she envied.

She fixed her customary boiled egg and toast, fed the cats, and left the house by eight o'clock. She could hardly imagine the Old Man closing the bank for anything short of a world war, but yesterday's events had interrupted the usual routine.

As she drove Abraham up Dover's Lane toward Elm Street the sun was already beaming down on the town, promising another hot day. The lawn sprinklers that had been illegally turned on during the night had been shut off. Everything appeared normal. And yet . . . there was the faintest shimmer on the air, like heat waves rising from the earth.

Evaporation, Bea thought with annoyance. My lawn's going to dry out and I'll have to water the geraniums when I get home.

She noticed Hooper Watson crossing his front yard; a stocky, bowlegged figure who walked as if he had just dismounted from a horse, though he did not ride. His round red face would have looked almost cherubic if not for the greasy ring of graying hair that encircled his bald dome. The former sheriff resented the encroachment of age and still made it his business to know what was going on in Sycamore River.

Some people said he was just plain nosy.

Bea pulled up at the curb and called, "Hooper!"

He turned a blank stare in her direction. His rumpled clothes looked as if they had been slept in.

Been hitting the bottle already, thought Bea. "Hooper, over here!"

He tottered to the car and leaned in. "How you, Bea?"

"I'm fine, but . . . do you know if the S and S will open today?"

Watson pulled back a grubby shirtsleeve and attempted to read his watch. "'S too early, Bea, way too early."

"I know that, but we had some difficulties in there yesterday that might have—"

"I'm not the sheriff anymore, I got voted out last year, remember? Did you vote for me? Hunh? Didja?"

"Did you hear about our problems?" she countered.

The puffy, unshaven face loomed close to hers. She struggled to keep from inhaling bad breath diluted with whiskey fumes. "I got my own problems, Bea. The wife's gone off with a traveling salesman or some such. Again. Y'know anything about that? Nadine come in to get some of my money, maybe?"

"No, but the bank—"

"Trouble's not limited to the bank. Nadine threw a fit yesterday 'cause her false teeth stuck in the bathroom glass. Like melted bubble gum, all that pink plastic. The bastard she's running around with prob'ly don't care, he might like her better without teeth anyway. He prob'ly . . ." Mumbling to himself, he weaved away down the sidewalk.

*There was a time when I thought Hooper Watson was an attractive man,* Bea recalled. *I certainly have a talent for narrow escapes.*

The employees' entrance in the parking lot behind the bank had a heavy steel door that gave access to the keypad in the security hallway inside. Bea had not yet programmed her new AllCom, so she opened the door using her old one. There was no other way to enter.

Once inside she discovered she was the first employee to arrive. She used the AllCom again, keying it with Oliver Staunton's private number. The Old Man's gruff voice answered—he hated being disturbed at home.

"Is the bank going to be open today?" she asked him.

"Unless hell freezes over. I'm leaving right now and we'd better not have any more trouble; you keep a sharp eye out, Bea."

*What does he think I could do about it?*

# 5

Shay Mulligan lived on the edge of town in an area where homeowners could have horses or a family-sized swimming pool. His son kept a horse in the stable at the rear of the property. Shay's veterinary clinic was adjacent to the house. It was life in the country without being fully committed. No one made a fuss about barking dogs.

Shay looked forward to his daily run; it was a self-imposed discipline. Five miles every day of the week, rain or shine, was a ritual with him. He preferred to go in the late morning, before lunch. Or instead of lunch. Running kept his head clear and his reflexes quick.

By eleven that morning no more patients were in his waiting room and the appointment book was empty until two. Shay left his veterinary nurse, Paige Prentiss, in charge of the clinic with instructions to contact him if an emergency came in. Tall, tanned and competent, in school she had been the captain of her soccer team. She wore no makeup, but her hair, the color of brown sugar, hung to the small of her back in a glossy braid.

"Before you leave," she said, "remember where we're going this evening."

"Hmmm?"

"The fund-raiser for the Daggett's Woods Conservancy. I told you about it last week and you said you'd join me."

Shay snapped his fingers. "Sorry, Paige, I guess it slipped my mind. I have a date for tonight."

"Angela Watson?"

"Who else? But I'll go to the next one, I promise."

"There might not be another one: you know what we're up against. This was important, Shay."

"Okay, I'll write a check for it as soon as I get back," he assured her.

His nurse looked dubious. For a man with a degree in veterinary medicine, her employer was lamentably absentminded. He never forgot anything pertaining to the animals and their welfare, but things like bills to pay and family birthdays to commemorate flew right out of his head.

Paige had concluded she could never be romantically interested in a man who would not remember her birthday.

Beginning at the grove of cottonwood trees that marked the boundary of the old Miller estate, Shay's customary route for running took him past the derelict Miller mansion with its graffiti-covered walls, across the fields to Nelson's apple orchard, two miles along the bike path that circled Alcott Park, and then back to the clinic, the long-established practice founded by his father. His parents now lived in a retirement community in Florida.

Today Shay's nearest neighbor, Gerry Delmonico, happened to look out a window and saw him go by. Gerry shouted, "Hold on and I'll join you!" In less than a minute he emerged from his house clad in cutoffs and a T-shirt. "I don't have to be in the lab until later," he said, "so I was doing some work on my taxes."

Gerry's long black legs took one stride for every two of Shay's, but when he tried to alter his pace to accommodate his companion, Shay protested. "Hey, pal, don't do me any favors."

"Don't worry," Gerry said amiably, "I wouldn't piss on you if you were on fire." They jogged in silence until he remarked, "Speaking of fire, we're having a barbecue on the deck on Saturday. Come on over, anytime. Gloria said to tell you to bring Angela."

"You're supposed to tell me? You can't just ask me, nice and polite-like?"

"My wife said tell."

"That's why you have a wife and I don't."

Gerry cast a sideways glance at Shay. "You don't have a wife because you don't know a good thing when you see it."

"I do too. Tonight I'm taking Angela to that new French restaurant, Chez Pierre, and I've got cash for a big tip. Remind me to tell you what happened while I was at the S and S, by the way. You'll never believe it."

They ran on.

Halfway down the bike path on the way home Shay slowed to a trot; a walk; then leaned forward and put his hands on his knees. Gerry turned and came back to him. "What were you saying about the bank?"

"Tell you in a minute. Stitch in my side." Shay took a deep breath and slowly straightened up. "That's better. First, let's agree not to talk about Angela, I already heard enough on that subject. I know a problem when I see it. If I married Angela I'd have to take the whole package, including her man-crazy mother, when the woman bothers to come home, and her alcoholic father. I can't set foot in their house without one or the other starting in on me."

"So don't set foot in their house. Move Angela into yours, you have enough room. Evan likes her, doesn't he?"

Shay gave a rueful smile. "I'm not sure how he'd feel about it, I don't discuss my sex life with my son, we'd both be too embarrassed. Besides, the only time I mentioned living together Angela made it plain she wanted marriage, so I haven't pushed her. I'm not ready for that."

"You're too soft for your own good, buddy. I don't know how you can stand the vet business, you must see a dozen things a day that make you want to cry."

"Not a dozen. Since the last recession if I treat a dozen patients in one day I'm ecstatic. But if I see some I can help—and I help a lot of 'em—then it's worthwhile. How about you out there in Bennett's Bunker in the forest; you helping a lot of people?"

"To be honest, Shay, I'm not quite sure what we're doing anymore. When Robert Bennett hired me his company was involved in producing packaging for the pharmaceutical industry. My job was to help develop containers for sensitive or volatile materials; real cutting-edge stuff. The lab was equipped for a wide range of testing and it was a pleasure to work there.

"Then Bennett started adding 'peripheral products,' as he calls them, and they're taking over. They're not, well—and this is between us—not strictly on the up-and-up. The other employees don't seem to mind, but I'm not sure I want to be involved anymore. The money's too good to turn down if we want to start a family, though, and we're trying. Gloria plans to take a leave of absence from the hospital when she gets pregnant."

"Family man, hunh?"

Gerry smiled. "We plan for two boys and a girl. Or two girls and a boy, either way, as long as they're healthy. I was an only child and so was Gloria. We want our own tribe."

Shay gave a whistle. "That's going to be some leave of absence." He was about to start running again when he noticed a photographer and his assistant setting up a photo shoot in the park. They were accompanied by a reed-thin young woman in a semitransparent crimson toga with a matching pair of designer sunglasses. When she realized Shay was looking at her she assumed an aloof professional smile—that faded abruptly as she began to paw at her face.

The designer sunglasses were oozing down her perfect cheekbones.

———

When they returned from their run the two men found a gleaming red convertible parked in front of the vet clinic. "Hey, look at that, Gerry! Jack Reece must be back in town. D'you know him?"

"Not personally, but I've heard the name. He's a . . . well, what *is* it he does?"

"No one knows exactly, but he's a hell of a guy. Come on in and I'll introduce you."

It was obvious that Paige Prentiss knew Jack. She was watching him the way a greyhound watches a rabbit.

A plastic pet carrier stood on the counter. The unseen occupant was complaining bitterly.

"Who do we have here?" Shay asked Jack.

"Plato, Aunt Bea's oldest cat. He's having trouble going up the stairs and she wants you to give him glucosamine."

"How old is he?"

"At least twenty. If she can't get a cat to live into his twenties she thinks she's a failure."

"So I guess you don't want him put to sleep."

Jack shook his head. "It would be more than my life is worth."

"My wife's that way about plants," said Gerry. "She even hates to kill weeds."

"She's a gardener?"

"She's a psychologist at Staunton Memorial."

Jack raised an eyebrow. "I'm impressed."

Shay said, "You two wait for me, I'll take Plato to the back and examine him before I decide on his treatment. Come on, Paige, I'll need you to hold him."

While they waited, Gerry told Jack about the model and the dissolving sunglasses. "Poor girl's probably going to need help from my wife."

"Think she has psychological damage in addition to being burned?"

"She wasn't burned, which makes it stranger. The glasses weren't any warmer than skin temperature, I touched them myself."

"But plastic won't dissolve at skin temperature."

"You won't convince me of that, Jack. I saw it with my own eyes; so did Shay. Some of the stuff even dripped onto the ground."

"Then I think you'll be interested in what my aunt saw at the bank. Listen to this . . ."

Shay soon returned, carrying the cat carrier with its now-silent contents. "Plato's unhappy about having a shot in his spine and one in his neck, but he's not hurting. We'll repeat the process in six weeks and it should last him the rest of his life."

"No glucosamine?"

"That's outdated, Jack: nobody uses it now." He noticed their expressions. "What were you two talking about, anyway?"

They told him.

"Aren't you both describing the same thing?"

"Sounds like it."

"We're having a hell of a hot season," Shay said. "Could the climate be responsible somehow?"

Jack shook his head. "You can't blame the climate for things dissolving inside an air-conditioned bank. I think there's something larger at work here."

"Based on what evidence?"

"Gut instinct, Gerry."

"That's a damned poor substitute for science. Tell you what, Jack; we're having a barbecue at my house on Saturday, and by then we'll probably know what's going on. Shay's coming, so why don't you join us? Bring a friend if you want to."

"I've only been back in town for a couple of days, there isn't anybody special."

"You never know, you might meet someone at the party. But I warn you; the most gorgeous girl there will be my wife, Gloria, and she's strictly off-limits."

By the weekend the inhabitants of Sycamore River knew their town was not unique. Similar incidents had been reported elsewhere around the country; plastic items were inexplicably dissolving. Small things; unimportant bits and pieces. News commentators began referring to the bizarre incidents as "the Change."

People made jokes about it.

On Saturday afternoon a good-humored crowd gathered on

the deck at the Delmonicos' house to enjoy the barbecue. The Change was the main topic of conversation.

"It's weird, but is it dangerous?" a woman wondered.

"Only if you're plastic," said a male guest, glancing at her breasts.

She snapped, "Everything you see is real!"

Most of the guests laughed, but one said, "I have a bad feeling about this, we don't know what's going to go next. It's like waiting for the other shoe to drop."

"Don't sweat it," advised Frank Auerbach, publisher and editor of *The Sycamore Seed*. "Crazy things happen all the time, but you never hear about most of them. Usually it's technology gone bad and they're trying to cover it up. This is just another of the petty annoyances of the twenty-first century."

Auerbach was an archetypal American, a blend of many generations of immigrants from the four corners of the earth. Average height, average build, medium brown hair, no distinctive features. His wife, Anne, who loved him and was annoyed by him in almost equal measure, once told him, "You wouldn't stand out in a crowd of two."

Now she asked, "Would you rather be living a hundred years ago, Frank? With no modern medicine, no wallscreens? No air-conditioning?"

"Of course not, but—"

Another guest interjected, "I think a Russian agent emptied—"

"A Chinese agent, you mean."

"Whatever. A foreign agent's emptied chemicals into our reservoirs and now the knobs on our cabinets are falling off. Some secret weapon that is!"

There was more laughter.

Gloria Delmonico, wearing a textured yellow sunsuit that contrasted with her smooth dark skin, emerged from the house carrying a tray of canapés. "It's not funny," she said as she set the tray on the redwood picnic table. "People are frightened by what they don't understand so they make up stories to explain it. At the hospital we have a patient who's seen a woman rise from the dead."

"Like a ghost?"

"The poor man was hallucinating. He's convinced she's come back from the grave to ruin his life, but the real problem is he's still suffering occasional flashbacks from a bad drug experience years ago. When he accepts that, I may be able to help him."

"The Change can't be a giant hallucination."

"It's a giant hoax and someone's going to have to pay for the damage."

Theories were batted around like tennis balls. Everything from a foreign conspiracy to the nation's propensity for alcohol was blamed.

"The government's going to have to do something about this."

"Sure they will. They'll form a committee the taxpayers will pay for, and the committee will form a subcommittee and put together a panel of experts . . ."

"That's all we need, a panel of experts."

Jack remarked, "The ordinary man in the street might be better than a panel of experts locked into their own viewpoints."

"Don't include me in that," said Gerry.

"You're a scientist, aren't you?"

"Industrial chemist, that's my job description. I got interested in science very early, when my granddad told me about smartphones that spontaneously caught fire years ago. In school I discovered I was like Marie Curie, fascinated by both chemistry and physics. But it's easier to make a living in chemistry."

"Did they ever find out why the phones caught fire?"

"Sure they did, science has an answer for everything."

"You have a lot of faith in science, don't you?"

Gerry grinned. "Faith and science are a contradiction in terms. Science is about what's real; faith is wishful thinking." He shot a glance in Gloria's direction. "But don't tell my wife I said that."

"I know what I saw at the bank," Nell Bennett insisted on Sunday evening.

"You should stop having those liquid lunches," her husband told her. A ruggedly handsome man, retaining the neck and shoulders that had made him formidable at college football, Robert Bennett dominated the dinner table. "Alcohol's going to start showing on your face."

Nell hated it when her husband made disparaging remarks

to her in front of the children. "I didn't have a 'liquid lunch' that day, Rob, I didn't have lunch at all."

"Another diet, Mom?"

"I'm not dieting, Jess, I don't need to."

"Yeah, sure."

A few minutes later Colin complained of a headache. Headaches had become a frequent feature of his teens. Rob dismissed them as attention seeking, but Nell worried. The specialist she consulted had sought to reassure her. "It's a normal occurrence in teenagers, Mrs. Bennett; their bodies are changing so rapidly. If Colin's headaches occur more frequently or the pain becomes worse, bring him back in and we'll run some tests, but I don't think it will be necessary."

The meal ended as most meals did in the Bennett household; like the breakup of a small constellation. Robert Bennett announced he was going to his office at RobBenn for a couple of hours. His son went to his room to play war games on the internet. In her room Jessamyn avidly followed the celebrity gossip on social media.

Nell was left to retire to the media room and seek electronic company alone, as she did most evenings.

When she activated the wallscreen a local broadcaster walked toward her from a surrealistic set. "A blizzard of potato chips swirled through Alcott Park today. The bags disintegrated as they were being unloaded at the refreshment stand. We also have unconfirmed reports of plastic pill bottles dissolving on drugstore shelves."

As if I needed this, thought Nell.

She switched the wallscreen to the international news to be greeted by an onslaught of violence and tragedy, interrupted at three-minute intervals by celebrities appearing to walk toward her from the screen, extolling the virtues of a new-model car or the latest energy drink.

She changed to a pay-for-view documentary channel where the past was brought to life again; the safe and distant past that held no surprises. A program on archaeology, one of her favorite subjects, absorbed her interest until bedtime. But she did not sleep well that night. When Rob finally crawled into their bed she was grateful for his bulk and solidity. Robert Bennett, to whom life had given all the prizes, was her bulwark.

He would keep her safe. Rob always kept his trophies safe.

# 6

On Monday morning Nell alluded to the destruction of the bank card while she spooned scrambled eggs onto her husband's plate. "I hope my new card comes in the mail today."

"Do you have to go on about trivia? I've got a lot on my mind, an important meeting this afternoon. And don't give me any yatata about your real estate business either. As if any intelligent person would give you their business," he added while helping himself to more sage-and-apple sausages.

"Rob, you shouldn't eat so much sausage. What about your cholesterol?"

"The same cholesterol you're trying to boost with all these scrambled eggs? Can't wait to collect on my life insurance, hunh?" Ten minutes later he strode from the house. As he drove away he decided not to come home that night but sleep at RobBenn—his usual response to any disturbance at home, particularly those he had initiated himself.

He had been in his office for only a few minutes when his personal assistant came in. "The grip on my handbag—I thought it was leather—stuck to my hand," Karen Moeller said, looking stunned. "It took ages to peel it off. See how red my palm is!"

"Don't you women keep any cream in your desk? Go put some on it and then bring me my calendar."

A mile away from the Bennett house Sandy and Buster Nyeberger were hard at work on schemes to liven up the summer. Mischief was their constant preoccupation. Any possibility was grist to their mill. As the oldest boy at fourteen, Sandy had a room by himself. Kirby and Buster were thirteen and eleven respectively and shared another room, while Flub and Dub occupied a third.

The wing of the house that contained the boys' rooms resembled the wreckage left by a passing tornado.

On this morning the two oldest boys had closeted themselves in Sandy's room and locked the door. They only emerged for a hasty breakfast and then retired again. Sometime later they summoned their brother Buster.

The twins, Flub and Dub, complained at being left out. "They're playing World War Four again and they won't let us!"

"You have a PC in your room," their mother reminded them. "Go on the internet and find—"

"It's just an old one and you've got all the good stuff blocked," Flub said. "It's not fair. Why can't we—"

"You just can't, that's all." Tricia Nyeberger pushed a stringy lock of hair back from her damp forehead and looked at her watch. It was not yet noon. Dear God. A long day still stretched ahead. Children used to play outside in the summer, she recalled with longing. You could shoo them out the back door and not see them again for hours. Now they're glued to machines and they speak a different language. They don't even talk to each other half the time, they just send texts, even from room to room.

She wondered if it would be safe to leave them alone for an hour while she went to the hospital. Dwayne was due to be discharged after lunch.

Just one problem after another.

As she entered the boys' wing to start changing the beds, she heard a whoop of delight followed by Buster's exclamation, "Awesomely fatal!"

Awesomely fatal. Tricia Nyeberger silently mouthed the words. It really is another language.

While she waited for her husband at the hospital she talked with his psychologist. "Dwayne's still somewhat withdrawn, Mrs. Nyeberger. Anything you can do to get him interested will be helpful."

"That's just it, Doctor; he's not interested in much outside of the bank."

"His children, surely?" Gloria Delmonico's warm brown eyes and sympathetic voice put Tricia at ease.

"Our kids are kind of . . . wild, I guess you'd say, but Dwayne doesn't want to know."

"Boys, aren't they?"

"Five."

"Do they have a play station at home?"

"Sure. Interactive virtual reality, they're crazy about it. They have their own computers too."

"Have you heard of neuroscience?"

"I think I saw the word on a game show once."

"It's the study of the brain and nervous system," Gloria explained. "The Chinese were the first to recognize that people were becoming seriously addicted to video games. Now we're using that same addiction to treat antisocial behavior. Games have been designed with positive and negative stimuli to help reprogram the mind and develop a disciplined cognitive process. In other words, they subliminally encourage mental maturity."

From the blank expression on the other woman's face Gloria realized she might as well have been speaking Sanskrit. "The process has been approved by the US Food and Drug Administration," she added comfortingly.

"Oh. Well, that's good."

"If you'd like I'll give you a few games to take home, Mrs. Nyeberger. Just remember to remove the information packet before you give them to your boys, and if you have any questions, let me know."

Jack Reece watched the chief executive officer of RobBenn impassively. From the other side of his desk Robert Bennett regarded Bea Fontaine's nephew with an equal lack of expression. It's like playing chess, thought Bennett. I make a move, he makes a move. Neither of us gives anything away.

That was what he most enjoyed about business. The game. Not even the winning, though he played to win with ferocious determination. The game itself was the ultimate thrill.

Bennett knew the rules and manipulated them to his own advantage. He had no compunction about dishonesty; no businessman ever got to the top without, as he put it, "coloring outside the lines." The proposal he had put to Jack Reece years earlier meant coloring outside the lines. Reece had gone along with it, helping RobBenn to make a sizeable profit from time to time.

But Bennett didn't trust Reece. Not an inch.

In their original discussion the two men had chosen their words carefully. Both knew what they were talking about without being dangerously specific. This afternoon they were facing one another across the same desk in the same office, but it was a new game.

Before opening the conversation Bennett tented his fingers and took a moment to study the man in front of him. He was good at reading body language. Reece appeared to be relaxed, but he had the intensity of a coiled spring. Like any good gambler, he knew when to play a hunch and when to walk away.

For Robert Bennett Jack's value lay in his contacts overseas.

Too many hours behind a desk and too many rich meals had taken their toll on Bennett. His youthful athleticism had been replaced by brute force. In the competitive arena of big business intimidation was his specialty. He often said, "Appear big to win big." Another of his slogans was, "There is no such thing as enough, believe me."

Bennett wondered if Jack Reece ever had enough. Of anything. There was something feral about that face.

He opened his hands and laid them flat on the desk. "Remind me, Jack; how many languages do you speak?"

"Five in addition to English: French, German, Russian, Mandarin and Farsi."

"Farsi. That's new for you, isn't it?"

"Fairly recent: I study anything that may come in handy. And I have translation apps on my AllComs."

Bennett, who spoke no foreign languages, refused to be impressed. "I detect a trace of an accent in your speech now."

"I'm like a navy blazer, I pick up traces wherever I go. In a week I'll be back to plain American."

"Let me guess . . . you've been in the Middle East, right? That's where you got that tan?"

Jack gave a noncommittal grunt.

"Doing any business for me over there now?"

Instead of answering, Jack swung around in his chair and gazed out the window.

Bennett tried another approach. "How about this trouble with plastic? The media's calling it 'the Change'; sounds menopausal, doesn't it?"

Not by the flicker of an eyelash did Jack react. Bennett's coarse streak was only one of the reasons he disliked the man.

He turned back to face him. "You think it might affect your business?"

Bennett ran one hand across the top of his head to smooth the thinning hair. His palm came away damp. "'Course not. Couple of pieces of plastic dissolved, that's all. I stay on top of things, believe me. That's why I asked you to come in as soon as I heard you were back in town. If you have any new—"

"You think that's all this is?" Jack interrupted. "A 'little problem'?"

"Sure it is, nobody's been hurt. The giants of the pharmaceutical industry have a massive financial cushion so our original market will always be there. But what about the market for RobBenn's more, ah, profitable products? Is that still there?"

"War is still there," Reece said tersely. "Or hadn't you noticed?"

"My business has nothing to do with war."

Jack said nothing.

Bennett cleared his throat. Leaned back in his chair to show that he was at home here. Confident. Very much in charge. "My grandfather started out working in a little dry goods store upstate, did you know that? Saved his money until the owners wanted to retire and bought them out. He had an instinct for what people wanted; he put in a soda fountain and began selling patent medicines. Granddad did well enough to send my dad to college to study pharmacy. In time Dad developed a few patents that were worth something; when he died he left me enough money to go into business for myself when I came back from the war. Took a while to get started, but I never gave up.

"And here we are. RobBenn." He spread his hands in an expansive gesture meant to take in the entire complex.

"It's quite an achievement."

"Damn straight it is! From the beginning I knew I'd have to diversify to make it work. Diversity is the name of the game in business these days. In pharmaceuticals the field was too crowded for me to compete, but I realized the corollaries could be almost as profitable for a smaller investment and lower overheads. That's why I went into packaging. New drugs are constantly coming onto the market and the demand for more is enormous, especially since the failure of antibiotics. Many medications are inherently fragile. Too much vibration, or the wrong temperature, even a little pressure can cause irreparable damage, so protection is vital.

"I hired people who could design and produce the necessary containers for shipping and storage—which was changing all the time, like drugs themselves. RobBenn also developed protective devices no one else had thought of, and along the way we started to turn out some very interesting—"

"Widgets," said Jack Reese. "The first time we spoke about this you called them widgets."

"Shorthand for small but versatile components," Bennett affirmed. "You understood what I meant."

"Of course I did. I also understood that you weren't applying for 'dual-use' export licenses because they're expensive and time consuming, but you had a more compelling reason. Your widgets could be employed in a wide variety of weapons systems. In other countries they can go into equipment that can't be imported but has to be built from scratch. By supplying those simple components—"

"That's all we do," Bennett interjected. "We supply small components that, as far as we're concerned, can be fitted into dishwashers or tractors. The whole world runs on machinery made up of bits and pieces: they're indispensible. I wouldn't do anything illegal, believe me."

"Then why are you hiding out here in the forest?"

"I'm not hiding. In a way, I'm continuing a tradition like the one Elias Daggett established. I've built something here that I can pass on to my son and his sons. If you had children yourself you'd understand, Jack." Bennett paused. "You don't have any children, do you?"

"I'm not married."

"What does marriage have to do with it?"

Silence.

Bennett leaned back in his chair and laced his fingers behind his head. "Let's get down to business. I know the international situation's complicated right now, but can you do any more business abroad for me?"

Jack said nothing.

Bennett tried to conceal his annoyance. "Well, then. With your contacts, can you at least discover who's behind the so-called Change? It's industrial sabotage, that's for damned sure.

The stunt's very clever, but there's greed written all over it. Someone intends to make a hell of a killing by marketing the solution to the destruction of plastic."

"You think there is a solution?"

"Of course there is; the whole thing's a gimmick—so maybe there's some way we could cut ourselves in on it. You know the shakers and movers; not the Gnomes of Zurich, that was last century. This is a different ball game now. Find out who's behind the Change and you could become a rich man."

"I'm sure plenty are on that hunt already." Jack cast a covert glance around the office, wondering if Bennett had the place bugged. For a heartbeat he was returned to the shadowy world of billionaire arms dealers and secret intelligence organizations controlled by forces playing deadly games with the future of the planet. "I'm not equipped to compete with them," he said aloud.

Bennett felt his blood pressure rising. "Okay, okay, I get it. You've lost your nerve, right?" Before Jack could respond he continued, "There is something else you can do for me. A pack of crazy tree huggers in this town is out for my scalp. I'd feel better if I had reliable personal protection, if you know what I mean. Is it something you could handle? You do have contacts for that sort of thing, don't you?"

After Reece left his office Bennett replayed their conversation in his head, looking for possible mistakes on his part and vulnerabilities the other man might have revealed. Then he sat for a while, staring into space.

No one appreciates how hard I worked to achieve this. Or how easily I could lose it. If I sweat blood, who cares? Nell and the kids spend money as fast as it comes in and never say thank you. Maybe Jack Reece has it right, don't tie yourself down with other people.

But I love them, damn it. They're *my* family.

I give them everything they want.


Fred and Louise Mortenson were anticipating their wedding anniversary. "Twenty-five years of wedded bliss," Fred announced as he entered Gold's Court Florist shortly after three in the afternoon.

"Isn't that lovely, Walt," cooed Martha Frobisher, a birdlike little lady in a rayon dress that hung halfway down her shins. "If only my Phil had lived, we—"

"I'm double-parked in the lane, Martha; mind if we get on with this? I want a dozen red roses delivered to my house this afternoon between four and five. No later. If they're any later I'll send them back. Got it?"

Her lips tightened to a thin line. "I have it, Mr. Mortenson." And I hope you spear your fingers on the thorns, you nasty old so-and-so, she said silently to his departing back as he left the shop. How could a sweet-tempered woman like Louise Mortenson put up with such an unpleasant man for twenty-five years? And there's my poor darling Phil up in Sunnyslope Cemetery. . . . She thrust two fingers into the sleeve of her dress and pulled out a wadded handkerchief. Dabbing her eyes, she looked out the front door of the shop to make sure no customers were approaching, then went into the back to check the stock in the walk-in refrigerator.

Nine red roses. Only nine. Martha did a quick mental calculation. There was not enough time to send for more from the commercial flower market in Nolan's Falls. By the time the order went through it would be tomorrow, knowing those people. As she returned to the shop area she noticed an elaborate flower arrangement in a celadon vase beside the credit card machine. The arrangement included several long-stemmed red roses, full blown and gorgeous. They were artificial, but in these days when flowers could be replicated so easily no one could tell the difference. Certainly not Fred Mortenson, who refused to have the basic eye surgery that people of his age usually did. "No kid fresh out of medical school's going to laser my eyes!" he declared.

The florist selected three magnificent blooms to be included in the Mortenson order.

Fred Mortenson stopped to compare his AllCom with the clock on the front of Goettinger's department store, nipped into the pharmacy for a bottle of antacid, then walked around the corner into Miller's Lane.

There was a parking ticket on his windshield.

"Damn that everlasting bitch to hell!" he cried, snatching the ticket and tearing it into tiny independent republics.

His outburst startled a mother passing by with her little boy. The child began to cry; the mother gave Mortenson a dirty look. "Language!" she reproved him.

"Bitch!" he shot back.

He was not referring to the child's mother, or the traffic warden who had written the ticket, but the wife for whom he had just ordered a dozen red roses.

For most of their marriage the two had shared an abiding passion. Even their closest friends were unaware of their true feelings. The tumultuous love that brought them together had faded to be replaced by a different emotion; one which brought just as much sustenance and would last longer. Both Fred and Louise possessed a talent for hating.

They hated everything about each other. Down to the smallest detail Louise loathed her husband and he loathed her. Their joint acrimony defined their lives and fueled a flame so steady they relied on it as an asset. Neither had a sense of personal responsibility. Anything that went wrong in one person's life was the fault of the other one.

A quarter century of such constancy deserved commemoration. Such as a dozen red roses for a woman who was allergic to flowers.

At four thirty a van bearing the name of *Gold's Court Florist* delivered a stunning floral arrangement to 29 Patterson Place.

Framed in cellophane were a dozen perfect red roses set off by green ferns and a large satin bow. The delivery boy admired them as he carried them up the sidewalk. He wished he could afford such a treat for his girlfriend. Maybe then she'd put out.

At five minutes after five Fred Mortenson opened the front door of his house and walked in.

At six minutes after five Louise Mortenson exclaimed, "Your phony flowers *melted*, you cheap bastard!" She hit her husband square in the face with her grandmother's cast-iron skillet, breaking his nose and knocking out three of his teeth.

# 7

Straddling a bend of the Sycamore River, the eponymous town appeared peaceful and superficially law abiding. Most of it was solidly middle class. Apart from RobBenn there was little industry; factories were reserved for Benning, the nearest large town. Sycamore River was almost but not quite self-sufficient. Its inhabitants mostly worked in offices, retail businesses and the service industry, providing a comfortable lifestyle for their families.

South of the river were busy shopping centers and leafy neighborhoods populated by those who could employ the less privileged to mow their lawns and clean their houses.

North of the river were discount shops whose customers mowed lawns and cleaned houses for a living, or struggled to stretch their welfare checks. There were also a few immigrant families that did not yet speak good English.

To the west lay Daggett's Woods, originally a forest containing over nine hundred acres of native hardwood. A sharp-eyed settler named Elias Daggett had laid claim to the land when the settlement on the riverbank was only a huddle of shacks. Elias did some timbering, made some money. Mostly he liked to camp out among his trees. Eventually his grandson, Ephraim, left the entire property to the expanding town of Sycamore River, to be held in perpetuity as a nature reserve.

To the environmentalists Daggett's Woods was a slice of paradise. Others saw it as a wasted asset that should be profitably exploited. For a few, Daggett's Woods was a temple.

Robert Bennett had spent a small fortune on lawyers' fees and bribes to politicians in order to carve out ten acres in the forest. There he had built a research and development center. Inspired by the plans for the Mars settlement, the architect had created a futuristic complex of cement and glass.

Except for RobBenn and the private access road that connected it to the main highway, the forest remained much as Ephraim had left it, its virginity slightly tainted by discarded beer cans, used condoms and festering heaps of rubbish. A slab of granite at the foot of the access road was carved with only two words: RobBenn Enterprises.

A local wag had nicknamed it the Tombstone.

Jack Reece was collecting information about the Change. Not because of Robert Bennett; Jack had decided he wanted nothing more to do with the man. But the puzzle was fascinating. Instinct warned him the Change might be the advance guard of an attack. For as long as he could remember there had been attacks on the American way of life: have-nots rebelling against the haves, political parties seeking to discredit their opponents, foreign powers jealous of America's position in the world.

"So far the Change doesn't seem to benefit any particular group," Jack commented as he sat with Bea watching the wallscreen. The latest world news program was almost over. Another would begin after a long interval of commercials.

The screen started to flicker around the edges. "Jack?" Bea said warningly. "Can you . . . ?"

"Sure, wait a minute." He fiddled with the controls until the picture steadied, though it seemed to have lost its third dimension.

The network commentator was reporting, "From Boston to Beijing to Botswanaland, storage containers are disgorging their contents as they collapse."

Bea said, "Do you suppose any storage containers are dissolving in the Pentagon?"

"I wouldn't be surprised, but we'll never hear about it."

"You don't have much confidence in the media, Jack."

"The same people who use war for entertainment value? We get 'real time' news from the wallscreen and we're supposed to accept it without question. Listen, Aunt Bea; I've been over there, I know what's going on. People used to believe what they read in the papers because journalists took time to investigate before they wrote. Now any sort of lie can turn up in print and we've lost the ability to discriminate."

"Frank Auerbach still publishes *The Sycamore Seed,* and I don't think he tells lies."

"That's a labor of love; how much longer can he keep it up?"

She took off her glasses and rubbed her eyes. "How long can we keep up anything?"

The wallscreen hissed. Jack began fiddling with the controls again.

Shay Mulligan told Paige, "I went to our supplier to restock pet supplies and found what looked like a nest of snakes in a drawer. All the collars and leashes had stuck together and turned slimy. They weren't real leather, but the bastard's been charging me for real leather. You can bet I'm changing suppliers!"

"The miracle material of the twentieth century is getting down-right dangerous in the twenty-first," Jack Reece said to Gerry Delmonico via AllCom. "Have you heard the latest news?"

"Bennett won't allow a wallscreen in the lab, not even a two-dimension without interaction. Says it's too distracting and he's probably right. Then when I get home Gloria and I share the chores, and so forth. You know. Tell me what's happened now."

"A ballerina with the touring company of the Bolshoi broke her ankle during a performance of *Swan Lake.* The hardened toe of her ballet slipper contained a small amount of plastic sandwiched with rubber to cushion the foot, and the plastic dissolved while the dancer was *en pointe.*"

"Ouch."

"I'll say. But listen to this one. Have you ever been to Bruges, in Belgium?"

"'Fraid not."

"You should, it's a UNESCO World Heritage Site. For five hundred years a brewery in the heart of the city has produced a famous barley beer that accounts for a big chunk of the nation's economy. To spare the ancient cobbled streets from thousands of delivery trucks, years ago a network of plastic pipes was run underneath them to carry the beer from the brewery to the distributors. Now those pipes are dissolving. The subsoil of Bruges is being saturated with beer!" Jack roared with laughter.

Gerry didn't laugh. "If the Change is extending to larger items . . ."

"Stories like this are popping up all over the place," said Jack. "You should see some of the ones I've found."

"If the Change is extending to larger items," Gerry continued doggedly, "it's really bad news. No one knows how much plastic is used in everyday life. Since this thing is advancing it might be moving from one set of polymers to another, or one molecular structure to another. Sort of like a disease. I hope they can stop it."

"'They'? Haven't you noticed we always expect someone else to do the heavy lifting?"


Bit by bit, drop by drop, decay was setting in.

Lines began to form outside of banks. Nervous depositors

wanting to withdraw their money were requesting old-fashioned paper bills. It was a new sort of run on the banks.

Bea Fontaine was embarrassed by the excuses she had to offer old friends.

"I'm sorry," she told Edgar Tilbury when he appeared at her window, "but for the time being we're limiting the size of cash withdrawals."

A lean, grizzled man in a plaid lumberjack shirt and faded denims, Tilbury might have been sixty, he might have been eighty. He was as sharp-featured as a fox and his eyes were very bright. "You know where I live?" he asked in a voice rusty with disuse.

"Of course I do. Out in the country."

"That's right, way out. No supermarkets. If I buy eggs or a couple of cabbages from my neighbors I have to pay them in cash, not cards, which is why four times a year I withdraw cash from your bank. I've always done it that way."

"And I've always said you shouldn't keep that much cash at home."

"It couldn't be safer in Fort Knox," he assured her.

Lila Ragland kept a wealth of information in the most sophisticated AllCom on the market, a top-of-the-line multitasking international communicator with an immense data-storage system guaranteed to thwart hackers. It was set in a handsome case made to resemble platinum, and included a retinal identifier concealed in the hinge. The device gave her access to enough skeletons-in-closets to bankrupt billionaires and bring down foreign governments.

Many people put their AllComs beside their beds at night; she put hers under her pillow.

The furnished apartment she was renting did not contain anything else that might tempt a burglar. She did not even own a gun.

She abhorred guns.

Waking one morning from a restless sleep, Lila slipped her hand under the pillow.

And felt something sticky.

Robert Bennett stormed into the editorial office of *The Sycamore Seed*. "What the hell's going on, Frank? Something's gone wrong with my personal AllCom and there are things out at RobBenn that'll be ruined if the Change isn't stopped. My employees are freaking out."

"What things?" Frank Auerbach inquired.

Oh, no you don't, thought Bennett. My business is strictly my business. "The equipment it takes to run this factory," he said blandly. "Like polycarbonate safety goggles for the assembly line."

Auerbach gave a contemptuous snort. "Cyber attacks and

chemical warfare and proxy wars around the globe and you're worrying about *goggles*? Get real, Rob; this is the world we live in."

"We who?"

"Us. The good guys."

"This 'good guy' isn't just talking about goggles, and I damned sure don't want to see any mention of my problems in your chickenshit newspaper! Just let me know as soon as you hear about a solution to the Change. Some of your money's invested in this place too, you know."

"Is that a threat?"

"Would I threaten you? Aren't I the guy who advised you to diversify because the Seed wasn't making enough in advertising revenue to keep food on the table?"


Robert Bennett stayed in his office late that night. Eschewing the company cafeteria, where he would have been asked questions he couldn't answer, he deliberately chose the highest-cholesterol items in the vending machines for supper at his desk. Potato chips, corn chips, salted peanuts and a sickeningly sweet candy bar in a neon blue wrapper that urged, "Try Me! I'm Good for You!" An obvious lie, he thought. No truth in advertising. Who should know that better than me?

At last he fell asleep on the seven-foot-long couch in the reception area of the executive suite. Upholstered in the softest Italian glove leather, the couch had been purchased in anticipation of interviewing female personnel but was rarely used for its intended purpose. In retrospect, Rob decided, the ploy had been too obvious. He had exhausted his limited supply of subtlety years ago, wooing Nell.

He awoke with a start shortly before dawn. Like a ghost, he wandered through the deserted offices surrounding the executive suite. Not a living soul in any of them. No one had looked into his office to wish him good night either—though he had never encouraged that sort of camaraderie from his employees. He recalled the time Nell had visited the complex with him shortly before it opened. He was proud of the place after the years of hard work, and eager to show his achievement to his wife. All she had said was, "It's hard to take it in, Rob. A manufacturing complex buried in the woods like this, far away from people . . . it seems so *impersonal*."

He had never invited her back. Except for the grand opening, of course, when the lavishly decorated lobby was filled with loud music and important guests, and pretty girls were circulating with trays of wine and canapés. He had wanted to show off his lovely wife, so he steered her by her elbow around and around the room, introducing her to the men and enjoying the expressions on the faces of their female companions; the false smiles of wariness and jealousy.

Nell had left early that night, summoning a taxicab from town. They had quarreled about it later. One of those unresolved arguments that would come to punctuate their marriage.

The complex was worse than impersonal now; it was eerie.

While Bennett was asleep the dissolution had spread. He went from one area to another, following its trail. In the business office the computer screens waiting on their workstations were supposed to transmit the slogan of RobBenn in red letters: We Package the Future! But the screens were blank.

He punched an on button.

Nothing happened.

He went from one machine to the next, punching buttons, holding them down, breaking into a nervous sweat.

Nothing happened.

An old joke ran through his head: If a bus station is where a bus stops and a train station is where a train stops, what happens at a workstation?

"Shit on a stick!" he said loudly. Into the silence.

He tried to restore normalcy by returning to his private office for a quick shower and shave. The adjoining bathroom contained a precise arrangement of mirrors that allowed him to see himself from every angle, to check on how far the creeping baldness on the crown of his head had spread. His daughter, Jess, had begun calling him Baldy. It didn't feel like a joke to him.

On the top shelf of a bathroom cabinet was a carefully drawn grid chart depicting his fight against alopecia. When it reached a predetermined point he would start having hair transplants. This morning he wasn't interested in his baldness problem. The haggard face in the mirror told him he had something worse to worry about.

Only slightly refreshed after his shower, Bennett called home. To his surprise his AllCom hissed when he thumbed the keys, but the call went through.

Nell's personal AllCom was inactive.

He switched to the house number. No answer.

Shit and fuck. Doubled.

As Rob drove out the main gate of RobBenn, he paused to speak with the night watchman in the security hut. At least there was one person he could talk to. "Everything all right out here, Jimmy?"

"Same as allus," the gray-haired man replied, "'cept for my coffee cup. I'm headin' home to the missus as soon as that new fella arrives for the morning shift." Noticing the expression on his employer's face, he added, "'S everything all right with you, boss?"

"What happened to your coffee cup?"

Jimmy held both hands palms up in a gesture of helplessness. "Just went whoosh! It's the cup on top of my thermos, y'know? I allus drink my coffee out of it. When I poured out the last bit this morning the cup went whoosh. Nasty mess all over my shoes. Go figure." He gestured toward his feet.

Looking down, Bennett saw that there was indeed a nasty mess on the other man's shoes. A revolting mix of viscous red jelly and coffee with cream.

Robert Bennett drove home well over the speed limit. The summer sunrise flooded the valley with light, but when he reached the main road there was scarcely any traffic. He did not even see a delivery truck, though within another hour the approaches to Sycamore River would be suffering from clogged arteries.

The Bennetts' mock-Normandy château was located in a gated enclave west of town, close enough to be convenient to the city but within easy reach of Daggett's Woods and RobBenn. Bennett parked his silver-blue Mercedes on the circular brick drive in front of the house and strode briskly to the double front doors with his AllCom in his hand.

Something was wrong with the chandelier in the entry hall. The flambeau bulbs were tilted sideways in the plastic cups that were supposed to simulate Waterford crystal. The decorator had assured Nell that "no one can tell the difference." Already one bulb had fallen out and smashed on the black-and-white–tiled floor that was supposed to be indistinguishable from marble.

A similar problem affected the light fixtures in the great hall, replicas of medieval torches arranged in clusters. A peculiar smear on the inner frames of the triple-glazed windows across the front of the room indicated the sealant was . . . was what? Dissolving?

"Nell?" Bennett shouted. "Cookie! We've got some problems down here!"

No answer.

Where was everybody?

It was far too early for his wife to go into town to that office of hers. Jessamyn and Colin were on summer holiday and undoubtedly still asleep, which explained why there was no sound from them. Bennett strode to the kitchen. Although Nell was an early riser there were no breakfast dishes set out on the polished granite countertop. No coffee was perking in the latest espresso maker.

Nothing was perking anywhere.

When Bennett opened the walk-in refrigerator the light was out. The recessed lights under the kitchen cabinets also failed to come on. He repeatedly thumbed his AllCom to restore electricity to the system, but nothing happened.

Unbelievable.

In the bedroom wing the master bedroom looked normal; their double-king bed was made up and the doors of the two walk-in closets were closed. When he opened Nell's and peered in the light didn't come on, but he could see that her clothes were hanging neatly on their hangers. But the beds in the kids' rooms were unmade. In their twin bathrooms the basins and bathtubs were dry to the touch. Unused towels hung on their rails with the monogram facing outward, as he demanded they must do.

The people who should have been in the house were nowhere to be found. Not even the dogs were there. The Irish setters were not shedding hair all over the carpets, nor was the Rottweiler barking in his chain-link pen outside.

The mock-Normandy château was as unnaturally silent as the complex in the woods.

He savagely thumbed his AllCom, trying to force a response from his wife wherever she was. No reply.

He hurried to the attached three-car garage to see if her car was still there. It was. He yanked open the door—she never thought to lock it in their own garage—and briefly inhaled the scent of Chanel that wafted out from the little two-seater sports car.

Bennett felt his anger spike.

How typical of Nell to buy a car that was too small to accommodate a man's legs! But where is she? And where are the dogs, for God's sake?

What the hell is going on? *Who the hell is in charge?*

# 8

Eleanor Bennett had awakened in a fog of depression. As she slept it had crept up on her; depression about her marriage and the effect it was having on her children, depression about the future . . .

The deep comfort of the bed was like a hug and she needed a hug. A glance at the luminous dial built into the nightstand told her it was too early to get up.

But action was preferable to lying there tying herself into knots.

Maybe I'm taking too many diet pills.

Rob's side of the bed was empty, and for once she was glad. If her husband were a different sort of man she could have discussed her feelings with him, but she knew what would happen if she tried. Rob would just say, "Early menopause, Cookie?"

A woman must stand on her own two feet and be able to look out for herself. Stubbornly, and against all the emotional roadblocks her husband put in her way, Nell had persevered until the proud day when she watched her name being painted on her office door. Assigning her a place of her own in the world.

It was time to face that world again.

In the bathroom she discovered that the handle of her electric toothbrush had dissolved. She stood beside the basin, staring down at the blue puddle on the edge of the sink.

Remembering the bank card.

She felt an irresistible urge to go someplace else. Anyplace else.

Do something different.

"To hell with it!"

Just saying that made her feel better.

Instead of her usual subtle makeup she applied a thorough coat of sunscreen to her face and the backs of her hands and dabbed lip gloss on her mouth. She replaced the tailored suit she had laid out the evening before with a pair of skinny jeans and a blue chambray shirt. A wide leather belt showed off her narrow waist. Well-worn loafers from the back of her closet had not seen shoe polish for years, but welcomed her feet like old friends. She did not activate her AllCom but tucked it into the pocket of her jeans; today she would not be at anyone's beck and call. The ensemble was completed by a wide-brimmed straw hat.

Then she went down the hall to awaken Jessamyn and Colin.

"Come on, kids! It's a beautiful morning, so I thought we'd go for a hike to Daggett's Woods before it gets too hot. We'll take the dogs. All three of them could use the exercise."

Agonized groans of protest greeted her announcement.

"I mean it! Roll out so we can make a start."

"Without breakfast?" Colin was scandalized.

"We'll walk more comfortably on an empty stomach, then I'll spring for blueberry pancakes at that restaurant on the highway. Perhaps your father will join us."

Jessamyn said, "You *know* I don't eat pancakes, Mom. Think of all those *calories*. Besides, I thought we were going on a shopping trip later. The summer will be *over* before I get a new bikini! That's not *fair*!"

"I'm not getting up for any hike in the woods," Colin added, "we don't do stuff like that. When did we ever do stuff like that?"

"When I was your age my dad took me for long walks."

"Why didn't you just go to the gym?"

Eleanor Bennett adopted her husband's tone of command. "You heard me. Up and at 'em. Now!"

Taking the kids on a hike today was not one of my best ideas, she told herself an hour later.

Her son and daughter complained every step of the way and there were far more steps than she had realized. In the car the access road to RobBenn seemed like a relatively short distance from the house. On foot it was miles, even with a shortcut through Daggett's Woods.

Colin claimed they had walked twenty miles at least.

"You don't know how far twenty miles *is*," his sister told him.

"You've never walked one mile," the boy shot back.

"Well, I don't intend to walk another one," said Jessamyn—loudly, for her mother's benefit. "I've got a blister on my heel and I hate the country, it stinks. And there's *bugs*. I hate bugs. What are we doing out here anyway?"

Nell could not admit to her children that flight was her response to anxiety. "We're here to surprise your father," she said brightly. "We'll appear out of nowhere and take him to lunch."

Jessamyn whimpered, "I hope he has some calamine lotion in his desk, I'm being eaten alive."

"You'll give some bug a bellyache," said her brother. "You better get used to 'em though, 'cause Mom's lost."

Nell gritted her teeth and kept walking. The two setters frisked around her, their russet coats gleaming in the sun. Her husband's overweight Rottweiler paced stoically behind them. Any sense of play Satan possessed had faded long ago.

They stopped when they reached a clearing in the trees. At its center stood a small dolmen made of rough slabs of stone. Nearby was a makeshift altar holding a few tiny animal figures and a stub of candle stuck in the neck of an empty glass bottle.

The smell of burned cloth was unmistakable.

The two teenagers giggled. Before his mother could stop him, Colin picked up the bottle and smashed it against a stone.

"What did you do that for?"

The boy gave his mother a blank look.

"That's vandalism. I won't have it, you understand?"

Colin scuffed the dirt with his toe.

Fuming inwardly, Nell gathered up the pieces of broken glass and pushed them far under a bush so the dogs would not step on them. She walked on, obeying one of her husband's many axioms: Act like you know what you're doing and people will believe you.

Her children followed her.

They emerged from among the trees to find themselves on the access road. The futuristic white bulk of RobBenn loomed to their left, like a spaceship tilted for takeoff.

Jimmy Haas, whom Nell knew, was not on duty in the small sentry cabin at the front gate. Instead there was a different man with cold eyes and bad teeth. He stared at the disheveled trio approaching him. "Do you have an appointment?" he challenged.

"I don't need an appointment, I'm Mrs. Bennett. Mrs. Robert Bennett," she added for emphasis.

"He's not here."

Nell was startled. "What do you mean, he's not here?"

The guard stepped out of the cabin to face her. "Just what I said. I been on duty since eight this morning and he's not here, so you better go now."

"Where is my husband?"

"How should I know? The boss don't have to report to me."

Nell squared her shoulders. She wasn't going to give an inch to this self-important nobody in an ill-fitting uniform. She was aware that her children were watching her. "Please ring his P.A. on extension nine and tell her we're here," she said frostily.

"How'd you know the extension?"

"Just ring it right now or you'll be out of a job by tonight!"

In a few minutes the three Bennetts were seated on the immense leather couch in the reception area of Rob's private suite. The panting dogs sprawled on the floor at their feet. After apologizing profusely for her employer's unaccountable absence, Karen Moeller went to fetch coffee for Nell, soft drinks for the children, and a large bowl of cool water.

While she was gone Colin said, "Hunh, I thought Dad's secretary would be younger than that."

"Mrs. Moeller's not his secretary," said Nell, "she's a personal assistant, that's almost an executive in her own right. Her looks aren't important, but her initiative and efficiency are."

Jessamyn giggled. "Or maybe that's what Dad wants you to believe."

Nell sat in silence, struggling to keep from scratching her own mosquito bites, until Karen Moeller returned with the refreshments. She offered to drive them home in her car whenever they were ready. As they reached the main highway they met Robert Bennett coming in. He slammed on his brakes and lowered his window.

Mrs. Moeller lowered hers.

Bennett shouted at Nell, "Where the holy hell have you

been?" Without waiting for an answer he hit the accelerator and zoomed off toward the parking lot.

In the backseat of Karen Moeller's car Colin Bennett said, "Mom's sure gonna get it now! Just wait till Dad comes home tonight."

With his thumbs hooked in the waistband of his jeans, Gerry Delmonico ambled around to the side of his house. In the twilight Gloria was fastening stakes to the tallest stems in a bed of irises. In spite of her busy schedule at the hospital, she managed to keep several flower beds blooming. "They're my children in waiting," she told Gerry.

When she saw him she smiled. "Who are you supposed to be, a fugitive from the OK Corral?"

"No, ma'am." Gerry withdrew his left hand, cocked an invisible pistol and sighted along the barrel. "I'm the only man left standing after the gunfight and I've come along to collect the reward. A pretty gal in a bed of flowers is just what I had in mind. What are doing for the next hour or so?"

She laughed again; the warm, easy laugh of summer. "How did your work go today?"

"Same as usual. Maybe more problems than usual, though. Just between us, I wouldn't put it past Robert Bennett to be involved with the craziness that's going on. He's always looking for angles; dissolving plastics may be part of some new scheme. Today Adele from bookkeeping came to me questioning an invoice for materials we've never used before, like magnesium carbonate. I asked Bennett about it but didn't get a straight answer."

"I never have liked that man," said Gloria. "Before you go in, would you bring me my gardening gloves? I think I left them on the deck."

Gerry returned with her gloves and a deep frown on his face. "Don't go around back."

She gave him a quizzical look. "Why not? What's wrong?"

"The deck's gone soft. If you step on it the boards will stick to your shoe. I'm afraid the whole structure might give way."

"I thought only plastic was dissolving."

"Porch decking is made of wooden planks, Muffin, but they've been permeated with plastic to make them last longer. Some of it's oozing out and dripping down; there's a puddle of it on the ground under the deck."

Gloria instinctively put one hand on her belly. Her beautiful brown face turned ashen. "This thing that's happening . . . is it something in the atmosphere? Oh my God, what if I'm pregnant at last?"

# 9

Contrary to his son's prediction Robert Bennett did not give his wife hell the evening after her walk to Daggett's Woods. He had stayed at RobBenn until what would have been his usual departure time, then drove home in a sour mood. He was relieved to see that the antique copper carriage lamps on either side of the front doors were lit, a sure sign that his wife was home and expecting him. She would have some excuse for her erratic behavior earlier in the day, but he did not want to hear it. Let the woman dither; he had real problems on his mind.

He found Nell in the dining room, setting the table, and gave her a perfunctory kiss on the cheek. Expecting trouble, she stiffened, but he did not notice. Nor did he observe the looks of anticipation on the faces of his children as they came in for dinner.

Bennett's face was a blank wall with turmoil behind it.

Napkins were unfolded; a basket of hot Parker House rolls was proffered, a platter of sliced ham and bowls of freshly steamed vegetables were passed. Conversation was sporadic, and mostly involved Jess and Colin insulting each other.

Nell ate only enough food to make it look like she was eating. Then she waited. The children waited.

When Rob finished wiping up the last of the ham gravy with the last bit of his roll he said, "Anything for dessert?"

"Is that all?"

"More coffee?"

"I mean is that all you have to say to me?"

"Don't start on me, Cookie, I've had a hard day . . ."

"*You've* had a hard day!"

". . . and when I came home this morning I found my house abandoned."

"You were here this morning?"

"And you weren't. Damn it, you shouldn't go off like that without telling me first. The light switches and the—"

"That's all you were worried about? The house?"

Rob leaned toward her. "I've invested a lot of money in this place, in case you're forgotten. You blithely waltzed out the door and left it to fall apart. Or be burgled. And that's not all; now the lunatic fringe is making threats against me. They even set up an altar in Daggett's Woods and burned me in effigy. Some of my employees took me out to see it: a scorched doll hanging from a tree branch. I tore it down and threw it away, but I got a letter saying they would burn the whole complex to the ground if I didn't restore the nature reserve to the way it was intended."

The color drained from Nell's face. "The children and I saw that altar, Rob. I had no idea . . ."

"Of course you didn't, you've never taken an interest in my business. This is just a small part of what I have to deal with. If

I don't get a handle on things PDQ you can wave good-bye to RobBenn and the lifestyle you enjoy so much. But I'm not going to roll over and play dead for anybody, believe me."

The momentum of the Change was increasing. Reports of it came from every direction. Concluding an edited report of one day's events in America, the commentator on the wallscreen reported, "In Maine the mannequins in a shop window dissolved, seeping out of their clothes; vinyl records in the collection of a symphony conductor in Seattle disintegrated; and at a Hollywood premiere the red carpet stuck to the soles of celebrity shoes and had to be scraped off."

"And your wallscreen's about to fail," Jack informed his aunt.

He called Gerry to relay the latest developments, concluding with, "The space agency's reporting massive solar flares."

"They couldn't be causing the Change, Jack. Solar flares are highly charged particles of energy that're carried to the Earth by solar winds, captured by our planet's magnetic field and safely conducted toward the poles. That's what causes the northern lights. But . . . wait a minute. There is something that might be related. Absorbing high-energy electromagnetic radiation *can* cause the nucleus of something to change by ejecting a subatomic particle. It's called photodisintegration. That could be another way of describing the destabilization of plastic. But why should it only happen to plastic?"

Before Jack could reply Gerry said, "And frankly, buddy, I have a more pressing question. D'you think the Change could hurt a pregnant woman?"

"Gloria's pregnant!"

"Not yet, but . . ."

"Don't worry, the Change isn't hitting anything organic."

"Maybe not, but the psych department in the hospital is overrun with people on the verge of panic. I'm worried about my wife being in there."

"Doesn't the hospital have adequate security?"

"For normal situations, but not this. Have you been to the bathroom recently?"

"What're you talking about?"

"Toilet seats. South of the river they're mostly wood to be fashionable, but in businesses and on the north side most of them are plastic. I'd guess the ratio is about thirty-seventy."

"You don't mean . . ."

"Yeah. First thing this morning most of the seventy percentile sat down on their toilets and stuck to the seats. It hurt like hell to rip their buttocks free, and the longer anyone sat the worse it hurt. People are flooding into the hospital. They called my wife to come in early."

Two faces on two AllCom screens gravely regarded one another.

"This could be a helluva time to have a baby."

"Yeah."


Pandemonium descended on the Nyeberger household when the boys had problems with their computers. They were taking too long to come on and arbitrarily turning themselves off again. One was emitting a thread of noxious smoke.

Amid howls of protest, the boys' mother banished the machines to the garage. She could not placate her sons with replacements. When she called the local supplier she was told, "I'm sorry, Mrs. Nyeberger, but we can't guarantee any of our PCs right now. Try us again in . . . six weeks, maybe?"

The Sycamore and Staunton Mercantile Bank was in a similar position. Their computers were becoming unreliable, beginning with the newest. Against his every instinct, O. M. Staunton was forced to close the bank while his staff tried to manage the accounts the old-fashioned way.

Which hardly anyone knew how to do anymore.


What the Old Man disliked most was any departure from routine. His longtime housekeeper, Haydon Leveritt, was under strict orders to serve roast chicken every Sunday, chicken croquettes on Monday, Swiss steak on Tuesday, spaghetti and meatballs on Wednesday, broiled fish on Thursday, Manhattan chowder on Friday, and ham on Saturday. She allowed nothing to alter this schedule.

Staunton could cope with the dissolution of toilet seats; when he was growing up his grandfather still used an outhouse. Shortly after the incident with the bank cards and pens he had arrived at the S&S with boxes of old-fashioned ledgers, reams of paper and scores of freshly sharpened pencils. The routines of business must be reestablished and maintained.

But sheer determination was not enough.

"Wall Street's got jittery," the Old Man confided to Bea Fontaine. "According to the news, fanatics are claiming to see visions ranging from choirs of angels to the end of the world."

"Don't believe everything you hear," she advised him.

"Hell, I don't believe anything I hear; not since the last election."

The first thing Edgar Tilbury did every morning was check his personal outposts for further signs of decay. Eyes. Hands. Shoulders. Hips and knees. Everything still work? What about his back? Sunnavabitch was the worst. The most difficult action he performed was sitting up in bed. Get that far and he could make it the rest of the way, even with a brain still cobwebbed by sleep. The fuzziness would not begin to dissipate until after the second cup of coffee. Jamaican Blue Mountain as strong as a mother-in-law's tongue. Then he could organize. What to do and in what order.

Hardest things first.

While he drank the coffee he repeated the lecture he gave himself daily. Not going to put up with any nonsense. Everything has to keep on keeping on. No future in getting old. No future in *not* getting old either, but I've got some good years left.

Let Ollie Staunton sock his money away in bank vaults. Putting machines in charge; machines don't care. When we were growing up I thought he was a damned fool and I still do. When things go wrong—and every damn thing goes wrong sooner or later—I'll be just fine. Had better sense than to connect myself up to something called the World Wide *Web*. That name alone should have been an indication of what could come down the road.

Maybe I ought to pay a personal call on Ollie, give him a bit of friendly advice.

Or maybe not. Ollie never took anyone's advice.

When Jack Reece said it was good to be home, his aunt remarked, "If you married and settled down here you could have a home of your own."

"That's not in the cards, so why keep bringing it up?"

"What have you got against marriage, anyway?"

"Absolutely nothing," he assured her, "it's a noble institution. Don't laugh. You may not believe this, but I'm really an old-fashioned guy. I believe marriage should include a commitment to monogamy. But monogamy is only three letters away from monotony. I won't marry because I have too much respect for the institution."

"If you ever did marry, would you honor your vows?"

"All of them," he said solemnly.

Bea knew Jack kept his promises—which was why he rarely made one. He was a rogue, but he was her rogue. She was quietly proud of his success with women. His virility reflected well on the family genes.

"You went out to RobBenn the other day and came back looking like the cat that swallowed the canary," she said. "Is there a new girl in the office?"

"Nothing like that; Robert Bennett is what put a smile on my face. It did me good to see that pompous bastard brought down a peg or two. People everywhere are having problems, but he thought he was exempt. Now he wants me to help pull his irons out of the fire."

"I didn't know you had business dealings with him."

"Not business: I don't 'do business.' I've acted as an agent for him on some deals, that's all. Things I could do as a freelancer. You'd be surprised how many freelancers—some call them rogue agents—there are in the world. They're involved in everything from import/export to equipping professional mercenaries. The days of having a pensionable job are long over, Aunt Bea. It's more profitable to float free if you're not averse to a bit of risk."

"I don't like the sound of that, Jack. Is Robert Bennett doing something illegal?"

"A lot of business is illegal one way or another."

"You think I don't know that? I work in a *bank,* remember? Long before the internet came along, banks kept the most astonishing secrets."

That evening Jack took his favorite suitcase off the top shelf in his closet and set it on his bed. One piece of luggage represented years of his life; years spent gaining the trust of strangers, acting on hunches, taking risks. The custom-made case contained those basics without which he never traveled; he could walk out the door with nothing else and go anywhere. The frame was steel, the covering was leather, lovingly burnished to a mellow glow. Subtle modifications had been made to the basic piece over the years, invisible to the casual observer. But no part of it was plastic.

Jack stroked the leather with a touch of nostalgia. "Good times," he remarked aloud. Then he hoisted it back to the top shelf.

If I'm going to stay here for a while I better find another way to make a living.

# 10

At one end of the main waiting room in the Hilda Staunton Memorial Hospital a massive wallscreen extended from floor to ceiling, wall to wall. For the safety of patients and their families it was not interactive, and was tuned to the blandest programming available.

Recently there had been an insistent demand for network news.

As Gloria Delmonico entered the room to summon her next patient a commentator was saying, "The Change is being reported throughout Africa, the Antipodes and Asia, but it's hitting hardest in the most technologically advanced areas. For once, the developed countries are on the front line of a calamity."

The word "calamity" sent shock waves through the room.

A massive woman perched on a king-sized pillowcase filled with crushed ice gave a shriek of hysteria. By the time Gloria reached her side the woman was flailing her arms. One of her fists hit the psychologist squarely in the stomach.

Lights flashed behind Gloria's eyes. She heard a roar like the sea. She started to say, "How irresponsible . . ." Then the sea rolled over her.

———

At first Gerry could not understand the message from the hospital. The AllCom was spitting static. When he realized Gloria had been injured he ran to his car in the parking lot at RobBenn. As he roared through the front gate the guard called out, "Hey, you just got here!"

"Wrong! I just left."

He found his wife in a private room, propped up on pillows and looking sheepish. "They shouldn't have called you, I'm fine. One of the patients was hysterical, that's all."

"You're coming home with me as soon as they release you." He took one of her hands in his. Her fingers were icy. "Are you sure you're okay, Muffin?"

"Better than okay, me and our baby both. She's tucked up safe inside me, that little accident didn't hurt her a bit."

Gerry's heart gave a leap. "Our baby! Did they tell you it's a girl?"

Her smile filled the room. "Some things a mother just knows. But let's keep it our secret for now, okay? I don't want to jinx anything."

By the time Gerry spoke to Jack again, Gloria was at home. Jack drove to their house with a large bouquet wrapped in florist's paper lying on the seat beside him.

"She's in the bedroom," Gerry said as he opened the door. "Go on in and I'll fix us some coffee."

His wife was sitting in an overstuffed armchair with a book open on her lap. Through the window behind her Jack could see Evan Mulligan's chestnut mare grazing in her pasture.

Gloria greeted her visitor warmly. "You shouldn't have bothered, Jack, but it's sweet of you to bring flowers."

"Nobody ever calls me sweet. How're you feeling?"

"Embarrassed over all the fuss. I'm going back to work tomorrow."

"That's good, I guess—if your doctor says it's okay."

"He does, and the hospital needs me. People are really . . ."

"Spooked?"

"Yes, some of them. Then there are the stalwart types who deal with whatever comes."

"That's me," said Jack.

"I know; I wouldn't expect to see you in my department. Sit down in the other chair and tell me what's going on outside. Gerry doesn't talk about it because he doesn't want to worry me, and our internet's down. That's why I'm reading a book."

Her brown eyes were pleading with him.

He tried to answer without conveying the unease he felt. "The media's still treating the Change like some sort of freak show. I suspect the authorities are trying to keep a lid on things as long as they can, but rumors are flying. We should take them with a grain of—"

"What's happening, Jack?"

"The Change has begun affecting computers."

"In Sycamore River?"

"Everywhere," Jack said bleakly.

Gloria unconsciously clutched her book. "What's next?"

"We'll probably lose our connectivity; perhaps the whole global network. Anything that depends on computers could fail, and that's just about everything we rely on."

"Everything?"

"A lot," he amended, "but it won't happen all at once, and in the meantime someone may figure out a way to stop it. Your husband thinks the Change may be attracted to differing molecular structures and is moving from one to another."

"Do you agree with him?"

"Gerry knows a lot more about science than I do. I have some theories of my own, but—"

"I can't take this in, Jack."

"No one can, not yet."

From the doorway Gerry said, "Care to make a guess as to how much time we have before the real panic sets in?"

Jack stood up and took the tray and cups from him. "I hope this is stronger than just coffee."

"My wife's off alcohol for the duration."

"Sorry, I forgot. Here you go, Gloria."

Cradling the warm cup in cold hands, she looked up at Jack. "Can you answer Gerry's question?"

"Not until we find out who's behind this."

"And how to undo the damage," she added.

Gerry sat down on the arm of her chair. "I don't think it can be undone, Muffin, we'll just have to find acceptable substitutes for what's lost. Already there's some experimentation with soft woods like pine, and especially willow. They can be flexible enough to do the job plastics do, but their reaction to heat is a problem. Plus wood's organic and permeable, rather than inert, so there are situations where it can't be used at all."

"Surely there are synthetics that—"

"Most synthetics are made from petrochemicals," Jack told her. "Even fabrics. That slipcover on your chair, for instance."

Gloria looked from one man to the other. "A hundred years ago nothing was synthetic and our grandparents got along just fine."

"That's because they didn't know what they were missing."

Jack was staring out the window. "Trillions of bits and pieces. A kid's model spaceship and the guidance system for an intercontinental ballistic missile. We're going to lose them all."

"Don't forget about cars," said Gerry. "Under the hood some now have enough electronic gadgetry to send a rocket to Mars."

A muscle twitched in Jack's jaw. "I'm not going to stop driving my Mustang."

"It's a classic car, isn't it? Don't they predate computerization?"

"Just barely. How much do you know about cars, Gerry? They started using computers in them before the turn of the century. If mine was a vintage automobile like one of the 1950 Mercs, it wouldn't matter."

Gloria spoke up. "So much medical equipment depends on computers too."

"Except bedpans, Muffin."

"Even bedpans. Their computers weigh output and report it to the nurses' station."

"Too much information," said Jack Reece.


Edgar Tilbury visited his wife's grave every Sunday. He did not comfort himself with the thought that Veronica was looking down on him; he did not believe in an afterlife. But he went to Sunnyslope Cemetery in every sort of weather and sat on a wrought-iron bench a few feet from her headstone. Sometimes for only ten minutes but never more than an hour. Then he would drive home again, a long, silent drive into deep country.

After leaving the cemetery that morning he saw the young woman. At least she looked young to him. She wore a poncho and carried a buckskin shoulder bag, and was standing by the bus stop.

None of my business, he told himself.

As he drove past he glanced in the rearview mirror and saw her face.

He slowed. Stopped. Backed up and lowered the window. "Want a ride?"

She didn't look at him. "No."

"Got it." But he didn't drive on. "You been to the cemetery?"

"My mother's buried there."

"You don't remember me, do you?"

"Should I?" Still not looking at him.

"I remember you," Tilbury said.

"Do you." A statement, not a question. She was looking at him now. Warily.

"It was a morning like this one, nice and dry. But your clothes were soaked."

"You were kind to me."

"You were dizzy and covered with bruises."

"So you took me home with you."

"You were only a kid; I never laid a finger on you."

"No, you didn't." She bent to look in the window without touching the car. "You look older now, Edgar."

"I am older. So are you."

A faint smile ghosted across her lips. "A thousand years older."

He touched a metal button on the dashboard. The door on the passenger side clicked. "Get in if you want to, Lila."

"You still live in the same place?"

"I do, but it's been extended; kind of unusual if you like that sort of thing."

She opened the door. "I'd like to see it."

"Come to lunch now and I'll give you some of my Blow-Your-Socks-Off Chili."

"That I remember."

Neither spoke for several miles until she asked, "What kind of car is this?"

"A hybrid."

"I've been in a lot of hybrids and they're nothing like this."

"Mine's part pickup truck and part Jeep; I put it together myself. It'll run on gasoline or used cooking oil or rubbish I find lying by the road."

"Are you still making reproduction carriages, Edgar?"

"It's a profitable hobby. Nostalgia sells. I just built a little trap that's supposed to be a surprise birthday present, and I have a brougham about half finished that really is beautiful. It would suit you, I think."

"Is that what you put on your tax forms? Occupation, carriage maker?"

"What makes you think I file tax forms? I keep my assets in a hole in the ground."

Tilbury's hybrid turned off the main road, drove over a rusty iron cattle guard and jolted down a rutted laneway. The fields on either side were pastureland sparsely studded with boulders. "You called them 'remnants of the Ice Age,'" Lila remarked.

The lane curved to the right. The view ahead was blocked by a dense stand of cedars. Beyond them was a rambling white frame farmhouse with the upper part of a storm cellar protruding from one side. The building nestled in a haphazard mix of evergreen and deciduous shrubbery that had not been pruned in years.

"Home sweet home," Tilbury announced. "Come on in."

The living room was papered in a muted blue-and-white stripe; the brick fireplace smelled of ashes. Bookshelves were crammed with volumes on every imaginable subject, arranged according to topic. Two full sets of encyclopedias, one American and one British, took up a whole shelf by themselves. A well-worn recliner upholstered in coppery velour waited beside a large floor lamp.

Lila recalled that Tilbury had been a widower, but in this room there was no visible hint of his personal life. No framed photographs, none of those flourishes described as "a woman's touch."

"You still don't have a dog, Edgar?"

"Had two since you were here. One got run over on the road, the other got shot for a sheep killer."

"Was it a sheep killer?"

"Nope. But the guy that shot him hasn't shot anything since. Would you like a drink before we eat?"

"Irish whiskey, right?"

"You have a damned good memory," he said.

"Thanks."

"You're economical with words, aren't you?"

In response she quoted, " 'Listen to everything, learn a little, answer nothing.' "

He gazed at her in astonishment. "Aristotle?"

She smiled. "Euripides."

They sat with their drinks on either side of the fireplace. After a while Tilbury cleared his throat. "Under the circumstances I'd like to hear the rest of your story, Lila. If you think I'm entitled to that much."

She gave him a measuring look. Slowly, some of the hard knots loosened inside her. It was getting too painful to hold up the shields which had protected her since childhood.

"Did I tell you about the party?"

"Just that it got too rough and some bastard who wouldn't take no for an answer hit you. Hurt you pretty bad."

"Knocked me out, I think, then threw me into the river. Maybe he thought I was dead; it's lucky I didn't drown. By the time I crawled out of the water he'd disappeared. Instead of going back to the party I just started walking." As she talked the words came more easily. "I was like a moth coming out of a cocoon. Dazed, you know?"

"I can imagine."

"I realized I'd been close to dying and I wasn't ready for that. I never knew who my father was, but I knew what my mother was and I didn't want to turn out like her."

"So you kept walking until I found you," Tilbury finished for her. "Buddhists would call that karma. We'd both had some life-changers, Lila; I'd buried my wife and you needed a fresh start. You know what? Every life's a hallway with a certain number of doors in it. When you go through one you can either leave it open or close it behind you. I tend to close 'em."

"So do I."

"Obviously. You stayed with me for three weeks and then

left without saying good-bye. After you'd found the cash I kept hidden," he added.

The wary look returned. "I'm sorry about that. I just . . . I was still running, I guess."

"Survival instinct; that's something I understand. Yet here you are after all these years. Why come back when you'd got away clean?"

# 11

"I had the best reason in the world to come back to Sycamore River," Lila told Tilbury, "at least I thought I did. I was going to make a dream come true." She hesitated, deciding how much to reveal. "After I dropped out of school . . ."

"How old were you when you did that?"

"Eleven."

"Was school too hard?"

"No, it was too easy, Edgar; I was bored out of my skull." Talking was getting easier for Lila by the minute. Perhaps it was the warmth of the whiskey in her veins; perhaps it was the need to let go after all this time. All the trouble, all the pain.

"My mother didn't care what I did, she had her, ah, men friends. Sometimes I crossed the bridge and wandered around on the south side. We always lived in cheap furnished rooms and those houses looked like palaces to me. Real homes with a mother and one father instead of a parade of dirty uncles. My favorite was one with a tile roof and blue shutters, and window boxes full of flowers that were changed with the seasons. There was a doghouse in the yard that was an exact replica of it, complete with the shutters and window boxes. I used to imagine living in that little doghouse."

"Why didn't you tell me any of this before?"

"It was part of what I was running away from. When I had your money—it seemed like a fortune to me at the time—I decided to use it for the one thing I could change: myself. I hitched a ride to New York, checked into a small hotel under a different name and began studying.

"In school I hadn't bothered to learn much, but if you want to teach yourself the place to go is the New York Public Library. I read up on all the things that interested me. And I sought out *people* I could learn from. New York's great for that too. I went to the best places and began rubbing shoulders with the best people. In Manhattan almost everyone's from somewhere else; they're not interested in your past, only in today and tomorrow.

"I was pretty spectacular, you should have seen me at my best. I learned to dress like a fashion model and talk like a university graduate. And eventually I hooked up with a rogue in the IT industry who showed me how easy it was to get my hands on other people's money.

"I discovered I was magic on a computer. I could uncover personal secrets and private financial data and siphon money out of any bank that wasn't adequately protected. There are still more of them than you'd think, Edgar, both foreign and American. That's why it's so hard to prevent cyber crime.

"In a cashless society with instant real-time money transfers wealth can be accessed across multiple platforms. There used to be a saying: 'If you have a smartphone you have a bank.' With the newest AllComs that's more true than ever. In a single day

I could transfer a fortune to an offshore account, exchange it for dollars if necessary, then transfer it again and again until it was untraceable. All the money I could ever want, right at my fingertips, accessed while I was wearing my pajamas and calling up room service.

"I could even come back to Sycamore River and buy the house with blue shutters. People will forgive and forget anything if you have enough money. So I stored what I needed in the best AllCom on the market and caught the train, ready to begin a new life.

"But nothing ever turns out the way you expect, does it?"

Her expression hardened. The green eyes were as opaque as glass. "The day after I arrived I went on one of those southside walks again. The houses I remembered are still there, but now there's bloody war in every one of them. When I looked through the windows I saw men and women—and children too—hypnotized by their wallscreens, watching people slaughter each other as if it were some kind of game show. And for what? No one wins. The junk people snort up their noses or inject into their veins is a minor poison; killing is a worldwide addiction.

"And to make matters worse, the crowning insult, Edgar; my irreplaceable AllCom with all the information in it doesn't work anymore. Now you know why I'm so upset."

"If the tools of modern technology are failing, a hell of a lot of people are going to be upset," he replied, "because they've put their faith in it. But the more complicated something is the more can go wrong. That's why I like to keep things simple."

He was wondering if the story she had just told him was as simple as it sounded.

By her own admission the girl—woman now—was far from honest. But her tale was intriguing to a man who loved a good story. She might be telling the absolute truth, but she also might have shaped her narrative to extract the last drop of sympathy from him. Acting was an innate ability. It could be developed and honed, but the best actors believed every word they said—while they were saying them. Working out of a backstory that was temporarily their reality.

"What are you going to do now, Lila?"

"I honestly don't know."

"You have a place to stay?"

"I do for a while; I'm not going to ask you to put me up again."

Their eyes met. They understood one another completely. "I'm not offering," he said bluntly. "But you can come back for a visit. I've got a real good workshop here; I'm not the techie you are, but maybe between us we could fix that AllCom of yours.

"Now, let's have a meal and then I'll take you back to wherever you live."

Jack Reece continued to monitor the progression of the Change. It was becoming more difficult as the vast network created for and sustained by the computer started a slide toward extinction. Electrical power in the national grid was undiminished, but the necessary portals, due to their vulnerable components, had begun to disintegrate.

According to the news it was happening all around the globe. Governments were growing frantic as they realized the implications for civil society and military might.

Yet it was the small details, not the big picture, that seemed to upset people the most.

Bea Fontaine stood in her bedroom doorway almost in tears. "My nylons, Jack! They've turned into soggy tatters. I can't possibly wear them to the bank in the morning and the Old . . . Mr. Staunton is very firm about—"

"The bank's going to be open tomorrow?"

"And every working day, he's firm about that too."

"Do you have any makeup? Fake tan, that sort of thing?"

She was insulted. "I never wear fake tan."

"I'll drive down to the drugstore and buy some. You can spread it on your legs in the morning and he'll never know the difference."

"You've been my problem solver since you were a boy," she said with a smile. "But I don't understand about my nylons."

"Nylon is a synthetic material, Aunt Bea, made of polyamides that have a high molecular weight and can be turned into a fiber. It was developed in the 1930s, I think; before that women must have worn cotton or silk stockings."

"Silk?" Her eyes lit up.

"If the Change is starting on nylon I'll buy you silk," Jack promised. "In the meantime I'm on my way to the drugstore."

As he backed his Mustang out of the two-car garage behind Bea's house, she watched from the front porch. "One of your tires looks low," she called to him.

Jack stopped the car and got out. If the tire on the driver's side was low it was only minimal. He gave it a hard kick.

"Son of a damned *bitch*!"

He drove to the drugstore very carefully, bought the fake tan and delivered it to his aunt, then drove with even greater care across the bridge to the north side.

When Jack was away for any substantial period of time he left the Mustang with Bud Moriarty, a gentle giant of a man who owned an automotive garage on the north side. Like Jack, Bud was a classic car enthusiast; the two had met at a vintage car show. Bud kept Jack's convertible in top condition until its owner returned.

Bud shared a house with Lacey Strawbridge, a former runway model going to seed. She claimed to have been a cover girl on the top fashion magazines. When Jack's car pulled up in front of their house Lacey came running out to meet him, shrugging into a white cotton cardigan to hide the slackness of her upper arms. "Jack Reece, you devil, are you leaving us so soon?"

"Not for a while. But I need to have a talk with Bud; is he inside?"

"He's down at the garage. Wait and I'll ring him."

"Is your AllCom okay?"

"Why shouldn't it be?"

Jack followed her into the house and waited while she rang the garage. The case of her AllCom was dull from long use, but the call went through immediately. After a minute's wait Bud Moriarty's blunt features, smeared with grease, appeared on the screen. "Sorry about that, Jack, I was down in the pit. What can I do you for?"

"There's something I want to show you. Are you coming back this way?"

"In half an . . . no, I can come back right now. It's almost lunchtime."

"We're having Chinese dumplings," Lacey told Jack. "Do stay, they're almost as good as sex."

Jack raised an eyebrow.

"I said almost."

Jack grinned. "You should try it with a man."

She stuck out her tongue at him.

Her relationship with Bud contained everything a marriage should—except sex. They were a fond pair but not a couple. Bud was interested in men. Lacey preferred women.

Asexual intimacy baffled Jack. For him any relationship with a woman—except for his aunt Bea—contained at least an awareness of sexual tension. The only time he broached the subject with Bud the other man had laughed. "If you leave sex out of the equation a woman can be your best friend."

The three ate their meal on a wooden picnic table in the backyard, with paper napkins on their laps. Bud's house was close enough to the river for a summer breeze to lessen the heat, but it was also convenient for mosquitoes. Although the air was thick with citronella, soon tiny dive bombers were attacking.

Jack slapped at his neck and arms. "Why in hell do you live here, Bud?"

"Cheaper property prices and lower taxes. I bought this place and the garage down the street for less than I would have paid for a house alone on the south side. There are a few inconveniences but nothing we can't put up with."

Lacey added with a wink, "At least we have a wooden toilet seat."

When the meal was finished Jack led the way to the gleaming red Mustang waiting at the curb, looking almost as perfect as when it left the dealer's showroom many years before.

"You put a set of brand-new tires on this for me," Jack said to Bud.

"Yeah, a couple of months ago."

"Pick one."

"What do you mean?"

"Pick any tire you like, and kick it hard."

Puzzled, Bud swung his foot and delivered the requested blow to a front tire.

The rubber was mushy.

Bewilderment was replaced by dismay. "Don't tell me they're all like that, Jack!"

"They are." There was a subtle change in Jack's voice; an edge that had not been there before. "Did you put synthetic rubber on my car?"

"It's just as good; even better," Bud said defensively. "Synthetic can wear longer."

"The invoice I paid specified premium high-performance rubber."

"Yeah, well . . . I mean . . ."

"Natural rubber," Jack continued in the tone Bea would have recognized as his lecturing voice, "is obtained by tapping rubber trees and using chemicals to coagulate the liquid into latex."

"But—"

Jack was relentless. "Natural rubber is resistant to heat buildup, which makes it invaluable for high-performance tires on racing cars, not to mention trucks and buses and airplanes. On the other hand, synthetic rubber is derived from petroleum and alcohol and is a helluva lot cheaper, so it's used on ordinary cars. But my Mustang's special. Did I ever tell you I wanted to do things on the cheap for it, Bud?"

"No, but—"

"Stop right there. 'No' was the correct answer."

"I've always taken good care of your car, haven't I? When that drunk ran into you and we had to replace the door I couldn't find an original anywhere, but I had an exact duplicate made. You didn't say anything at the time."

"You didn't tell me it was a substitute. And don't look so worried, we're still friends. Except now I know I need to keep an eye on you." Jack flashed his sudden dazzling grin—which did not totally reassure Bud Moriarty. "Unless I miss my guess, soon you're going to see a lot of unhappy people complaining about their tires. Synthetic rubber contains petrocarbons."

"I'll replace your tires immediately, Jack, I have some high-perf tires in the garage."

"How many?"

"Maybe a dozen, I don't get much call for them."

"Where'd you get them from?"

"A wholesaler in Benning. Why? You won't need more than five."

"Call right now and tell them you'll take all the high-perf tires they have in stock. Get a firm commitment before the rush starts."

"Are you crazy, Jack? I can't afford that!"

Jack lifted one eyebrow. "How do you know? You're going to have a partner; me. A disaster can be an opportunity in a cheap suit."

Acrylic paint was not immediately vulnerable to the Change, but in a matter of weeks people noticed that the protective covering on their walls, both inside and outside, was wet. Was beginning to run.

Since the twentieth century contemporary artists had used acrylics to produce the intense colors. Occasionally they were used surreptitiously in restoration projects of the utmost delicacy. The Change evoked memories of the dreadful summer back in 2016 when the Seine flooded and priceless works of art had to be relocated from the basements of the Louvre and the Musée d'Orsay. Fearing a similar disaster, museum staff began packing their modern masterpieces into hermetically sealed vaults in hopes of protecting them.

Then the *Mona Lisa*'s inscrutable smile sagged into a jowly grimace.

At about the same time America's asphalt roads began to soften; the secondary network that helped connect the country.

If Robert Bennett was right in assuming that industrial sabotage was behind the Change, it was sabotage on an unprecedented scale.

Shay Mulligan awoke promptly at five thirty every morning. It was his habit to lie very still at first, eyes closed, breathing shallowly, reluctant to let the world know he was available for more heartbreak. Then he'd take one deep breath, throw off the covers and spring to his feet as if he had all the optimism in the world.

He had just thrown off the covers when he realized he was not alone in the bed.

Shay froze, waiting for memory to return. Too much to drink last night. A blue-lit bar in an alley off Spring Street, and a girl he once knew . . .

He eased himself to a sitting position on the edge of the bed. The rumpled sheets reeked of sex and sweat. A hundred horses were galloping through his skull. Slowly, to keep his head from falling off, he turned to look at the other occupant of the bed. "Lila?" he said tentatively.

"Hmmm?"

He knew she wasn't asleep. Like a cat, she was fully awake and waiting.

"Is that really you?"

"Let's see."

She sat up and stretched. Arms extended to their utmost, fingers curling like claws. The mattress adjusted to her weight as she crawled over to sit beside him, letting the covers fall away from her naked body. He watched as a single drop of sweat rolled down the slope of her breast, dangled from her dark pink nipple and trembled there.

Shay wanted to lick it off. He licked his lips instead.

The drop fell to the quilt.

"It's me, all right," she confirmed. Her voice should have been husky, but it was clear and sweet. "I don't think we had much conversation last night; you were bombed out of your skull. I wasn't even sure you'd recognized me."

"I had, all right, but I couldn't believe it. And I never expected to find you—"

"In your bed? I suppose not, but I didn't want to be alone last night; all the weird stuff that's going on. You know?"

"I know."

"You offered to bring me home because you didn't have a pet."

"Did I really say that?"

"You really did."

He needed to clear his befogged mind. "Okay, wait a minute. Let me fix a cup of coffee . . . fix us some coffee . . . and then . . ."

Wrapping the lower half of his body in a bedsheet, he made his unsteady way to the kitchen. With his left hand he reached for a jar of instant coffee and two cups. He heard her come up behind him. He could feel her warm breath on his back but did not look around, in case she was a drunken delusion.

It might be better if she was. Suppose Evan woke up and found his naked father in the kitchen with . . . "Lila?"

"Hmmm?"

"You are Lila Ragland, aren't you?"

"And you're a veterinarian."

"I'm a man with a teenage son who's likely to walk in on us any minute."

"I heard someone leave the house a while ago."

"That must have been Evan, going out back to feed his horse," Shay said. "Why didn't you wake me up?"

"I would have, if I'd wanted to get up myself, but I didn't. And now look at you." She lowered her eyes and smiled. "You're up already."


For the first time since she took the job Paige Prentiss had been in the veterinary clinic for an hour before her boss arrived. She called him on his personal AllCom, but it was turned off—either that or the device was no longer working. Paige assured the Reed-Johnsons that Dr. Mulligan would attend to their bulldog's erratic breathing as soon as he arrived. "Your dog's probably just too fat," she said.

Mrs. Reed-Johnson bristled. "Chauncey only eats what I eat," she retorted icily. "Are you saying I'm fat?"

Paige regretted her words. Half of the dogs who came to the clinic were too fat, but their overweight owners didn't want to hear it.

By the time Shay entered the clinic the Reed-Johnsons had left with their bulldog and without paying their overdue bill, as Paige was quick to point out.

It's going to be that kind of day, Shay told himself. My clients don't pay, and when I wake up with Lila Ragland she won't tell me when I can see her again.

Two of the Nyeberger boys were rushed to the Hilda Staunton Memorial Hospital when Styrofoam cups containing Cokes dissolved into white goo. Flub and Dub mistook the goo for marshmallow whip and gobbled it down.

On a sweltering, overcast Saturday morning Bea Fontaine answered her doorbell to find an unexpected visitor standing on the porch.

Bea unlatched the screen door and ushered the young woman

into the house. "I've been almost expecting this. Dwayne Nyeberger saw you outside the bank a few weeks ago and had a nervous breakdown."

"Serves him right."

"I never thought you were dead."

"Neither did I," Lila Ragland said with a wry smile.

"Why come to me?"

"I thought it would be better to explain to you privately, rather than in the bank."

"This is about money, I assume."

"Isn't everything?"

"Not in my experience, no." Bea's voice was cool. "If you want to talk, come into the living room and sit down; I'll be right back." She went to the kitchen for a pitcher of iced tea and a plate of vanilla wafers. The conventions of hospitality were as much a part of Bea Fontaine as her gold-framed eyeglasses. She would have done the same for Jack the Ripper.

After taking a sip of tea Bea removed her spectacles to give the younger woman the Look.

Which had no effect.

"Do you want to open a bank account?" Bea queried. "You've picked a bad time for it."

"I don't have any money to deposit."

"We couldn't give you a loan, even if you had collateral."

"I don't; at least I don't think so, but I'm trying to get my assets together. Did my mother have a safe deposit box in your bank a long time ago?"

"I have no idea."

"Could you find out for me? Her name was Treasie Ragland and she died before I . . . went away."

"Do you have a death certificate for her?"

"I'm not sure."

"You can get a copy of one from the courthouse. Then you'll need a court order requesting us to give you the box. Don't worry, it's pretty straightforward." Bea was beginning to feel sorry for Lila. She was well dressed and well groomed, but there was something almost forlorn about her.

At that moment they heard the front door open. Footsteps sounded in the hall.

# 12

Jack Reece paused in the living room doorway with a copy of *The Sycamore Seed* tucked under his arm. His aunt had a guest, a not uncommon occurrence on Saturday morning. Bea's house was in a long-established neighborhood. Friends often stopped by to chat with her when she was not at work.

This visitor did not resemble Bea's usual friends.

Jack shot a quizzical glance at his aunt.

The height of Lila's notoriety had coincided with Jack's most prolonged spell of globetrotting. By the time he returned the town's interest had been captured by another tumultuous presidential election followed by a steep recession. Bea was uncertain how much he had heard about Lila—if anything. She believed old scandals were best left alone.

Fortunately she had the old courtesies to fall back on. "Lila, this is my nephew, Jack Reece. Jack, Lila Ragland."

Bea was watching her nephew's expression. It was obvious the name meant nothing to him. "Do you want some iced tea, Jack?"

"No thanks, I just brought you a copy of the paper. *The Seed* has the local news, and our wallscreen's not working," he explained to Lila.

"I've always liked newspapers myself," she said. "And real books with hard covers."

"You and my aunt have something in common, then. She loves to read thrillers."

Bea reached for the newspaper. "Is there anything in here about the Change?"

"It's all about the Change, but not much that's really new. A physicist in California did suggest that the squeezing and stretching of gravitational waves was affecting the planet."

"How would that work?"

"Don't ask me, I'm not a physicist."

"He knows something about everything, though," Bea boasted to Lila. "Jack of all trades."

"And master of none," he added. "Now tell me something about you, Lila. Where do you—"

She stood up. "I'm sorry, but I have to go now. I have a lot to do."

"When you have that certificate bring it to the bank," said Bea, "and we'll help you."

After Lila left Jack commented, "That's an attractive woman. Have you known her long?"

"I don't really know her at all. Her mother may have been a customer of the S and S, but as you saw for yourself, she's not very forthcoming. Now, let's see what's in the paper."

She read aloud, "'Mitchells Motors on Davis Street reports that new automobiles equipped with android boosters are not selling, even with real rubber tires. Customers are asking for old-model used cars with manually operated windows and door locks.' Hunh! Abraham's not for sale at any price."

Jack said, "The AllCom market's suffering too. The newest ones seem to be failing first."

"And listen to this," Bea went on. "In the competitive world of online shopping, business has slowed to a trickle. Telesales employees are looking for other work. Advertising revenues generated by data gathering from high-end consumers are dropping alarmingly."

Jack shook his head. "No wonder people are freaking out."


Frank Auerbach knew a lot about advertising revenues. A fourth-generation newspaperman, he had watched with a heavy heart as social media decimated the industry he loved. The attention span of the public had been shrinking by the day. Few would take the time to read an entire page of newsprint anymore. The once-healthy circulation of *The Sycamore Seed* had dropped to a few hundred diehards who did not provide enough income to keep the presses running.

Frank Auerbach had not given up.

As the Change progressed he sought to provide a positive voice for a town teetering on the brink of a panic. "We are in an undeclared war," he wrote in a front-page editorial, "which is imposing a new sort of rationing. We have endured rationing before, we can adapt. Toothpaste containers have failed, but we can mix salt with baking soda and continue to care for our teeth. Beginning with this issue, *The Seed* will be offering helpful hints to its readers. Please send us your own discoveries for the benefit of your friends and neighbors."

As components of his printing machinery began to fail Frank was fighting back. He improvised where he could; found or fashioned replacements. In desperation he dragged outdated equipment out of storage until what he had looked like something out of the nineteenth century, but was still serviceable. No plastic parts.

A member of his staff showed up one day with an ancient typewriter. Frank appropriated the relic and set it up on his desk beside his computer. He sent his wife halfway across the state on a bus in search of typewriter ribbons.

His employees teased him at first, then began looking for typewriters of their own; Royals and Underwoods from the last century, constructed of metal. They made a terrific clatter, but they worked.

The redbrick building that housed *The Sycamore Seed* began to smell the way it had smelled when Frank Auerbach was a small boy; an amalgam of metal and ink and physical labor performed by men with their shirtsleeves rolled up.


"The Change is happening faster now," *The Seed* reported. "The outskirts of Sycamore River are being littered with the corpses of consumerism. People are dumping nonfunctional, big-ticket appliances on curbs and along roadsides. Freezinfridges, washing machines, even supercycles and ride-on mowers—we urge you to retain these items for spare parts. You will need them in the future."

The calm editorial voice of *The Sycamore Seed* had a steadying effect on the town, though a barely contained hysteria was building beneath the surface.

As social media sites faded ghostlike from their computer screens, Nell expected her children to respond with adolescent histrionics. Colin was outraged that he could no longer communicate his feelings directly to the sports stars of the moment, who he assumed were eager for his critiques of every game.

Jessamyn had revealed an unsuspected maturity. "I don't think I'll miss it very much, Mom. The internet's, like, awful for self-esteem. If anybody's going to call me fat I'd rather they said it to my face. Lots of snot-clots are hovering over their keyboards waiting to destroy other kids."

Nell frowned. "I hope you haven't been doing that."

Jess dropped her eyes and pleated the sleeve of her blouse instead of answering.

The nation received a shock when two high-speed passenger trains on the East Coast found themselves on the same track but going in opposite directions. The carnage was massive.

In the Oval Office at 1600 Pennsylvania the president complained to the secretary of state, "Is everything on God's green earth dependent on computers? How the hell did we let that happen?"

The small annoyances which had heralded the Change were as nothing compared to the discovery that a large part of the nation's ground transportation network was compromised. The national highway authority predicted that automobile traffic in the United States could be cut in half by Christmas.

With a corresponding decrease in carbon dioxide in the atmosphere, as meteorologists pointed out.

To the average American male, whose automobile was emblematic not only of his financial status but also of his manhood, the situation was personal. "Road rage has taken on a whole new meaning," the *Seed* reported. "Those who can still drive their cars are becoming the victims of those who cannot." At first they were punched and cursed; soon they were being shot and stabbed.

Shay Mulligan and Gerry Delmonico still went for occasional runs together. The Change had been their major topic of conversation until Gerry announced, "We're pregnant."

A smile furrowed the meadow of Shay's freckles. "Gloria must be thrilled."

"She is and she isn't. We've waited so long, and now it seems to have happened at just the wrong time."

"How can there be a wrong time for something you've

wanted so much? The Change is a big mess, I know, but we'll get through it."

"Will we?" Gerry asked glumly. "I've lost my job at RobBenn. 'We're sorry, but . . . ' You know the drill, Shay. Bennett's not sorry about anything but losing business. They don't need anyone in the lab now, the assembly line's shut down. So I'm unemployed and there's a baby on the way. I've put money aside over the years, but it won't last forever."

"There must be plenty of other things you can do."

"An industrial chemist in a town with no industry? We love our house, we don't want to sell it; it's ideal for raising children. But if I do find another job how will I get there? My tires have a whiff of rotten eggs and the ones on Gloria's car are shot. I can run a few miles on shank's mare, but that's no way to commute to work. Or get to the grocery store or the doctor . . . the doctor, for God's sake! Do you know any local doctors who still make house calls? I've put my name down at my car dealer's for a set of high-performance tires, but there's an eight months' waiting list and it's getting longer every day. You don't know how lucky you are to have your place of business attached to your house."

"You think so? How are people without tires going to bring their pets to me? This thing's having a tremendous ripple effect, we're all stretched to deal with it. The town's hoping to add more buses, but the mayor says there's no money in the budget. Even if there were, what's to prevent the buses from . . . say, how do you feel about dealing with the black market?"

"What does a straight arrow like you know about the black market?"

"In times like these a guy can't afford to be a straight arrow. You know Eleanor Bennett?"

"Not personally, but of course I know who she is."

"She's been a client of mine for years. When she brought her dogs to me for their annual inoculations I commented on the fact that she was still driving her car. She told me her husband bought high-performance tires from a 'private source,' as she put it, a garage on the north side. Bud Moriarty and a pal of his had realized what was going on before the rest of us did, and cornered the market. Tell them Rob Bennett's wife recommended them; I suspect you'll get your tires."

"How do I pick them up?"

"Problem solved. Day after tomorrow, my boy Evan is taking delivery on the slickest bit of transport you ever saw. It's what used to be called a pony and trap; a light cart that can carry two or three people and be pulled by a pony or a small horse. It was made by a retired fellow this side of Benning who builds reproductions of horse-drawn vehicles as a hobby. I ordered this one for Evan's birthday present not long before the Change set in. That chestnut mare of his is in foal and I thought it would be easier on her than carrying my big lug of a son on her back."

"Pony and trap," Gerry repeated. "I like that. You, my friend, are either prescient or a certifiable genius."

"You may be right. I've just ordered a full-sized carriage that can carry more passengers. It could be the start of the River Valley Transportation Service."

"Do you plan to issue stock?" Gerry asked hopefully. "And hire a driver, maybe? There's enough room for a barn at the back of my place: I'm tired of mowing all that grass anyway."

By late summer the World Wide Web had gone down. A bit at a time, but down. For Americans born and bred in the computer era, the larger world ceased to matter. Focus narrowed to Here.

As it became impossible to hide behind an enhanced image, individuals were forced to deal with each other in person. Millions discovered that electronic friends were actually strangers. Internet-addicted urban dwellers experienced something akin to rural isolation.

Frank Auerbach felt it was time for radio to stage a comeback. With his usual resourcefulness he located an ancient crystal set that had no suspect components and could be coaxed by a skillful ham operator into providing satisfactory short-wave reception. Soon he was making contact with similar enthusiasts who kept him supplied with news from beyond the Sycamore River Valley.

He made the announcement in *The Sycamore Seed*, adding, "Although it is a catastrophe with global ramifications, the failure of computers puts an end to cyber crime and the scourge of internet trolls. Sadly for retailers, the ability to influence consumers through social media has been lost, and the end of shopping online and internet banking is a massive inconvenience. We can be thankful that the US Postal Service has I-Roads for its mail carriers. Those one-person vehicles use special tires so the mail still goes through. Commerce in this great nation is badly wounded but not destroyed."

Standing on the southeast corner of Elm Street, Jack Reece observed how different the town looked with so little traffic. Within his range of vision and prematurely bedecked for Halloween with black and orange crepe-paper chains were Goettinger's department store, Deel's hardware, The Magic Carpet, Ye Olde Booke Wurm, and Gold's Court Florist.

So far the Corner Pharmacy (Open Till Ten), the Fletcher Building, the Sycamore and Staunton Mercantile Bank, Ralph Williams's insurance agency and In-a-Minnit dry cleaners had been spared the spiderwebs and witches on broomsticks, but it was only a matter of time. What Sycamore River did last year it intended to do this year. If possible. A lot of ingenuity would be needed to find satisfactory replacements for inexpensive plastic decorations.

The town looked better without them, Jack decided. Nineteenth-century brick and stone buildings still standing in the twenty-first century, as solid and confident as ever, were mellow in the slanting sunlight of autumn.

Why did I used to hate Sycamore River? There must be some truth to the old adage about familiarity breeding contempt. At sixteen I was bored to death with the ordinariness of it. I felt trapped among thousands of other people who were as bored as I was. Where was the excitement? Where was the adventure? I couldn't wait to escape.

Which shows how much a kid knows at sixteen.

He strolled down Elm and turned left at the drugstore, into Miller's Lane. There were even fewer Halloween decorations there. Just ahead Arthur Hannisch was adjusting the striped awning above the display window of his jewelry store. When he noticed Jack he said, "Hi, buddy, long time no see. You been abroad again?"

"Not recently; you might say I'm in and out. Seems like I can't stay away from the high life of Sycamore River for very long."

"Yeah. Well. What you see is what you get."

"How're things with you, Art?"

Hannisch tugged at an earlobe. "Could be better, we're struggling through every day and trying to keep things working. Betty Ann's not teaching in the middle school anymore."

"I thought your wife loved teaching."

"She did; she does. But that high-tech equipment the board of education spent our tax dollars on has disintegrated and taken a lot of jobs with it. The schools will be going back to pencil and paper, but my generation's finding it hard to cope. Facebook was the way Betty Ann viewed the world, y'know. She's like the kids, nothing's real if they don't see it backlit on a screen. Without social media my wife doesn't know what to do with herself."

"Is she helping you out in the store?"

The other man gave a hollow laugh. "You must be joking. As it is I'll have to let my only employee go. You remember Maude Foley? A widow with grown children? She can sell fleas to a dog, that woman, and she's been with me for years. I'd like to keep her through Christmas, but we aren't making enough to cover our overheads, never mind her salary. I'm worried about her, the suicide rate's gone up since the Change started."

"She wouldn't do that."

"How do we know what anyone might do these days? It's like . . . it's like a tide's coming in, Jack. We can see it creeping toward us, getting higher and higher, but we're on an island with no place else to go."

"If that's true, the whole world's an island."

"Yeah. Do you think the tide'll go out again?"

Jack forced a grin. "Sure I do, Art. This is a crisis, but every crisis has an end."

"If we live to see it. Sales of firearms are up, way up. They're no good against the Change, you can't force plastic to keep its shape by shooting at it, but you can let off steam by shooting at someone else if you're frightened enough and angry enough."

# 13

A generation was still alive that remembered the US Postal Service at its best. These men and women knew how to lick stamps and stick them on envelopes. They spelled "quick" with a *qui* rather than a *kw* and could construct declarative sentences. Without email they were not lost; handwritten letters began to flood into Washington, D.C. The great army of the Silver Foxes demanded the government reopen closed post offices, hire thousands of new postmen and get back to business.

In spite of all the obstacles created by the Change, America was determined to move forward.


Returning to his desk after a period of "convalescence," Dwayne Nyeberger feared others might see his breakdown as a weakness. He became more of a martinet at the S&S than his father-in-law. He roamed the bank openly criticizing the employees, knowing they feared for their jobs because of the uncertainty of the times. He stood too close to female customers and insulted male customers to their faces. On the increasingly rare occasions when a beleaguered individual sought to apply for a loan, Dwayne accused them of being financially irresponsible.

If he had set out deliberately to ruin the Old Man's business he could not have done a better job.

Shortly after lunch the president of the Sycamore and Staunton Mercantile Bank paid an unannounced visit to his daughter. She lived in a large white house in the symmetrical Federal style, set on a professionally landscaped lot in a desirable residential neighborhood. Patricia's father had given the house to her as a wedding present, although he retained the deed. He also neglected to mention that the house was a bank foreclosure.

The wing the Nyebergers had added after Kirby was born looked like an ill-advised afterthought. So, Staunton thought, were the rest of the children.

No matter how many times he pushed the bell no one responded. In exasperation he took a brick from the border of the nearest flower bed and banged it repeatedly against the door.

That got results.

When she appeared, Patricia's hair was tangled and her eyes were puffy from sleep. She served her father diluted grape drink in a jelly glass, with a plate of stale cookies. "The boys've eaten everything else," she said wearily. "I haven't had time to go to the store yet . . . I don't know where the day goes . . ."

The glass was not clean; a faint corona of crumbs was embedded in dried saliva around the rim.

Staunton cleared his throat loudly to interrupt the spate of apologies. "Pat, sit down here and listen to me. We need to talk.

Your husband is not happy at the bank. I've been speaking with some friends of mine and they're willing . . . I mean they'll . . . offer him a place in politics. It would be a high-profile position with one of the public service committees; a real plum that might lead to better things when all this 'Change' business gets sorted out. What do you say? Will you help me persuade him?"

As she always did, the Old Man's daughter said yes to him.

In the vice president's office later that day Dwayne Nyeberger told Staunton no. Emphatically, no. "You want to dump me on a committee of talking heads like some worn-out government flunky? I won't do it! I'm going to stay right here in the S and S until the roof falls in. When I married Tricia you promised me a job for life and I'm damned well holding you to it!"

Staunton returned to his own office to consider his options.

An envelope with an official seal was waiting on his desk.

"The president of the United States wishes to inform you that the military reserves are being put on standby. The nearest garrison to you will be in Benning. All banks are to reenforce their security systems and notify the military authorities of any suspicious behavior."

Staunton read the letter twice. "What the hell constitutes suspicious behavior?" he asked the stern faces gazing down at him from their portraits. "This damned thing's been suspicious from the beginning!" He stomped out of his office and called across the lobby, "Miz Bea! Come in here and explain to me what in hell's going on."

She read the letter gravely, then handed it back to him. "At least somebody's doing something."

"*We're* doing something, woman. I'm proud of this town. People are trying hard to keep going."

"Most of them are," she agreed. "What choice is there? Besides, after 9/11 the New Yorkers didn't panic. They kept their heads and helped each other, we've all seen the films."

"I'm surprised that a foreign country didn't attack us then."

"I don't think we need to worry now," she said reassuringly. "Other governments are no better than ours at dealing with the Change, they all have layers of entrenched bureaucracy. China's not making its problems public and the Russians claim they have 'everything under control,' but the Swiss and Germans have admitted defeat. Like us, they're just trying to maintain civil society."

The young Nyebergers had become addicted to their new games and were going through the early stages of withdrawal after their machines failed. Their mother had been relieved to pack them off to school when the autumn came.

The school staff was frantically busy trying to adapt to the altered situation. No single aspect of education was without its problems. Even the check-in system had failed.

The young Nyebergers took advantage of the opportunity for permanent truancy.

Relieved of any adult oversight Sandy, Kirby and Buster Nyeberger, with Flub and Dub in tow, roamed widely. On an afternoon fragrant with burning leaves their energy carried them as far as RobBenn.

A couple of cars at one end of a parking lot designed for hundreds looked like castaways on a beach. Robert Bennett had done away with the expense of a security guard at the front gate. The sentry cabin was padlocked, as were the other gates in the high chain-link fence that embraced the complex.

The young Nyebergers followed the fence around the perimeter, searching for an easy way in. They had no plans but endless optimism. In such a large place there were bound to be opportunities for mischief.

An hour earlier Gerry Delmonico had left RobBenn for the last time. After weeks of putting it off, he had returned to collect a few personal items he had left behind. He found Robert Bennett still in the office, shuffling through papers. Good manners had compelled Gerry to say good-bye, but not before Bennett extracted one last service. "Before you go, take this swipe key to the laboratory wing and make sure all the doors are locked," he ordered. "You never know when some cokehead will come looking for drugs."

Gerry had nodded absentmindedly. His thoughts were concentrated on Gloria, their unborn baby and the increasingly uncertain future.

Buster Nyeberger stared at three stories of blank concrete un-like the rest of the complex, which displayed more glass than walls. "Hey, lookit this," he called to Sandy. "Whaddaya think they got in there?"

Sandy scratched his head. Like all but one of his siblings he had a dense, scruffy mop of straw-colored thatch atop a pudgy face. "It's a top-secret lavratory," he ventured.

"Laboratory," Kirby corrected. The nicest thing O. M. Staunton had ever said about his grandsons was, "They look like a tree full of young owls." Kirby was the exception, an attrac-tive youngster with angelic features and thickly lashed eyes. "Jimmy Deel's in my class in school," he told his brothers, "and he says they make stuff out here to store gunpowder in. His dad sells them hardware and stuff so he knows all about it. If we get hold of some gunpowder we can make terrific fireworks and stuff for Halloween."

They headed for the nearest panel of chain link and began to climb.

The fence was no challenge to the young Nyebergers, who could swarm over obstacles of almost any description. All five made it without so much as a skinned knee. Their delight was compounded by the discovery of a small service door at the side, with the kind of lock they understood. Assiduous application of determined boyish muscle and a Swiss army knife were enough to do the trick.

The Nyebergers entered the laboratory wing alight with ex-citement. Their footsteps echoed on polished floors lined on either side by framed photographs. Robert Bennett in football gear, Robert Bennett graduating from university; Robert Bennett turning the first sod for RobBenn; Robert Bennett, almost invisible in a pack of dark-suited business leaders, meeting the president at the White House.

Buster dismissed the entire display with a single word of contempt. "Assholes."

The boys went from one room to the next, but their search was thwarted by locked filing cabinets, books of technical jargon and storage closets stuffed to the ceiling with boxes. When they discovered several inoperative computers they hooted with laughter. "It's no better than our junk," Sandy sneered.

Then they hit the jackpot.

In a cornucopia of shameless bribes for good behavior—which never worked—the boys had once been given a child's chemistry set. Only Kirby had shown any interest, though after the liquids were spilled and the powders scattered he abandoned it. In a large room at the end of the hall he recognized its adult version. "This is where they do the serious stuff!" he gleefully informed his brothers.

The laboratory was well organized. A double-width island of gray metal tables ran down the center of the room. It held both Bunsen and Fisher burners and a variety of glass test tubes and vials, as well as numerous bottles and jars. The latter were identified by labels that mostly resembled hieroglyphics. Tall stools were ranged around the tables. Shelves laden with more supplies and teetering piles of file folders covered the walls. In one corner stood a large glass water cooler on a metal tripod.

The older boys edged around the tables, reading the labels aloud to each other.

"Sodium something," Sandy reported. "That's just salt. You think they put it on their hamburgers?"

His brothers laughed.

On one of the highest shelves Buster spied a large glass container filled with what looked like water. Something floated inside. A shrunken head maybe? He climbed onto a stool in order to examine the label on the jar. "Phosphorus," he called over his shoulder.

"That's just what we need for the fireworks!" Kirby cried. "Let's get it down!"


Everything was right with Evan Mulligan's world. He was driving his new cart down a country lane, enjoying the autumn sunshine and the rhythm of trotting hooves. His chestnut mare, Rocket, was as content as he was. A brisk currying and brushing and a manger full of oats were waiting for her back in Sycamore River. Life was good.

Several weeks earlier Evan had ridden Rocket seven miles to meet Edgar Tilbury, who taught the youngster how to harness the mare and instructed him in driving a pony and trap.

"Don't go too fast until you get the hang of it, and swing wide on the corners. Remember it's a two-wheeled cart and you can turn it over pretty easy. As for driving, it's like a tele-graph, son. Those long reins in your hands telegraph your thoughts to your horse; she telegraphs hers back to you. Don't pull at her or saw on her mouth, just talk to her through your fingers. Ask her to do something new and maybe she won't like it at first. Horses don't care much for change; I'm like that myself. Give her time, she'll come 'round if you're kind to her."

Thanks to Rocket, Evan Mulligan felt independent. Many of his friends had their own cars, but the automobile had be-come problematic. Rocket was not problematic. She was warm and alive and carrying more life within her swelling belly.

"Rocket," he said fondly. She flicked an ear back in response.

"You and me zooming through space all on our own. Next stop, Mars Colony. What d'ya think of that?"

A shadow passed overhead. Evan glanced up. A single-engine airplane was descending in the direction of Nolan's Falls. One small silhouette in a wide sky that until recently had been crisscrossed with jet trails. Earlier in the century international terrorism had curtailed air travel, but with massively improved security measures it had been recovering—until the first pas-senger jet crashed after the onset of the Change. While the wreckage was still smoldering in a field outside of Cleveland the aeronautical world had changed.

Now the only passenger aircraft that dared fly were small private planes constructed with canvas and sizing and relying on human eyes for guidance.

No area of commerce was as vulnerable as the aircraft

industry. The malfunctioning of computers was only part of the problem. Flight was one mode of transportation that dare not use improvised parts. Manufacturers were frantically re-tooling and retrofitting to replace polymeric components wher-ever possible. "We explored the whole world with ships and sails," Evan informed the unseen pilot overhead, "and horses. Horses can take you almost anywhere if you're not in a hurry."

He was still young; he only viewed life from his own perspective. Evan was not much interested in airplanes, but he harbored a secret fantasy about being one of the first colonists on Mars.

If there was still a chance of going there; if They could stop the Change.

But maybe They caused the Change. And who was "They" anyway?

"Since the Change began Rob's become paranoid," Elea-nor Bennett complained to her widowed mother, Katharine Richmond. "I mean it, Mom. He thinks the whole thing's a plot against him personally."

Because the dishwasher no longer worked the two women were doing a sinkful of dishes by hand. Mrs. Richmond al-lowed them to pile up when she was alone, and Nell did not often get time to spend with her mother. Rob's silent but evi-dent disapproval was an obstacle she rarely challenged. She felt guilty about it.

She was wearing her mother's red-and-white–striped cotton apron in the kitchen of the apartment where she had announced her engagement to Rob with a lot of blushing and a Big Ring. The ring had impressed Nell's father, who regretted he did not make enough money to give his pretty daughter the finer things in life. The things her beloved Dad had taught her to expect as her due.

"Businesses are switching to wood products these days," Nell continued as she dried the teak salad bowl. "If RobBenn controlled the timber rights to Daggett's Woods we'd be set for life. I suspect Rob knows what strings to pull to make it happen, but he's focused on what is rather than what could be. He'd never listen to me anyway, he's convinced I have no head for business."

Nell's mother sighed and made sympathetic noises; urged her daughter to change her hairstyle and do more home cooking. "Take home some of my cookbooks," she suggested. "Nothing improves a man's mood like coming home to the smell of muffins baking."

"Muffins baking," Nell muttered under her breath as she left the apartment. "She has no idea." Wasn't there an old song about the road getting lonelier and tougher? Nell understood perfectly. Especially the lonely part.

Was Rob lonely too? He must be, he had no gift for making friends. She decided to make one more effort to reach out to him. She didn't call it "one final effort," though in the back of her mind she knew it was.

Thankfully her car was still operable. She drove to the Golden Peacock to make a dinner reservation for that evening. Another reconciliation dinner.

Over the years Rob had become increasingly detached from their marriage. Hoping to sever the umbilical connection between her husband and his work, Nell had booked reservations in one restaurant after another. She knew that Rob liked fine dining. Used to like fine dining.

Before the Change Rob had always brought at least one All-Com with him whenever they went out together, as well as a laptop in its case. The moment they sat down he would begin talking, texting, answering emails. Sorry, Cookie, I have to take this call. Send this memo, look up these stats. Sorry, Cookie, sorry.

He wasn't sorry. He scarcely knew she was there.

All but the old metal AllComs were useless now, and laptops of every age were being thrown away. Nell hoped that without them dinner would be different at the Golden Peacock. If only half of what the new restaurant advertised was true it would be hard to resist the atmosphere. The owners offered Edwardian luxury to create a sense of the past; the safe, pre-Change past. Private booths with lush upholstery and heavy curtains that could be drawn to suit the mood of the diners. Mood music, requested in advance, played by a string quartet. A six-page menu and the best wine list in the state.

For weeks Nell had been dropping hints about the Golden Peacock until finally Rob shouted at her, "For fuck's sake, get us a reservation at the damned place and stop going on about it!" His voice was so loud the Irish setters had fled the room.

He was at the breaking point: Nell knew it even if he didn't. Her pity was as great as her love had been, and more tender.

# 14

"Life," a lugubrious Hooper Watson informed the occupants of Bill's Bar and Grill as he entered, "is a misery."

No one disagreed. There were only three other people in the place: Bill Burdick, who was polishing glasses behind the bar, and a couple of out-of-work salesmen in a corner booth, sharing a pitcher of beer and making up stories about nonexistent sales to impress each other.

The former sheriff of Sycamore River expected to join his longtime drinking buddy, Morris Saddlethwaite. The two spent many evenings in Bill's, discussing the chaotic state of the world and trying to drink one another under the table. Friday and Saturday were sacrosanct, however. Hooper Watson wanted to be home on those nights to see who his daughter, Angela, went out with and how late she returned.

Saddlethwaite had not yet arrived, so Watson perched his bony behind on a wooden barstool. "Rock and rye, Bill."

"Can't," Burdick replied. "No rye, not today."

"Whaddaya mean? You been keeping rye for me since the time I didn't run you in for selling hard liquor to a minor."

Burdick continued polishing glasses. "That liquor wasn't so hard, Hoop, and she was no minor."

"Sez you. What about my rye?"

"The distributor can't get any. Trouble at the distillery, faulty equipment, he said."

The door opened and Morris Saddlethwaite entered. Blowing on his hands, he announced, "I swear there's a blizzard coming. At least the wife'll turn off the air-conditioning, it's costing us a fortune. When it works, that is."

Watson swung around on his stool. "Y'know what Bill just told me, Morris? Damned distiller's got faulty equipment. Fuckin' Change's ruining everything."

Saddlethwaite carefully hoisted his 230 pounds onto the adjoining barstool. "I won't let no Change drive me to drinking water," he declared, "no matter how bad it gets. Some things are more'n a man can tolerate."

"I'll drink to that," said Watson, "soon as Bill gives me something fit to drink. I was just saying life is a misery. No rye whisky to be had and my girl's at home weepin' her eyes out over a loony tree hugger."

Saddlethwaite prodded his ample posterior with thick fingers, trying to fit more of it onto the hard wooden stool. He missed the plastic-covered cushion that used to welcome his buttocks. "Which tree hugger? Town's full of 'em, putting up posters and collecting money on street corners."

"I'm talking about that redheaded son of a bitch out on Pine Grove, the one with the vet practice. Angela thinks he's seeing someone else now."

"I thought you hated both sides of him."

"I do, Morris, he's not near good enough for my girl. But I don't want her bawlin' in her bedroom, neither. You got anything behind the bar that even *smells* like rye, Bill?"

Try as he might, Colin Bennett could not get to sleep. His mother had given specific instructions to his sister: "I'm meeting your father for dinner and I expect you to take care of yourselves tonight. It's important. Jess. See that Colin's in bed at a reasonable hour, and you too. No having friends over, do you understand?"

Jessamyn had no trouble with Colin; the boy was suffering from one of his headaches and was willing to go to bed early. As soon as he was quiet she left the house to walk to a girlfriend's home several blocks away.

His sister had given Colin an aspirin before she left, but it did not seem to be having any effect. The boy tossed and turned in bed, his brain a jumble of thoughts. Until a few months ago his world had seemed normal—as normal as it could be, for a pubescent boy with raging hormones and erupting pimples. Now every day brought a new crisis for which he was unprepared. His sister was no help. Didn't Jess realize their parents were on the verge of divorce? What would that mean?

The house sold, a custody battle, the kids having to take sides, maybe even dividing up the dogs? What if they wound up going to school miles away from Sycamore River and his friends? He would have to start battling all over again to make the team, in a place where his father's college sporting reputation cut no ice. Maybe never get another coach like Coach Lonsdale, who let the guys get away with so much stuff . . .

When Colin heard a distant boom he thought it was thunder.

He waited, expecting Satan to bark his familiar challenge to the Storm Gods.

Satan didn't bark.

Carried on a rising night wind, the noise came again. Not thunder; it was a furious rippling growl that rose in volume as if a giant beast was slavering over its food. And moving closer.

Satan in his kennel began to howl.


Throwing back the covers, the boy slid out of bed and padded barefoot to one of the casement windows on the west side of his room. With an effort—something was sticking—he raised the bottom half of the window and looked out.

A clear, starless night greeted him. He could not see the moon, but there was a faint pink halo around the big holly bush in the yard, like a light shining on it from behind. Colin wondered where the light was coming from.

The growling beast exploded into a roar.

Colin hurried to the next window. An angry red glare suffused the sky in the direction of Daggett's Woods.

The boy gasped. RobBenn was over that way.

Could there be a fire at the complex? Was anyone calling the fire department? *Could* anyone call the fire department?

His parents were supposed to be having dinner somewhere, but where?

The blast that followed was louder than all the other sounds together. "Daddy!" Colin screamed in terror. "What's that?"

Robert Bennett could have told his son what was happening. But the CEO of RobBenn was fully occupied with dying.

At the Golden Peacock Nell was tapping her fingers on the tablecloth. She had finally managed to get through to Rob on one of his AllComs and tell him about the dinner arrangements. He had texted back, "I'll be there, just finishing up here . . ." Then the device failed.

At least he had not offered an excuse. Nell was grateful for small blessings.

In the restaurant she had no option but to sit and wait as the minutes crawled by.

The maître d' bustled over to her. "Is everything all right, Mrs. Bennett?"

"Yes, of course. I'm sure my husband's just tied up at work, but he'll be here. In the meantime, may I have another glass of wine?"

She sank back into the plush upholstery, sipped her wine and waited. And waited. Trying to concentrate on the good things about Rob and recall early, happy days together.

———

There had been a time when Dwayne Nyeberger rarely lost his temper with his wife, or if he did, she did not know. He had limited himself to subvocal mutterings well out of her hearing. These inaudible conversations had let off a fair amount of steam.

Since his breakdown—which he referred to as his "little episode"—he made no effort to tiptoe around other people. When he came home late from the bank and his sons were not there, he was enraged. "How could you let them wander off, you fucking imbecile!" he shouted at his wife. "You're dumber than a fucking sack full of hair!"

She cringed. "They didn't 'wander off,' Dwayne. They were outdoors playing."

"On a school day?"

"They've been skipping school a lot lately, I told you about it. Sometimes the school calls, but these days . . ." Tricia made a futile gesture with her hands.

"Have you called the police?"

"Not yet. My AllCom . . ." She made another futile gesture. "I took the bus to do some shopping and when I got home . . . how much trouble could they get into, Dwayne? In a nice town like this?"

"You really don't know anything, do you?" he shouted. "If I wanted smart kids I should have married a smart woman!"

Tears welled in her eyes.

Dwayne doubled his fist.

Her fear affected him like gasoline poured on a fire.

"D'ja hear that?" Hooper Watson asked abruptly.

Morris Saddlethwaite removed his hand from the bowl of peanuts. "Wha?"

"Sounded like the siren at the fire station."

"I didn't hear any . . . oh yeah, now I do."

"It was the fire alarm, all right," Bill Burdick confirmed. "And there it goes again. Must be something big."

Watson slid off the barstool. "Put that last drink on the tab, Bill, I better get over there."

"You don't have a tab, Hoop."

"Yeah, great, just put it on." Hooper was already hurrying out the door.

"A man with that much alcohol in 'em gets anywhere near a fire," Saddlethwaite remarked as he reached for Watson's unfinished drink, "he just might combust."

Nell checked her wristwatch every few minutes while the tiny hands sliced away sections of the hour. The solicitous maître d' inquired if she would like another glass of wine, but she refused. On an empty stomach it would make her dizzy and she wanted to keep her head clear for Rob. Perhaps it would be a good idea to order a plate of canapés, something to nibble on. Edibles she could substitute for a meal if she had to. In case she needed to drive home alone. In case there was ice on the roads.

The cold was gathering outside.

And Rob wasn't coming after all.

Another ten minutes, she told herself. I'll give him another ten minutes.

The cork soundproofing of the Golden Peacock muffled the scream of sirens on the highway.

# 15

Sunnyslope offered the best view in the Sycamore River Valley. Beyond the wrought-iron gates an expanse of manicured lawn descended by gentle degrees to the river. The parklike atmosphere was enhanced by carefully selected shrubbery, mostly evergreens that still had leaves in November. To keep them company a few treasured specimens of the nearly extinct American elm tree raised prayerful arms to heaven.

Only a few automobiles were parked on the paving at the end of the drive. Two black limousines waited among them. With the hearse.

For the rest of her life Nell would remember that the people of Sycamore River had made a pilgrimage to the cemetery on foot out of respect for her husband.

That was the way she chose to remember it.

She and her children had been assigned seats in the front row of wooden folding chairs beneath the funeral marquee. Beside the grave. Nell remained standing to greet the mourners and introduce them to each other. So many people. The family: Mom and the elderly cousins; the friends—mostly hers, not Rob's—and the numerous acquaintances; the business associates; a scattering of strangers . . . I'll never remember all their names, she thought. But Rob would expect it.

Rob.

Rob.

For once Colin and Jessamyn were subdued. In the funeral home when the director handed their mother the bronze urn containing her husband's ashes, Jessamyn had broken into uncontrollable sobbing. She was quiet now. Too quiet. Jess had thought of herself as "Daddy's little girl," and she was taking this very hard.

Colin's expression was frozen. To his mother he looked both older and younger than a week before.

A tall, thin man with an acne-scarred face approached Nell and extended his hand. "I'm Tyler Whittaker, the chief of police, Mrs. Bennett. I'm sorry about what happened." He spoke softly, as befitted the occasion.

"You're very kind." The response had become automatic.

"I'm in charge of the investigation, and I'd like to talk to you after—"

"Yes. After. Tomorrow, maybe."

"As soon as possible, while memories are fresh," he urged.

"Yes."

He wondered if she heard a word he was saying. "We don't have much in the way of forensic capabilities so I'm calling in a team from the state capital."

"Yes." Nell looked past him.

"It will take some time, though."

She shifted her eyes to meet his. "Everything takes time, doesn't it? Except dying. Death can happen in an instant."

Jack Reece had escorted Bea Fontaine to the funeral. They traveled in her Volkswagen with its new high-performance tires because she insisted his scarlet Mustang was too flamboyant for the occasion. As they approached the marquee Bea kept one hand firmly on his arm. She knew herself to be a strong woman, but recent events had upset her balance.

A lot of people in Sycamore River felt that way.

"I'd like to speak to Nell before the service begins," she told Jack, "but I don't know what to say to her. There aren't any words for a situation like this."

"Remind her that her husband died a hero," he suggested.

Bea frowned at him. "Do you have a shred of sensitivity? Sometimes I wonder."

"Well, it's true. There are five little boys in the hospital who might be having their funerals today if Robert Bennett hadn't tried so hard to save them. I never liked the man, but I'm willing to give the devil his due."

"Please don't say that to Nell Bennett. She's a friend of mine and I can only imagine what she's going through."

"Is she the blonde over there, in the dark blue coat? She looks like a deer caught in the headlights." Jack made a quick decision. "Wait here a minute."

He disengaged Bea's hand from his arm and walked briskly

toward the marquee, where a line of people was forming to speak to the widow. Jack elbowed his way past them as if he had every right to go to the head of the line. He interposed himself between Nell and the police chief and said to Tyler Whittaker, "Mrs. Bennett needs to sit down *now*. You can wait for another time."

A moment later Nell was seated in her chair with a printed sheet for the funeral service in her hand. She would remember this too: the sense of being gathered up and swept away by a force of nature.

Jack deftly maneuvered the disconcerted chief of police out from under the marquee. Tyler Whittaker had the authority of his office behind him, but Jack Reece radiated a different kind of authority; a steely confidence that dared a man to challenge him. The situation put Whittaker at a disadvantage. He could not make a scene; protocol must be observed at the funeral of one of the town's prominent citizens.

When they were out of earshot of the others Whittaker demanded in his normal tone, "Do I know you?"

"Jack Reece. Bea Fontaine at the S and S is my aunt; you probably know her."

Whittaker was mentally running through a list of names. "Do you have any connection with Mrs. Bennett?"

"Only the desire to protect a woman from being harassed."

"I wasn't harassing her, I was . . . Jack Reece?" Whittaker narrowed his eyes. "Bennett's P.A. told me he tried to hire a man called Jack Reece for some security work."

"Tried, yes, but I declined the offer."

"Any particular reason?"

"Security work isn't really my line."

"Then why did he offer you the job? What is your line, anyway?"

Before Jack could answer—if he intended to—Bea Fontaine interrupted them and pointedly asked Jack to take her to a seat. She did not like to see the chief of police questioning him. His habitual evasiveness was enough to make anyone suspicious and there were too many suspicions already.

Since the explosions and fire at RobBenn the local rumor mill had gone into overdrive. The extensive damage had uncovered disquieting aspects of the operation. Robert Bennett's policy of secrecy was responsible for suppositions and conspiracy theories that could ruin reputations before the truth was discovered. If it ever was.

Gerry and Gloria Delmonico were the last couple to be seated under the marquee, and then only because Gloria's pregnancy was becoming obvious. Eleanor Bennett had introduced them to the other guests as if she were sleepwalking.

"You needn't be here, Muffin," Gerry whispered. "No one expects it of you."

"I expect it of me, darling. He was your boss."

"Not by the time he died," her husband said.

"It began in your laboratory, didn't it?"

"According to the *Seed* the fire department thinks the original explosion was in there, yeah. By the time the Nyeberger boys ran out of the lab it was in flames, and the fire spread fast.

The kids were in serious trouble; at least one of them had set his own clothes on fire. Their screams must have alerted Bennett, the poor bastard. We won't know the exact sequence of events for a while, but he got the boys outside. One of the little ones was the last, he'd been hiding under a table. Bennett apparently went back for him and then something else exploded. He took the full force of it." Gerry paused. "An open casket wasn't an option. Cremation was the best choice."

Gloria briefly closed her eyes. "Poor Mrs. Bennett." After a moment she asked, "Was the Change responsible for what happened?"

"It's too soon to tell, Muffin, but I don't see how. The lab wing contained a lot of volatile material. All those boys had to do was expose phosphorus to air to ignite it."

"Surely no one will blame the children after what they've been through."

"Youngsters that age aren't children anymore," said Gerry, "and they haven't been for a long time. They've been seduced into a whole new category in order to sell them overpriced technology. If I'd been in Bennett's place, would you forgive them?"

Gloria's response was immediate. "If one of them was our boy, would you want him charged with murder?"

When people began to leave the cemetery Nell stayed where she was. She could not turn her back on the mound of flowers with the bronze urn waiting on top. Could not walk away.

Katharine Richmond hugged her as if she were made of glass. "Are you all right, dear? Are you too cold? I brought a heavier coat for you, just in case."

"I'm fine, Mom." To Nell's ears her own voice sounded like that of a stranger.

"Jess and Colin are coming home with me now in one of the limousines," her mother said. "You come when you're ready. I'll have beds for all of you. You and Jess in the guest bedroom and Colin on the rollaway in the dining room. You don't want to go back to . . . you don't want to go back yet."

Mrs. Richmond remembered burying a husband.

My mother's taking me home, Nell thought in an abstract way. That's nice. But she did not feel it, did not feel anything.


Jack Reece had remained at Nell's side throughout the funeral service. She knew of him in the general way people in Sycamore River knew about other people; he was Bea Fontaine's nephew. Aside from that he was a stranger. They were all strangers, the people under the marquee and on the lawn beyond. Faces with no one behind them.

When the workmen began to move the floral arrangements, Jack put a hand on Nell's arm. She did not feel its warmth, only its weight. "I'm here with my aunt Bea, Mrs. Bennett. We can take you anywhere you like."

"I have my own car," said Nell. In that faraway voice which wasn't hers.

His sudden smile surprised her. "I know you do; I supplied your tires."

Bea Fontaine insisted, "You're in no condition to drive right now, Nell. Leave your car here and we'll bring it to you later."

Later Nell would recall being in the front passenger seat of a Volkswagen driving along the riverbank. Her eyes were drawn to the moving water. Indifferent to life and death; obedient to another purpose. *Rob is gone, but the river will still be flowing tomorrow.*

She knew she should be grieving. All she felt was free.

And despised herself for it.

As he drove Jack kept a covert surveillance on the woman beside him. He knew before Nell did when she relaxed slightly. "I think a brandy might be in order about now," he said over his shoulder to Bea. "How about the Chatham Hotel?"

"In the back of the dining room, where it's quiet," she agreed.


Colin and Jessamyn were waiting for Nell at the door of her mother's apartment. Colin stepped forward and put his arms around her in a tight hug. "I love you, Mom."

Warmth began to flow through Nell's veins.

Jess said shyly, "I made up your bed myself. I took the best pillow from Gramma's bed."

*I would kill for these children,* Nell thought. *Nothing must ever, ever be allowed to hurt them.*

*I would kill for them.*

———

At the veterinary clinic Paige Prentiss was not favorably impressed by Tyler Whittaker. The chief of police had too much starch in his shirt and too little give in his attitude. "We've been informed by a reliable source," he said in clipped tones, "that Robert Bennett's firm was threatened by members of the Daggett's Woods Conservancy."

She bristled. "That's not true! None of us would do such a thing, we believe in peaceful protest. We certainly never blew up any buildings. Who's your reliable source anyway, a witch with a Ouija board?"

"I'm not at liberty to give you that information. Now, if you don't mind, I'd like to examine these premises for incendiary materials."

"I mind very much! Show me your warrant." Paige clenched her jaw.

Sheriff Whittaker was not a native of Sycamore River. When he took the job he had been warned that small-town people did not react kindly to the sort of tactics used in the city. "Ask 'em nicely, don't demand," was the advice he received from the former incumbent. The disaster at RobBenn was his first really big case, and proving to be a steep learning curve. "I don't have a warrant with me, Miss Parsons." He gave her a wooden smile. "I was hoping you'd cooperate."

"Well, I won't. Go get your warrant."

As he left Whittaker heard her hiss, "Fascist."

He wheeled around. "What was that?"

"Ashes," Paige said with wide-eyed innocence. "You have ashes on the seat of your pants. Do you want me to brush them off for you?"

Forensic investigation into the RobBenn disaster confirmed that Robert Bennett had been using unstable materials in the production of questionable merchandise. The mystery was officially resolved when Kirby Nyeberger, suffering from excruciating phosphorus burns, recounted from his hospital bed the part he and his brothers had played in the tragedy. The badly damaged boys would be paying for their hour of mischief for the rest of their lives. But no charges were filed. No judge in Sycamore River would hear the case.

Nell began to suffer nightmares about the last few moments of her husband's life. There must be some way she could have saved him, if only . . .

If only . . .

She awoke in the grainy light of dawn to pace the floor and smoke cigarettes, a habit she had abandoned when she met Rob. He would not kiss her if she tasted of tobacco.

"Mom," said Colin, "I wish you wouldn't smoke. What would we do if you got lung cancer?"

"You're like your father, you always see the bright side."

"Is that a joke?"

But she threw the cigarettes away.

The tobacco industry was one of thousands crippled by the Change. In the manufacture of cigarettes the highly specialized machines were constructed of metal, but every step of the production process involved parts made from hard plastic. Packaging ceased. Distribution ceased. Smokers would have to roll their own from now on.

There would be fewer deaths from lung cancer in the future.

Hospitals were struggling; no institutions were more reliant on plastic products. Patients were beginning to die due to failed technology. Medical professionals worked alongside lab technicians trying to discover usable substitutes.

As soon as the problem with stents was realized, doctors began replacing them with thin tubes of steamed and sterilized bamboo. But bamboo was not readily available everywhere. Three-D printers had been used for decades to replicate human organs with a plasticine material, but now some other substance must be found. In the ongoing battle against cancer, oncologists accelerated the development of antibody technology, but it would take time. Scientists who had pioneered the field of synthetic biology using manufactured DNA claimed it would be possible to replace all petrochemicals . . . within another decade.

———

Sycamore River could not decide how it felt about the Nyebergers. At one time RobBenn had provided employment for a number of people and was the pride of the town. That time had passed. Robert Bennett had very few friends to mourn his passing, but his widow was from one of the Old Families and had connections. Those connections could be resented by the less privileged; some thought the Bennetts had gotten what they deserved. In spite of the official report printed in full in *The Sycamore Seed,* there were rumors of a conspiracy on the part of the Daggett's Woods Conservancy.

"The Nyeberger family's going to sue for damages," Bea Fontaine informed her nephew. "Dwayne's been talking about it at the bank, he seems to think he's going to be rich for life. RobBenn had commercial liability insurance and Bennett carried a large personal liability policy, but I doubt if the combined sums will amount to the fortune Dwayne's anticipating."

"That greedy bastard," Jack said in disgust. "Kick her while she's down, why not? And especially with Christmas coming up."

"I don't think anyone's expecting a very festive Christmas this year. A lot of my friends are planning to go to church, though. More than usual," Bea added.

"You think the Change is a ploy on God's part to get people to pray? Put your glasses back on and don't look at me like that, Aunt Bea; I was being facetious."

"Then who do you think is behind it?"

"I'm not sure that's the right question," he told her. "Not who, not even what. But why? Why out of all the things on this planet destroy only items made from petrochemicals? It's too deliberate to be accidental. There's a cold logic behind the Change if we could figure it out. There must be some clue we're missing."

There were times when Finbar O'Mahony, the late Robert Bennett's personal attorney, wished he had gone into any other profession. He was thinking that now as he stood at the door of Katharine Richmond's apartment with his finger poised over the bell.

The balcony across the front of the second-story apartments was an obstacle course of bicycles, scooters and barbecue equipment. Some of the front doors could use repainting, but at least they were made of real wood, which had been considered a luxury detail half a century ago. The majority of doors and window frames used in modern construction were disintegrating. Lumberyards were swamped with more orders than they could handle.

While he waited for someone to respond to the bell O'Mahony noticed the balcony floor in front of the adjacent apartment, where brightly colored plastic toys had dissolved. Red, yellow and blue had flowed outward together to the edge of the wooden balcony, where they presumably dripped onto the ground below.

Yet unless the lawyer's eyes were playing tricks on him the balcony canted toward the apartment doors. Sagging supports, he guessed.

He took a coin out of his pocket and stood it on edge on the floor.

It rolled downhill. Toward the doors.

The edge of the balcony was uphill.

"What on earth are you doing?" Katharine Richmond asked behind him, breaking his concentration.

He whirled around. "I, ah, was conducting a little experiment, nothing important. May I come in? I need to talk to your daughter. I believe she and the children are staying with you for a while."

"Indefinitely," she corrected. "I couldn't let her go back to that house after the funeral, not even for Christmas. I don't think she wanted to anyway. I took them all to church with me and then we had a quiet dinner here. It was very pleasant, I found an old Monopoly board and we played games."

Rob Bennett would have loved that, the attorney told himself.

The Richmond living room was decorated in shades of beige and rose, with no Christmas tree but a slight odor of dog in the air. When O'Mahony sat down on the couch the odor enveloped him. "Nell brought the dogs with her, I assume?"

"Only Sheila and Rocky," Nell said as she entered the room. "Hello, Finbar. Three dogs would be more than the landlord would tolerate; as it is he's making a big concession."

Widow and lawyer faced each other across a low coffee table. A neatly arranged stack of glossy magazines sat in the exact center of the table. There were no flowers, no coasters and no ashtrays. O'Mahony did not disturb the arrangement by adding his briefcase.

The widow was pale and had lost weight; her plain dark dress looked as if it had been bought for someone else. Her hair was outgrowing its style; the roots were showing. She was wearing very little makeup.

"I'm here to fill you in on what's happening with the Nyeberger situation," O'Mahony began. "There's good news and bad, Eleanor; which do you want first?"

"Give me the bad news first, Finbar, and let's get it over with."

"I admire your courage. Dwayne Nyeberger's hired a high-powered legal firm that specializes in industrial compensation, and the accident at RobBenn is right up their alley. If they get what they're asking for it will clean you out; not only what's left of the property in Daggett's Woods but your house and cars, any other investments you and Rob held jointly, probably even your personal jewelry. They're professional asset strippers."

"I see. Well, I'm not surprised. And the good news?"

To Nell's surprise the lawyer's eyes twinkled. If she did not know better she would have thought he was about to smile. "The Change is the good news," he said.

"I don't understand."

"If this had gone to court a year ago . . . but this is now. Deeds, trust documents, insurance policies, bank records, the

Change is throwing priceless information out the window. Tons of data that was routinely digitized can't be accessed anymore. In many cases the paper originals have been destroyed; they were thought to be obsolete. Everything was done through the computer, but online is going offline." He made the last remark with obvious relish.

"Eleanor, I assume you know that the Cloud is the world's largest information bank, a virtual reality that was supposed to be safe. It's become the repository for just about everything important. Presumably the information still exists, but the micronized infrastructure is failing and so is the hardware to reach it. All that valuable material, lost in the clouds." The lawyer smiled at his little joke. "Without access to it lawsuits like the Nyebergers' are merely fodder for the wastebasket."

Nell's eyes brightened. "You mean they can't . . ."

"Precisely. Not for years or decades, maybe even centuries. IT engineers are working to circumvent the problem, but they're not making much headway." Finbar O'Mahony folded his hands atop the briefcase in his lap. "Nobody's saying this out loud, but it could destroy the legal profession. Didn't Shakespeare write, 'Let's kill all the lawyers'? I predict chaos in a matter of months. Frankly, I prefer to be well out of it.

"My wife'll be delighted if I retire. Carol enjoys fishing almost as much as I do; you should taste her grilled trout with herbs and bacon. We might get us a nice little boat and start drowning worms in Crystal Lake. Didn't Rob buy a vacation home up that way some years ago?"

"He did, a lovely cabin right on the lake. All the latest improvements and a small boathouse. Then he could never find time to go up there and he resented it if I went alone with the children. So there it sits."

"Ah. Yes. It's just as well; the cabin will go into the portfolio of assets Nyeberger's after. In the meantime I'm sure you can use it if you want to; you must be a bit crowded here. Carol and I would love to have you join us on our worm-drowning expeditions," he added. "You and the children and your lovely dogs too, of course."

"That would be nice, Finbar, thanks."

After he left the apartment O'Mahony spent several minutes fussily brushing silky red dog hairs off of his coat and trousers.

# 16

Edgar Tilbury did not visit his rural mailbox every day. He was superstitious about it. If he went to the mailbox too often he believed it would encourage more mail. Earlier in life when he was running a successful business he had endured unrelenting communication; constant bombardment from people who wanted something from him and wanted it *now*.

In retirement he preferred quiet.

His tin mailbox with its red metal flag stood on a dangerously leaning wooden post at the end of the laneway. On a cold morning Tilbury ambled down to the mailbox to see if anything worth reading had arrived. A single envelope awaited him. Not brown like a government envelope, or windowed like missives from the bank. This one was plain white with no return address.

"Personal letter," Tilbury informed a mockingbird sitting on the rail fence beside the laneway. Creosote had been liberally applied to the fence at one time to protect the wood, but now was nothing more than a stain on the earth.

The mockingbird cocked its head. Man and bird were old acquaintances. Sometimes it would imitate his out-of-tune whistle, but today it had nothing to say.

Recognizing the handwriting—an unusual combination of printed and cursive—Tilbury glanced at the postmark. The official stamp was smudged but still legible.

The mockingbird turned its head and precisely rearranged a single wing feather.

Tilbury examined the postmark more closely. When he rubbed it with his forefinger the red ink smeared.

" 'Neither rain nor snow nor dark of night . . .' " he remarked. "Something will keep the postal authorities from their appointed rounds, and damned soon too, if ink is going to dissolve on paper. Better read this while I still can; find out when she wants to come. Fly on off, bird. There'll be seeds in the feeder later."

Half an hour later Edgar Tilbury emerged from his house and went to the barn some distance behind it, perched on the rim of a hill near the rear of the property. He had more work to do on the coach he was building for Shay Mulligan, a custom design that was presenting him with several challenges. If Shay and his son, Evan, were not such engaging people he would have refused the commission, but Tilbury could not say no to people he liked—which was why he thought it best to avoid people.

Shay had been confident he could find a team to pull the carriage. "Several of my customers have retired hunters and event horses whose teenage riders grew up. They might be happy to sell their animals to a good home. But what about a harness for them?"

"Ordered a set for you from a fellow over in Coldbrook, the man who made a set for your son. Grumbled a bit; don't think he really wanted to get back into leatherwork."

"Is he retired in the same way you are?"

Tilbury gave him a lopsided smile. "Trying to be, but these days anyone with a practical skill's in high demand. Notice how the definition of practical has changed? Time was, people liked to live next door to a cyber nerd in case the home PC crashed. Now they want to live next door to a plumber."

"My nextdoor neighbor's an industrial chemist," said Shay.

"Any use to you?"

"Nope. And he's out of a job too. I'm thinking of offering him one driving the new carriage. Could you find time to show him the ropes?"

"Nobody *finds* time, son," stated Edgar Tilbury.

The Change was relentless.

The nation's trucking industry made every effort to keep business going; millions of tons of merchandise needed to be delivered every day. A percentage of high-performance tires was still intact, though no one could forecast how long they would last. Unfortunately the trucks themselves had been dispatched through a complex network based on computers.

Meanwhile another official missive arrived on Staunton's desk. "The United States government plans to withdraw all paper money in future. Coins will be minted in denominations from one dollar to five hundred dollars, and distributed throughout the banking system. You will be notified of the date in due course."

The Old Man didn't need to ask Bea to explain this one; he already knew. As usual, Frank Auerbach had heard first, and shared more details.

*The Sycamore Seed* reported, "The Change has destroyed the insulators in machines employed by the US Treasury to stamp out coins, but an enterprising federal employee has tracked down several nineteenth-century stamping machines that used cotton and silk for insulation. They are being rushed into service while new ones of the same model are manufactured."

An unanticipated consequence of the return to coinage would be a boost to the leather industry. Even before paper bills were withdrawn, designers were promoting masculine handbags with reinforced leather bottoms.

When the petroleum naphtha in newspaper ink dissolved, the effect on paper stock was equally catastrophic. The national dailies claimed to have discovered acceptable substitutes, but the public did not agree with them. India red was made of ferrous oxide, a reddish substance that came off on everything it touched and often left the text unreadable. In Sycamore River only the *Seed* retained a customer base: diehards who felt that even red news was better than none.

Against the odds the printed word struggled to survive.

Eleanor Bennett closed her office in December. No real estate was moving anyway; coming to work was only a face-saving exercise. She went in to collect her mail—there wasn't any—then checked the newspaper dispenser in front of the bank in hopes of some snippet of heartening news. She wasn't ready to go back to the apartment and make small talk with her mother.

The smeared headlines did not improve her state of mind.

### PEACE TALKS FAIL
### AMBASSADORS SENT HOME
### WAR THREATENS

*Plus ça change*, Nell said to herself, *plus c'est la même chose.*

She dumped the paper into the nearest trash can and walked the short distance to Bill's Bar and Grill in the lane behind the Williams's insurance agency. Fortunately Bill's was open. Many businesses in town had closed. Shuttered, boarded-up, deserted. It was getting hard to find a nice café or cozy coffee shop.

In normal times the wife of Robert Bennett never would have gone to a place like Bill's.

She paused at the heavy glass door, then pushed it open.

The dimly lit interior of Bill's Bar and Grill had been a welcome relief to Jack after the icy glare of the street. He usually carried a pair of aviator sunglasses with him, a habit born of necessity in the Middle East, but today he forgot them.

Getting careless, he warned himself. Better keep the old senses sharp.

The last time Jack was there the place had been almost empty. This afternoon quite a few people were at the bar or sitting in the booths. A number of changes added up to an entirely new look. Much of the illumination came from scores of strategically placed candles. The barstools were padded with folded blankets. Imitation leather upholstery in the booths had been replaced by two-seater couches and plump cushions.

Jack caught the bartender's eye. "I like your new décor, Bill."

Burdick grinned. "Y'know, I kinda like it myself. We had to replace the old fixtures because of the Change, so I said hell with it and went out and bought this stuff. Quaint is in."

A voice from one of the booths called, "Jack Reece!" Gerry Delmonico raised an arm and beckoned to him. "Come on over. We just dropped in for a hot meal; join us."

"I don't want to intrude."

"Don't be ridiculous, sit down."

They were examining the limited menu chalked on a blackboard when Gerry exclaimed, "Look who just came in! Muffin, you remember her, you met at the funeral."

Eleanor Bennett stood just inside the front door, gazing uncertainly around the room.

Jack stood up and went over to her. "Are you waiting for anybody?"

"No, I'm here by myself."

"Have a meal with us, then," he urged.

Since the disaster at RobBenn not everyone had treated Bennett's widow so warmly. She sensed hostile eyes following her on the street and tried to tell herself they were her imagination.

While Nell seated herself in the booth Jack and Gerry went to the bar to place the orders. First a round of drinks: craft beer for the men and a vodka sour for Nell, which she requested "plain, no fruit." Fruit in drinks reminded her too much of Panama City.

"Orange juice okay for you, Muffin?" Gerry asked his wife.

While the women waited for their drinks Nell said, "Your husband calls you Muffin. Mine used to call me Cookie. There must be something Freudian about that."

Gloria laughed. "It means they were both weaned too early."

The food was not fancy, but it was delicious. Marla, Burdick's sister-in-law, prepared it in the kitchen behind the dining area. At Jack's suggestion the party ordered two baskets of fried chicken with double hot chili fries. Bill added a large pitcher of ice water. "Trust me," he said. "You'll thank me later."

Nell began picking through the basket with her fork. "There aren't any wings in here."

"Buffalo wings with hot sauce?"

"No, just plain fried chicken wings."

"Who eats those?"

"I do; I learned it from my grandmother. My father's mother

came from a large family and I adored her when I was little. Nana preferred the wings because when she was growing up there were no arguments over them. She used to say, 'If you'll eat the wings or the neck you'll never leave the table hungry.' "

"When you think about it, we're all made up of bits and pieces," Gloria remarked. "Part of what makes us *us* comes from people who were gone before we were born."

"My kids aren't much like either of us," said Nell, "but they're great. I don't know what I'd do without them."

"Are you homeschooling them now? A lot of people are."

Nell shook her head. "Mine are staying in school whether they want to or not. Children need consistency and rules to make them feel secure; that's how I was raised."

Jack helped himself to a handful of fries. "Me too, but I'm a born rule breaker."

Nell said, "All rules, or just some?"

He was about to give a glib answer when her level gaze stopped him. "Only the unimportant ones," he replied. There was a discernible thread of sexual tension between them. He wondered if she could feel it; he certainly could.

Whoa, boy, Jack warned himself, don't go there. A new widow, vulnerable as hell. That's not your style.

Gloria wondered, "Who knows what the important rules are? There was a time we thought we did, but the laws of nature are breaking down."

"What are your thoughts on the Change, Gerry?" asked Nell.

He put down a well-gnawed drumstick. "Recently there's been speculation in the scientific community about a universal solvent, but I know a thing or two about containers. By its very definition no container could hold a universal solvent without being dissolved itself. It's only a myth, like the alchemist's stone that's supposed to turn lead into gold."

"I've always believed myths have a seed of truth in them."

Jack agreed with Nell. "We humans aren't clever enough to create something out of nothing." He ate a handful of fries and quickly took a drink of water. Setting down the glass, he said, "We haven't done that this time either. Any item is either a solid, liquid or gas depending on how tightly its molecules are bound together. The petrochemicals used in plastic contain hydrocarbons, which means they're composed of carbon, oxygen and hydrogen. Perhaps there's a variation on the universal solvent: a factor we don't know about. Maybe Factor X only dissolves the molecules connecting matter in hydrocarbons."

Gerry sat back and folded his arms. "That's not it."

"In theory it could be."

"No chance, Jack, for one irrefutable reason. There would have to be some almighty profit involved to incentivize developing your 'Factor X.' The Change is all about loss, not profit."

Another round of drinks and a second pitcher of ice water were ordered.

Gloria said, "If scientists all over the world aren't able to find the answer, what makes you two men think you can?"

"They're on the inside looking out," Jack replied. "We're

on the outside looking in. The view's better from here. I'm half-afraid there really isn't an answer, though. Maybe it's like a black hole. Or maybe an unknown agency is extracting hydro-carbons for a purpose we can't begin to imagine."

"An agency—you mean like the CIA?"

"No, Gloria, this would be beyond even them."

Gerry was looking more skeptical by the minute. "You think little green men from Mars are robbing us? Why? To prevent our continuing with the plans for a Martian settlement? Come on, Jack, get real."

"Did you never read Sherlock Holmes? 'When you have eliminated the impossible, whatever remains, however improb-able, must be the truth.'"

None of them admitted to wanting dessert, but when a des-sert menu was proffered all four made selections. It was the only graceful way to conclude a debate that could not be won.

While they waited, Jack swirled water rings on the tabletop with his fingertips. Watching the patterns they made. Teasing out his words before he spoke. "There's something about this . . ." he began. The others looked at him. "Something to do with the sun. . . . At one time cultures all over the world worshipped Old Sol."

"The ancients may have discovered that the sun had powers beyond light and heat," Nell interjected. "I've been reading a thought-provoking book on archaeology. We don't understand the calculations behind the construction of Newgrange in Ireland or the Great Pyramid in Egypt, but obviously the builders thought they could make the sun work for them in some way."

Jack grinned approval. "That's the kind of thinking we need! Let's explore this. In America everything changed with 9/11, but in Egypt the pivotal point was 2011. The Arab Spring was like a starter's pistol going off. The fractured tribalism that undermined the Middle East for so long came boiling to the surface. Iran's deep pockets had been funding terrorism for decades, then all at once everyone was getting into the act.

"Now the barbarians are no longer at the gates, they're sitting on top of the walls and giving the orders. And their roots—their wisdom, if you will—go back beyond the dawn of history. Let's suppose their scientists—and don't kid yourselves, they have some brilliant minds on their side—have discovered a *selective* 'universal solvent' that's activated through solar power. It's like being the only ones to have nuclear weapons. They can focus it on whatever they choose and hold the world to ransom if they want to."

"That's quite a hypothesis," said Gerry, "but I'd have to see definitive proof. I don't believe in anything that can't be verified through the five senses."

Gloria gave his arm a fond squeeze. "My husband is the original Doubting Thomas; that's what makes him so good at his job."

"Good at my former job, you mean. It ended with—" Gerry bit off the words. "I'm sorry, Nell, I didn't mean . . ."

"It's all right," she assured him. "What happened at RobBenn affected the whole town. Don't think you have to censor your words because I'm here."

"You're very brave."

"No, I'm not, I'm realistic. Talking about it hurts less than not talking about it; sort of 'the elephant in the room' syndrome. If I try to pretend it never happened I think about it all the time. Does anyone else want some of this chocolate cake?" Nell interrupted herself brightly. "It's delicious, but I don't think I can eat the whole slice. Bill's very generous with his portions, isn't he?"

Undeterred, Jack returned to the principal topic. "Remember that the rise of ISIS in 2014 caused former enemies to join forces to combat the scourge. The geopolitical map of the world was redrawn. Traditional protocols and methods of warfare were thrown out the window. The Kremlin even opened a Department of New Threats, something like the Cyber Command George Bush authorized after 9/11. I'm reminded of H. G. Wells's novel *The War of the Worlds* and the science fiction it inspired."

Gerry said, "I stopped reading science fiction when I was twelve."

"You've missed a lot, then. The best writers of speculative fiction have proved to be the prophets of a new age, miles ahead of hard science. They foresaw that mankind needed a common enemy in order to unite—and now we have one."

"Perhaps, but I'm not convinced about the uniting part. We're very much a tribal species."

Which started a new debate.

Eventually the last cup of coffee was consumed and the four prepared to leave. "It'll be getting dark soon," said Gerry. "Do either of you need a ride home?"

"Thanks," Nell replied, "but I'm living within walking distance now."

"Come on, you shouldn't pass up the chance of an inaugural ride."

Jack raised an eyebrow. "What do you mean, inaugural ride?"

"Something special's waiting at the end of the lane. Come see for yourselves."

# 17

"I think I just fell in love," said Nell Bennett.

Standing patiently in the shadows were a pair of dapple gray horses, warmly attired in red woolen blankets. They were hitched to a carriage complete with a tarpaulin cover, side curtains and headlamps fitted with candles.

The nearest horse lowered its head and gravely accepted Nell's gentle caress.

Gerry said proudly, "Allow me to introduce the River Valley Transportation Service, featuring the first two-horsepower bus in the state, powered by Jupiter and Juno. Shay Mulligan's extended the stable behind his house to give them a home, and I've built a barn for the carriage."

Nell's eyes were sparkling. "They're the most beautiful animals I've ever seen. Tell me about them, Gerry."

"Well, they're Quarter Horses, a mare and a gelding, and—"

"What's the other three quarters?" Jack interrupted.

"Quarter Horse is the name of the breed. They were developed in the Old West for racing a quarter of a mile, but they can do almost anything and they have great dispositions."

"Last year my husband didn't know a martingale from a nightingale," Gloria said. "Now he's an expert on horses."

"I'm not, but I'm learning more every day. A martingale is a piece of horse equipment; there's an interesting piece of trivia for you. My wife didn't know it either. Leaving RobBenn was the best thing that could have happened to me. I've gone into business with Shay Mulligan and it's a whole new world, a hundred times better than being cooped up in a laboratory eight hours a day breathing fumes that would poison me in the long run. In the beginning I spent several weeks walking all over town, selecting the most likely routes, but now I ride in style."

"What are you using for tires?"

"You would ask that, Jack. No tires; the wheels are iron and wood, same as they were before the discovery of rubber." Gerry put a proprietary hand on a blanket-covered flank. "Old-fashioned, the entire rig. No steering wheel, no radio, no GPS. But it works, even on asphalt."

"You don't mind the smell of horse manure?"

"At least breathing it won't harm my lungs," said Gerry, "and my wife puts the manure on her roses. She says it's the best fertilizer there is."

"Is this horse-bus idea actually going to make money?"

"I sure hope so. We're doing it by subscription. Frank Auerbach printed up advertising leaflets and I distributed them along the route, telling people they can buy a ten-ride or a thirty-ride ticket. The money's coming in already. A lot of it's in coins, but that's okay, we'll even take barter. Harriet Deane's paying two dozen eggs for a ride into town tomorrow to buy chicken feed."

Nell turned to Jack. "If you have money for the tickets I'd like to take my inaugural ride now."

In the gathering twilight Sycamore River looked peaceful. Without their wallscreens some of the townspeople were going to bed earlier. Others stayed up reading. Or talking. Discovering the pleasure of after-dinner conversation.

The *clip-clop* of hoofbeats in the street brought curious faces to windows. Jack and Nell waved.

All of the children and most of the adults waved back.

Louise Mortenson ran out with a handful of carrots for the horses. When Gerry explained the bus service she went back into the house for money to buy tickets. "I like to do my grocery shopping on Thursdays," she said. "Can I be a regular customer?"

Gloria fished a pencil and notebook out of her handbag and jotted down the information.

Meanwhile Gerry struck a match to light the headlamps. "Candles aren't really necessary," he told his passengers, "because horses can see in the dark better than we do. Gloria thinks they're a nice touch, though."

"So does Bill Burdick," said Jack, "but I wouldn't put much faith in those, if I were you. Commercial candles are made of paraffin and that's a petroleum product, so sooner or later . . . fill in the blanks. Beeswax candles would be a better option if you can find them."

"These are burning just fine."

"Now they are; many things are still working 'just fine.' But more and more are giving out on us every day, that's all I'm saying."

"Beeswax candles, huh? Where would I get those?"

"I'll look into it," promised Jack Reece.

When the carriage halted in front of the apartment building he accompanied Nell up the stairs to her door.

"I enjoyed that a lot," she said. "Would you . . ."

"Would I what?"

"Like to come in for a nightcap? Or is that too old-fashioned for words?"

"It's been an old-fashioned evening, Nell, and there is nothing I would enjoy more, but I . . . well, some other time, okay?"

Jack Reece had never turned his back on an invitation before.

He was surprised at himself.

Lila Ragland was not troubled by the problem with tires. She hitched a ride with a truck driver making deliveries from Sycamore River to Benning, and told him to leave her at the foot of Edgar Tilbury's road. The demand was not what he had expected. The trucker had been given the impression that he would be rewarded with sexual favors at the end of the trip.

When he reminded her of this she gave him a look that chilled the man to his marrow.

"I would sooner slit your throat," said Lila.

He could not open the door of the truck cab fast enough.

The red flag was up on the mailbox. Lila capriciously flipped it down before she entered the lane. The fields on either side of the fence contained nothing but grass. She might have been miles from any other human being.

She stopped long enough to run a comb through her hair and lick her lips. She did not plan to use feminine wiles on Tilbury; the gesture was automatic. No matter what façade she presented to the world she had her pride.

Pride had sustained Lila when nothing else did.

When she knocked on the front door Edgar Tilbury opened it at once.

"The bad penny's back, Edgar."

He squinted at her from beneath tangled brows. "Not a bad penny; maybe a tarnished silver dollar. I got your letter with your address, I was planning to come into town for you. You know what's been going on?"

"People are getting very tense. It's happening everywhere, I imagine. Fistfights are breaking out for no reason, even in the middle of town in the middle of the day. People expect something awful's going to happen and they're keyed up for it."

"That's a pretty accurate assessment," he affirmed. "Come on in and we'll talk. You bring anything with you? Any luggage?"

"I've only got my essentials in my handbag, I didn't expect to stay. I just wanted to see if we could do anything with my AllCom."

"There's an old Chinese saying, Lila: Save someone's life and you're obligated to care for them forever."

"You didn't save my life," she pointed out. "I dragged myself out of the river."

"The money you took was a lifesaver at the time, wasn't it?"

"Point taken."

"Well, you're here now. Maybe you'd like to see the extension I told you about. Come on out with me."

He led the way to the barn on the edge of the hill. The size of the building was out of proportion to the house. It was more like the huge barns common to New England or Pennsylvania Dutch country. Tilbury did not slide open the heavy main door that accommodated carriages and hay trucks, but opened the small one to the side. A rush of chilly air welcomed them when they went in.

"You know much about the First World War?" he asked.

"Only what they taught us in school."

"You learn the really important things on your own, Lila, but you already know that. What I'm about to show you was taken from the plans of the world's leading authorities on building underground. During that war the Germans constructed an elaborate system of tunnels below the surface while the allied forces were floundering around in flooded trenches aboveground. The German troops had more than safety; they had comfort. Light, heat, ventilation, sanitation and good food. I spent months studying the blueprints the Allies discovered after the war. The Great War. The War to End All Wars. Ha!

"That war's principal contribution to mankind wasn't peace, it was military mechanization on a grand scale. And the genius of the tunnels. I can't find fault with mechanization because it made it possible for me to build my own version of them; never could have done it with a pick and shovel. Not that I needed muscle power; everything was purchased, even the silence of the contractors. You said it yourself; people will let you do anything if you have enough money. I was grieving and I was lonely and I wanted something to keep me occupied. Not just building carriages, but a real *big* project."

Lila gazed at the hay-strewn floor of the barn. "Do you mean that's *here*? Is this your 'hole in the ground'?"

"No place better. Who's going to suspect anything underneath this barn? Originally my tunnels were fitted out with their own power system and two large generators, but the Change is playing havoc with so much, I don't trust them. The German tunnel builders allowed for every contingency and I'm going to do what they did: provide myself with alternate sources of light and heat."

"You're amazing."

"What I am is too old to be taken in by flattery. I'm not amazing, I just use my head. When I was looking for land to buy I learned this acreage has an unusually deep artesian well, and that decided me. The water tests almost one hundred percent pure. The tunnel nearest the house goes straight to the well, so fresh water is available all the time. The most distant tunnel has little chambers based on the 'sleeping pods' in Japanese hotels, and eventually leads to the garderobe."

"Which is?"

"Was. The toilet in a medieval castle. They worked on gravity, one natural law you can't break. Behind the barn the land falls away sharply before rising to the next hill. The toilet is positioned over a slanting hole that empties into a fast-flowing stream between the two hills. The whole setup's too far away to pollute my well or any of my neighbors'."

"Very clever, if not original."

"You want original? I've adapted the ventilation system prairie dogs use in the Nevada desert. Outside the barn are aboveground apertures concealed in dead trees, behind bushes and so forth. They're set at different heights so fresh air blowing over the higher ones forces stale air out of the lower ones."

"I'm a survivor and I've heard of survivalists, but you're the real thing, Edgar. Aren't you afraid I might give away your secret?"

He picked up a wisp of hay from the floor and tucked it in the corner of his mouth. "You want to know the most important difference between dogs and cats? Dogs are pack animals, they do what their leader does. Most cats act in their own self-interest, which is why they'll still be around when this is over—if it ever is. I think you're part cat, Lila.

"Since the Change struck it's obvious to me that we're in an apocalyptic scenario. Mankind's been teetering on the edge of another global war for years, revving up for it like lemmings getting ready to jump off a cliff. Now they have their excuse to go crazy. If you don't want to go with them, your best bet is to stick with me."

"Are you serious?"

"I am."

"Why me?"

"I've been asking myself the same question and I don't have an answer. Maybe I see something of me in you. Maybe I just don't want to die alone."

"Like I almost did in the river," she said in a whisper.

"Something like that, yeah."

At his request she helped him transfer some supplies from the house to the tunnels and store them away. "Might as well do it now," he said, "since I have help. I do have help, don't I?"

"It looks like it. What you said about global war, Edgar— do you think it's imminent?"

"I doubt it. We've got enough nuclear bombs and intercontinental missiles to blast us all to eternity, but—and the defense department will never admit this—the Change is destroying vital parts needed to operate them. It's bound to be happening in other countries too."

"I never thought I'd be glad for the Change."

"It's only a temporary reprieve, Lila; that's why we're putting this stuff in the tunnels. Sooner or later the munitions manufacturers will come up with satisfactory substitutes. They have too much at stake not to. Then . . . boom."

After lunch they started in on Tilbury's books. The printing in some was showing the results of the Change, with smeared ink and damp pages, but the older ones were still good.

"What do you like to read, Lila?"

"Almost everything; I told you, I'm self-educated."

"You're an autodidact. Some of the world's most successful people have been autodidacts."

"Don't include me in that. The only real success I've had was with the computer and that's not worth much anymore." Lila thrust her lower lip forward and blew a coppery strand out of her eyes. She was letting her hair grow.

Tilbury said, "You never can tell, it might be valuable again someday."

"This from a man who's prophesying the end of the world and equipping a giant fallout shelter?"

"I'm hedging my bets, that's all."

Her green eyes filled with shadows. "You're betting against all of humanity."

At his direction she began stacking up books she had never read but thought she might like to read. Every now and then he would add one to the pile. "*Swiss Family Robinson*?" she queried. "This looks old."

"It is, I know it belonged to my grandfather when he was a boy. It's about a family who had to start over and build a life out of nothing. On an uninhabited island, as I recall."

"You definitely want to keep this one close to hand, Edgar. Survival guide."

"Don't worry, I have plenty. Wait until you read *Five Acres and Independence*."

A few minutes later Lila said, "Surely we're not going to need all of those," indicating the thirty-three volumes of the *Encyclopedia Britannica* he was pulling from the bookshelves.

"No way of knowing when I might need to refer to them."

"Can't you download the information from the . . . Oops."

"Yup. Oops. The same with the complete works of Shakespeare. Let's get these big sets into cartons for safekeeping below."

They were both aware that "safekeeping below" was a tenuous concept. So far nothing in the tunnels had been affected by the Change, though Tilbury could not explain why.

Over dinner Lila asked him, "How many guests can you accommodate in your hotel down there?"

"Hotel; that's a good one. Bolt-hole, more like. Covers a lot of territory, but the resources are pretty limited."

"How many people?"

"You and me."

"We're not Adam and Eve."

"Certainly not, and I'm not a dirty old man. I thought we'd invite somebody nearer your own age."

Lila put down her cutlery and pushed her plate away.

"What's wrong?" he asked anxiously.

"Nothing, I'm just not hungry anymore."

"Why not? You coming down with something?"

"An advance case of survival guilt, maybe. When you told me about the tunnels and your plans for them it sounded like a fairy tale. Like when I first started amassing money. But now I'm taking a look at reality. This is reality, isn't it? You propose to rescue a very few people in your own version of the ark while God knows what goes on in the rest of the world?"

He frowned. "I wouldn't put it like that."

"I'm putting it exactly like that. And I can't be part of it, Edgar."

"If that's true you're not the girl I thought you were."

Lila stood up and pushed her chair away from the table. "I'm not the girl I thought I was either."

# 18

According to the local phone books—which had been superseded by computer search engines that had since surrendered to the Change—there were no beekeepers in the Sycamore River Valley and no commercial suppliers of honey. But a label on an almost empty jar at the back of the shelf in his aunt's kitchen had given Jack a clue: "Privately Labeled for Benning Beekeepers Suppliers."

When he drove to the neighboring town of Benning he learned the suppliers had been out of business for several years. "Everything comes through commercial distributors now, or it did," the former proprietor lamented. "As I recall, the last guy I dealt with on a personal basis was an old grump with rural pretensions. We used to get them every now and then, starry-eyed dreamers who wanted to go back to nature and make their own honey, grow their own vegetables. Damned fools who thought they were too good to eat supermarket food like the rest of us."

Jack could have pointed out that the quality and availability of supermarket food had declined drastically, but he didn't. "Do you happen to remember where the old grump lived?"

Following the directions he was given, he drove almost back to Sycamore River before turning north onto a gravel road.

He saw only a few small farms on a distant hillside. When he came to an unpaved lane identified by a rural mailbox atop a leaning post, he stopped the Mustang and got out. Looked around. Saw nothing of interest.

Whoever lived in this godforsaken spot probably died in his bed and had to be scraped off it.

Jack was unable to abandon a search without a conclusion. He got back into the car, put it in gear and jolted along the rutted laneway. At a bend in the lane he slammed on the brakes.

The woman walking toward him was carrying a large black cat in her arms.

He lowered the window. "Lila Ragland?" he called incredulously.

"Jack Reece," she responded. "How are you?"

"Flabbergasted to see you out here. Is this where you live?"

"A friend of mine does. I come to read his books."

"You bring your cat to the library?" Jack was trying to find a pattern in unrelated shreds of information.

"She's not my cat, she's a stray who wandered in here. I named her Karma; do you like it?" The long-haired black cat in Lila's arms lifted her head and fixed Jack with blue-green eyes. "Edgar can't keep her because he's allergic to cats."

"Edgar? Edgar Tilbury?"

"That's right, do you know him?"

"I'd like to," said Jack. "I'm looking for someone who can supply beeswax; I'm in the market for all I can get."

"Then he's your man; he has a field full of hives on the other side of the barn. Come to the house and you can talk to him about it. Do I tell him you're a wholesaler?"

Jack raised an eyebrow. "What do I look like?"

She regarded him thoughtfully. "A pirate."


"I *can't* put my life together again, Mom!" Eleanor Bennett insisted. "Stop telling me to. It's never going to be the way it was and . . . and I wouldn't want it to be. But if you're tired of having us living with you, just say so."

Katharine Richmond looked offended. "I didn't mean that, dear, you know I love having you here. All of you. I only meant it's not healthy for you to keep on mourning Robert."

"Is that what you think I'm doing?"

"Well, of course you are. In a way I'm still mourning your dad after all this time. But life goes on."

Nell was exasperated. "Haven't you noticed? Life isn't 'going on,' it's completely changed. The whole damned world's changed."

"There's no need to swear."

"There's no need for clichés either." Nell folded her arms across her chest. "Maybe we should start looking for a place of our own. Finbar feels certain the Nyeberger lawsuit will be hung up indefinitely, perhaps forever, so there's no reason I shouldn't access whatever funds I can."

"Now, dear, don't do anything drastic."

"What's happened to us has been drastic." Nell knew there

was no point in arguing with her mother, or even trying to explain. They lived in different realities. She went to the bedroom and began organizing her belongings.

Finding another home for herself and the children would not be easy. Rental property was scarce on the south side, which was solid homeowner territory. As Nell knew all too well the real estate business was moribund. In a time of such uncertainty people preferred to sit tight.

There was always the other side of the river, but Nell never considered it. She was not a snob, but she was a native southsider. She had never carried northside properties on her books. Without putting words to the thought, she knew where she belonged.

Until the Change.

When she tried sounding out her son and daughter about moving into another school district, they reacted as if she were suggesting going to Borneo. "Aren't things bad enough?" Jessamyn wailed. "You want me to go to school with slutty girls who wear black nail polish?"

"Don't be ridiculous, Jess. No one wears nail polish now because the polymers—"

"*I* know *that*. I was just using it as an *example*."

At the veterinary clinic the oldest AllCom was still working, though not reliably. When Paige answered it a fuzzy image came up on the screen. "This is Eleanor Bennett," said an equally fuzzy voice.

"Mrs. Bennett! What can we do for you? Is one of the dogs—"

"No, the setters are all right, and I want to thank you for rehoming Satan. When our housekeeper said she didn't have enough room for him I was worried. Did he get a good home?"

"I took him myself," said Paige. "I live alone and he's my security blanket. I've renamed him Samson—I hope you don't mind—and we're great pals already. He sleeps at the foot of my bed. Did you know he snores?"

"You don't happen to need two more, do you?" Nell inquired.

When Shay entered the clinic Paige told him about Nell's call. "She wants to move out of her mother's apartment and it's hard to find a place for the two setters. I told her we could board them here for a while, just until she gets settled. Was that all right?"

"We really don't have boarding facilities for dogs," said Shay. Then he grinned. "But for Nell Bennett, sure."

"What do you have for cats?" a voice asked.

Lila Ragland stood in the doorway of the clinic. Behind her was Jack Reece, carrying a large wicker hamper. From within the hamper came a scratching noise.

When Paige Prentiss saw Jack she lifted her chin and tucked in her tummy.

Lila told Shay, "We've come to solve your pet shortage."

It took him a moment to recall their last conversation. "I'm in and out all the time," he said, disconcerted. "It wouldn't be fair to a dog."

"This isn't a dog," Lila said, "this is Karma." Reaching into the hamper, she lifted out a big black cat and put her in Shay's arms.

"What am I supposed to do with a cat?"

"Love her and feed her and keep her safe; she's a precious gift. You aren't one of those tiresome people who return gifts, are you?"

"No, I'm not one of those people." He shifted his arms to snuggle the cat against his chest. Karma began to purr; a deep rhythmic buzz that made her whole body vibrate.

Shay grinned with pleasure. "Is this thing going to go off?"

"Not unless you've pulled the pin," Lila retorted.

Watching the byplay between them, Paige said stiffly, "I don't think jokes about bombs are very funny."

Shay gestured toward the wicker hamper. "Where'd you get that? Our customers are asking for something to replace plastic pet crates."

"I found this in Edgar Tilbury's barn," Lila told him. "I believe he's done some work for you, a cart and a carriage? He never throws anything away, so why don't you come and see what he has out there?"

Shay looked down into the triangular face turned up toward his. The aquamarine eyes were preternaturally wise. "Karma," he said softly.

Nell Bennett was pleased about Satan's—Samson's—new home. If only all changes could be so easy. Her mother, whom she had expected to remain sympathetic, had chosen instead to play the martyr. Nell was dusting the living room when Katharine came up behind her to complain, "If you move out, how am I going to get around? I'm not as young as I used to be and I have all those doctors' appointments. With my arthritis you can't expect me to climb into a horse-drawn carriage."

Nell put the dustcloth down on the end table. "There's no guarantee my car will keep running. The GPS doesn't work anymore and the steering wheel is starting to—"

"I'm not interested in your steering wheel, dear; I'm talking about safety. My safety. At my age it's best not to live alone."

Nell was amused. Her mother had always been fiercely independent. "You're not that old, Mom, and you're as spry as a cricket. Yesterday you were up on the stepladder cleaning out the kitchen cabinets."

"Suppose I fall and nobody's here?"

"Suppose I hire a live-in companion for you," Nell countered. "Someone with a car, if possible."

"I already have companions. I have you and the children."

Nell had a sudden depressing vision of the future her mother anticipated. The young widow would remain with the older widow; constricted lives revolving around housewifely chores and repetitive chitchat; grocery shopping the high point of their week. Colin and Jess would grow up and embark on lives of their own while two doddering old dears in lockstep waited for the grave.

The arrangement of her mother's living room had not

changed in years. She knew every detail. The row of pottery ducks on the mantel, a souvenir from her parents' honeymoon in Mexico. The photograph of her father as a young man in his military uniform, immortalized in a silver frame. The symmetrical arrangement of floral watercolors above the sofa.

If she took the pictures down from the wall discolored squares would remain on the wallpaper.

Nell felt something snap inside herself. Actually felt it snap, like the last straw breaking. "I can't please everybody all the time," she announced abruptly. "Maybe I can't please anybody anytime. But I have a lot of unlived life ahead of me, and if I'm going to enjoy it, I'll have to leave my comfort zone."

Before her startled mother could respond they heard the sound of sirens. The two women exchanged alarmed glances. Katharine put one hand over her mouth while Nell ran outside.

The man who lived in the apartment next door was hanging over the balcony, looking down the street. "I heard gunshots and no mistake. A rifle, I think. It's somewhere in town, but I don't know where. Go back inside, Nell, it may not be safe out here."

Other people were crowding onto the balcony. A middle-aged woman with an elderly AllCom pressed to the side of her head reported, "I'm talking to my son-in-law. There was a shooting right in front of Goettinger's. He saw it all. A man was walking up the street with a rifle on his shoulder and this woman came out of the store and he shot her. For no reason! He just shot her!"

Eleanor Bennett felt as if her blood were congealing.


Sheriff Tyler Whittaker had been interrupted during his afternoon coffee break, which consisted of something more substantial in the home of a young woman named Lynnda Gibbs. He was not in a good mood by the time he reached Goettinger's. What he found there did not improve his humor.

There was no automobile traffic on the street, but pedestrians were huddled at a distance from the department store, gawking.

Patricia Staunton Nyeberger lay face down on the sidewalk in front of the store. From inside terrified customers gazed out at her through the revolving doors. Her arms were outflung, one hand sparkling with rings still clutched a validated ticket for the store parking lot. Blood and blobs of brain matter were sprayed across the cement. A puddle of urine was seeping out between her sprawled legs.

There had been no time for her bowels to evacuate.

The top of her head had been blown off.

Whittaker regretted the chocolate cake he had eaten at Lynnda's.

In the service alley beside the department store was a man wearing a khaki jacket and cargo pants. He was holding a rifle. "They ought to pin a medal on me!" he shouted, drawing the sheriff's attention. "You hear me? They ought to pin a medal. She was passing our military secrets to the enemy, but I stopped her. Didn't I stop her? Didn't I? They ought to pin a medal!" For emphasis he raised the rifle and fired again.

The pedestrians screamed and scattered.

By evening the entire town knew what had happened without benefit of any form of electronic communication. The unidentified shooter was in jail, Tricia Nyeberger's body was at Staunton Memorial awaiting postmortem and Sheriff Whittaker had performed the unenviable task of informing both her husband and her father. Old Man Staunton had taken the news with apparent stoicism. His son-in-law had gone in search of a weapon of his own, vowing to "restore justice." Sheriff Whittaker interpreted this as a threat to enact vigilante law and sought a restraining order against Dwayne Nyeberger. From a civil court that had grown increasingly dysfunctional.

Staunton went to Bea Fontaine.

He found her at home, waiting for Jack to come back. When the news about the murder at Goettinger's spread through town he had gone in search of more information, leaving his aunt to worry.

"Miz Bea?" said the stooped figure standing on her porch in the twilight. "Can I come in? I've got a favor to ask."

She gave him a stiff brandy and her sympathy. "I can't imagine what you must be going through, Oliver."

"I can't imagine it either. There are pictures in my head . . . you know I had to identify her body?"

"Don't think about it."

"I'll never think about anything else. But I have to, for the sake of—"

"Your grandsons, of course! Do they know yet?"

"Unh-unh, they're still recuperating and we don't know how this will affect them. Right now my housekeeper's with them at their house, but that's not going to work out. If and when Dwayne shows up he'll do what he always does, order Haydon around like she's his slave. I need her in *my* house, damn it. Besides, she doesn't even like children. I'll have to find another solution, one that cuts Dwayne out of the picture and won't involve making them wards of the court."

He fixed his eyes on Bea's. "You know I can't take on five rambunctious boys, Miz Bea; the bank takes all my energy. You raised your nephew and did a damned good job, would you consider . . ."

She had seen this coming. She held out her hands, palms facing him, and shook her head. "I'm too old to cope with five little boys, Oliver. Don't you have any relatives?"

"A couple of cousins in New Mexico and a few others in Canada; distant cousins, we've never even met. That's how America is these days. The way things are, I can't send my grandchildren hundreds of miles away to strangers."

His lower lip was trembling.

# 19

Shay called from the back door of the vet clinic, "Hold this open for me, will you!"

Paige hurried to help. "What are you going to do with those boards?"

"They aren't boards, they're planks. And two-by-fours and . . . never mind, help me get them inside. We're going to start boarding up our windows."

"Do you really think we need to?"

"We keep drugs in here, Paige, but more than that, there are kooks in town who are beginning to go off the rails. I got these supplies from the lumberyard and brought them back in Evan's cart. A lot of people are starting to buy timber."

As Paige watched him carry an armload of two-by-fours inside, she said, "I think I'll keep Samson with me all the time from now on."


Bill Burdick was not boarding up anything. Bill's Bar and Grill remained defiantly in business, though Bill was keeping a couple of guns under the bar.

Business was brisk. The usual regulars were always present,

their number increasingly augmented by others in search of sanctuary.

"The good old days were good," Hooper Watson intoned, "because folks didn't know how bad they were. They lived their lives and just got on with it . . ."

"Listen to the philosopher of Bill's Bar and Grill," said Morris Saddlethwaite.

Watson in full flow was not to be interrupted. ". . . and just got on with it. They didn't know where the Ukraine was or what was happening in Korea and they didn't want to know, nothin' to do with them. Then along came the internet and instant communication and we were run over with information. Knocked down flat in the street and run over."

"Don't be such a Luddite," said Bill Burdick.

"A wha' ?"

"Someone who hates technology."

"I don't hate it," Watson rejoined, "I'm as modern as you are. But I've seen the damage it can do. My wife, Nadine, just went on a shopping spree on the internet and ran up bills I'll never be able to pay off. Then she took off with some salesman she'd met on social media and left all her debts in my lap."

"Has she come back yet?"

"Naah, why'd you think I'm in here drinking in the afternoon? Speaking of drinking, how long has it been since you refilled this glass?"

"Your daughter was in here only yesterday asking me not to

let you get loop-legged again. Angela's a good girl, Hoop, she's trying to look after you."

"She should mind her own business."

There were days when Watson irritated Bill Burdick. A man behind a bar should be sympathetic, but he might also have his own problems and be sick to the back teeth with hearing about someone else's. "She doesn't have much business to mind since you scared her boyfriend away," he told Watson.

"I didn't do that! Sunnavabitch is a two-timing liar and she caught on to him, that's all. If he ever comes around her again I'll put a bomb down his britches."

"Plastic explosive, maybe?" Burdick asked sarcastically.

"You know what I mean."

"I know that kind of talk is dangerous, Hoop. People are hair-trigger enough as it is. The town's been hemorrhaging jobs since the Change began, and now people are taking the law into their own hands. They say the Nyeberger murder proves we don't have enough law enforcement."

"That's the bloody truth," a customer interjected. "Hey, Jack!" he called to a man who was just entering. "You think we got enough law in this town?"

Jack Reece sat down at the bar and nodded a greeting to Burdick. "Is this an argument I should get into, Bill?" he asked in a low voice.

"It's harmless, they're just blowing off steam." Burdick cast a glance around the room. "With the exception of you and me there's not a person in here who still gets a salary, thanks to the Change."

"I work for myself," said Jack. "Which reminds me—I've taken on another sideline."

"In addition to tires, you mean?"

"Premium-quality tires are gone anyway, but this is one you'll appreciate. Beeswax candles. You're using candles in here already; let me put you on my list."

Burdick chuckled. "You have a finger in every pie, don't you?"

"Just the ones that are likely to remain profitable. Banking and IT are seriously crippled and so is retailing. About the only business with a future is war."

"That's a grim thought."

"But a realistic one, Bill. War's been the biggest business on earth since the Middle Ages, and big business has to be preserved by whatever means possible. It's in our genes."

The man who had mentioned law enforcement only overheard a portion of this conversation, but he agreed enthusiastically. "I've got plenty of guns!"

Jack ordered a double.

He had spent much of his adult life on the fringes of the military/industrial behemoth that spanned continents. By now he knew his abilities and limitations. He accepted that he would never rise to the top, lazing in a luxurious retreat on a private island while he pulled invisible strings. That would not suit his disposition. He preferred being in the heart of the action.

In the past if a payout was sufficiently lavish he had used it to take a chunk of his retirement, indulging himself while he was still young enough and healthy. Or sitting on his aunt's front porch with his feet propped on the railing, watching the world go by until restlessness seized him again.

Being a small-town entrepreneur was not what he had envisioned as a lifetime career.

Lifetime . . .

Jack set down his glass.

For a supposedly smart man you've been a damned fool, he told himself. You never really thought about how you'd spend the rest of your life. What a bloody jackass. You assumed you'd always be young and the world would be the same forever.

Until Nell Bennett came along. That gentle woman who just might complete the riddle of me.

At a time when it looks like all hell's going to break loose.

Bea Fontaine had not discussed Oliver Staunton's proposal with her nephew. She knew what he would say, and he would be right. Chaos was lurking on the horizon; it would be ridiculous to add five unmanageable children to their household. For once she was thankful for Jack's basic selfishness. He would not let her take them even if she wanted to.

Which was a good thing. What those boys might do to her cats didn't bear thinking about.

Yet while she was cooking supper she did think about it. And about five children, all of them still suffering from injuries both physical and emotional, who now had no responsible parent. Waiting for someone to decide their future.

Gerry and Gloria Delmonico wanted to keep the world at arm's length, but it was no longer possible. Gloria was on leave from the hospital, but she could not just sit at home and worry about her unborn baby. She rode with Gerry in the new carriage, which meant that the paying passengers were able to give her all the news she did not want to know.

She was waiting.

They were all waiting. For an event, an enemy, a nightmare. Something they could feel in the atmosphere but not see.

Evan Mulligan was worried about Rocket. "She's off her feed, Dad. I've given her oats and bran mash and alfalfa . . ."

"Alfalfa's too rich for a mare in foal, I've told you that."

"But she has to eat! What d'you think's wrong with her?"

"Animals are more sensitive than we are, Evan. Even that Rottweiler of Paige's is refusing his food; not all of it, but some. Don't worry about Rocket, I'll give her a feed supplement tonight and an appetite stimulant. She's going to be a mother and she has good instincts; she won't let her foal starve."

While Lila Ragland lay on the narrow bed in the Spartan chamber Edgar Tilbury called his "guest quarters," she ran a parade of favorite scenes across the screen of her mind. It was her favorite way of unwinding and courting sleep. Trees in a Swedish park, black against a startlingly bright sky. Sipping a mug of hot chocolate on the topmost platform of the Mont Blanc ski lift. A marble sculpture in the Musée d'Orsay, depicting the nature god Pan as a little boy playing with two bear cubs.

The next image came unbidden. Shay Mulligan cradling a black cat.

Since the afternoon when Jack and Nell met the Delmonicos there, Bill's Bar and Grill had become their frequent meeting place. All over town people were forming little groups, tribes composed of friends rather than relatives. Bill's exercised a magnetic attraction and not just for Hooper Watson and Morris Saddlethwaite. The central location combined with good food and a relaxed, convivial atmosphere encouraged other patrons to linger.

As Bill remarked to his sister-in-law, "Funny thing, Marla; people don't seem to be in as much of a hurry as they used to be."

"But you want me to hurry up with that last order, right?"

"Right," he affirmed.

When Shay Mulligan brought Lila Ragland to join the band of regulars, Hooper Watson glowered fiercely at him. Unabashed, the younger man gave him a cheery wave. "Hi, Hoop! How ya doin'?"

Under his breath Watson muttered to Morris Saddlethwaite, "Not gonna let him drive me outta my place." He spent the entire evening firmly planted on his stool, like a frog on a log.

When the regulars ordered a round of drinks Shay made a point of having one sent to "Sheriff Watson."

That set the pattern for subsequent occasions.

The group discussed regular meetings. Perhaps on a Wednesday. "I go to my office every Wednesday morning to check my mail," Nell said, "but I wonder why I bother. No one's making any offers on property; almost the only letters I get are from people trying to sell theirs, and I can't help them. It would be easier to visit the office in the afternoon and then drop by here for an early supper. Jess and Colin want fish fingers or hamburgers and my mother fixes those for them."

"I thought you were planning to move," said Shay.

Her expression was rueful. "I am; I just don't know where. Much good it does me to be in real estate."

"I can make this the regular stop for my supper break," Gerry decided. "Now that we have Danielle I can pick up Gloria and the baby and bring them too . . . if Bill's not averse to one of his customers breast-feeding."

Bill Burdick responded with a thumbs-up. "Only if you'll let me be her godfather."

The group took a proprietary interest in the newest Delmonico. Gerry enjoyed boasting, "She's the first baby in Sycamore

River to be born in a pony and trap; the hospital's only working ambulance was on another call. Young Evan Mulligan
helped with the delivery. That boy has a great future as an ob-
stetrician ahead of him," he added with a chuckle.

Among Rob's effects at home Nell had found a very early
AllCom that still worked. Battered and grimy, it had been in
the bottom of Colin's sock drawer. Gerry Delmonico had another reclaimed from a locker at RobBenn; Shay's son had a
third he had been given on his tenth birthday. Joined with the
AllCom at the vet clinic they formed a sketchy network not to
be trusted, but better than nothing.

On the strength of his AllCom and his assistance with
Danielle's birth, Evan Mulligan was invited to join the group.

And Lila invited Edgar Tilbury.

"Those youngsters won't want an old fart around," he
told her.

"You're the most interesting man I know, and they talk about
things that would interest you. Don't be a hermit, Edgar."

"I'm not a hermit," he said indignantly. And accompanied
her to the next meeting.

The Wednesday Club commandeered the largest booth and
augmented it with a table pushed against the end. If he was not
busy Bill himself was invited to sit in. He enjoyed the conversation and often had something to contribute.

Watson and Saddlethwaite retained their familiar stools,
but made no secret of the fact that they were listening too.
What was happening in Bill's was more interesting and more

entertaining than anywhere else. When it was time to buy a round of drinks the two men began to chip in, which entitled them to call out, "Say what?" if they missed something.

Conversation was the glue in the Wednesday Club.

One evening Shay said, "Thanks to the Change we know less and less about what's happening abroad, it's like the expanding universe after the Big Bang. Other countries are becoming distant galaxies."

"But we know more about what's going on in Sycamore River," Gloria interjected. "The *Seed* is down to only two pages a week, but the paper has more subscribers than ever; I know because we deliver a lot of them. We're taking more interest in our neighbors because they've become our world."

"Which is no bad thing," said Lila. "People were almost surgically attached to their electronic communicators. I'll bet whole families went to bed without ever speaking to each other."

"I liked it better when the wife didn't speak to me," Saddlethwaite volunteered. "Long as she was busy with her social network she wasn't finding jobs around the house for me. Being retired is hell on a man. But tell me, Jack: What did you mean about an expanding universe? I never heard of that. Are we blowing up?"

On another evening Edgar Tilbury asked, "Has anyone considered the Change may be natural?"

"What do you mean by 'natural'?" Bill inquired.

Tilbury cleared his throat. "The discoveries of Darwin, Mengel, and Watson and Crick have demonstrated that all life on Earth is connected and is subject to natural law. And natural law is determined by nature."

"The Change can't be natural, Edgar. Someone's behind it, everybody knows that."

The older man gave a lopsided smile. "Don't believe anything everybody knows."

Gloria, with her sleeping baby cradled in her lap, asked, "Don't you think there's something rather hesitant about it?"

"What do you mean?"

"Well . . . when I'm introducing new things into my garden I try them out first to see if the site and the soil agree with them. If I'm doing a bedding arrangement I start seeds in several different places and watch how they grow before I commit to a mass planting. With expensive shrubs I put them in pots and move them around until I find a location where they thrive. The Change is like that. It's as if somebody's trying ideas out, not destroying everything at once."

Jack raised an eyebrow. "What have you been drinking? That's like saying a tornado can choose what town to strike."

"How do you know it can't?" asked Hooper Watson. "When I was a kid we lived in the Midwest, that region they call Tornado Alley, and I can tell you there's something fiendish about those storms. One can turn a man's entire house into splinters but leave the front porch untouched with the swing still swinging and the cushions on it. I've seen it myself. It's like the damned wind's laughing at flesh-and-blood people."

# 20

The article in *The Sycamore Seed* occupied the entire front page:

## BREAKTHROUGH!

"Last week a team of microbiologists in Sweden announced a major discovery that could lead to a Nobel Prize. They claim that a hitherto unknown life-form, a bacteria so minute its existence has been undetected until now, could be the cause behind the Change. Its near relative, saprophytic bacteria, performs an ecologically indispensible role in the breakdown of organic wastes."

The Wednesday Club had their topic for the evening.

Jack was elated. "I had a hunch the sun had something to do with the Change, and here's proof. Bacteria use photosynthesis to generate energy."

"Whoa there!" cautioned Gerry. "Only some bacteria do. They're called phototrophs and they're totally different from saprophytes. The bacteria kingdom's divided into groups; any one of them's a specialized field of study."

"Why hasn't this new bacteria been discovered before now?" Nell wanted to know.

"Maybe it's like black holes," said Evan, proud to have something to contribute. "We studied those in school last year. They were only detected when their effects were noticed."

Gerry looked thoughtful. "By God, Jack, I know I laughed at the time, but maybe you weren't far off the mark when you talked about an unknown factor dissolving the molecules in hydrocarbons."

"An amateur's guess," Jack said. "But if the Swedes are right about this it means someone's developed a chemical super-weapon. The next question is, who's behind it? Every country seems to be targeted. Are we talking about a mad scientist with a grudge against the whole human race?"

Nell laughed. "You've been reading too many comic books."

"No, I'm serious. What do you think the atom bomb was to begin with? A mad scientist's dream. We'll need to find a poison that will kill the bacteria, then develop a way to administer it."

"Like spraying antibiotics over the entire globe?"

"The cure would be worse than the disease," Shay said grimly. "Remember DDT? It wiped out a whole slew of species."

The Wednesday Club ordered another round of drinks. Strong ones for everybody but Evan. Who took a gulp of his father's when no one was looking.

———

With people unimpressed by the Swedish discovery, wars large and small continued to expand or erupted afresh, among nations and allies and strangers. Anger was bubbling to the surface everywhere. The weapons employed were changing too, becoming less technical but no less lethal. Plastic-free equivalents of earlier weapons of mass destruction were being designed and rushed into production. So were the many weapons that had marked mankind's climb up the evolutionary ladder.

Jack Reece was more disturbed by the Change than he wanted to admit, even to himself. Disturbed by the change *in* himself. From being a freewheeling risk-taker he had become cautious, like a man who had something valuable to protect. Yet in spite of the chaotic global situation nothing had changed in his own life, except . . .

After a determined search he located two simple pagers, one for himself and one for Nell, and asked her to keep hers with her at all times. Being much less complicated than AllComs, pagers were not failing as frequently. Yet.

Jack hated that word "yet." The implications behind it were profound. Nothing was certain, nothing was permanent, the most felicitously arranged life would end.

His.

Nell Bennett's.

And there was nothing he could do about it.

———

"Aunt Bea, do you believe in God?"

Bea Fontaine was barely inside the front door after yet another difficult day at the bank. The First Federal in the new shopping center had cut its staff to the bone and was only open on two mornings a week. She suspected O. M. Staunton was planning a similar arrangement. Thank God for the weekend; at least she'd have time to brace herself.

She paused long enough to take off her coat while she digested Jack's unexpected question. "I suppose I do," she told him. "I still go to church sometimes—and I took you to Sunday school when you were little, in case you've forgotten." When she opened the closet door to put her coat away a tangle of wire hangers clattered to the floor. Jack always was careless about hanging up clothes.

Bea let them lie there.

"You go to church at Christmas and I don't go at all," Jack said. "That's not what I'm asking. Do you believe in God? God, heaven, an afterlife . . ."

"What brought this up?"

"The international situation's ominous, Aunt Bea. There's going to be another world war in the near future and America won't be safe, not this time. We'll be in the front line and a lot of people are going to die. I want to know if there's a heaven they can go to."

"What a cheerful greeting! I'd have preferred a cup of hot coffee."

"I'll fix one for you if you'll answer my question."

In the living room they sat side by side on the couch, facing the dead wallscreen. After Bea had drained her cup she gave a deep sigh. "I needed that."

"And my question?"

"Well. Yes." She set down the cup and turned to face him. "Here goes. Humans have grappled with the idea of God, or gods, for thousands of years. It appears we're hardwired to have faith in *something*, but in the end people believe what they want to believe. They worship God or sorcery or sports stars . . . to our shame, anything will serve. Perhaps having faith is more important than what we have faith in. The journey rather than the destination. I must say I never expected to have this conversation with you, Jack. You've always seemed so sure."

"That's down to you," he acknowledged. "You gave me such a solid grounding nothing could shake my confidence. But now . . ." He hesitated, reluctant to make a revelation about his private feelings.

She took off her glasses to study his face at close range. "You're scared, is that it?"

He was grateful to her for making it easier. "I guess I am, but not for myself." The old grin flickered but did not hold. "Well, maybe a little for myself. I have this sense of"—he struggled to find the right word—"of foreboding."

"Because of the Change? We're not plastic, we're not going to melt."

"This isn't about the Change, Aunt Bea. It's like when you

go into a dark room and you're aware of danger before you turn on a light. That's what I'm feeling now. Intuition's always been my stock-in-trade; if a deal's going to go sour I usually know ahead of time. I can't tell you how often that's saved my neck. It's my only real talent, but it's a good one."

"You're lucky, the rest of us have to rely on hindsight," she said drily. "From the direction of this conversation I guess you're worried about a special person?"

"Perhaps."

Bea's face lit up. "Does she feel the same about you?"

"I didn't say it was a woman."

"Don't tease me, I know you too well. You've been chasing girls since middle school."

"Since before that, Aunt Bea."

"And this one is serious?"

"When I'm certain I'll tell you."

The light went out of Bea's face. "That's the problem: Nothing's certain anymore."


At the next meeting of the Wednesday Club Jack announced, "I've been doing a little experimenting around the house and found some materials that can replace plastic. Cork is a good one. Leather's another. And when our high-perf tires wear out we'll have natural rubber too."

Marla Burdick spoke up from behind the bar, where she was stacking clean glasses. "Wool might work if it's thickly packed."

"How about felt?" Morris Saddlethwaite asked unexpectedly.

"I went back to RobBenn and did a little scavenging in the ruins of the laboratory before the bulldozers came in," Gerry admitted. "I had the company ID with me; no one tried to stop me. I brought home things I thought might be useful and I've been doing some experimenting myself. Several of the silicates could substitute for plastic under the right conditions."

By now Jack was grinning. "Just listen to us! If we can get this far on our own, the human race can go all the way!"

As they did almost every Sunday, Gerry and Gloria Delmonico attended the church on the corner of Pine Grove and Alcott Place, where their daughter, Danielle, recently had been baptized. Although the morning had dawned bright and clear, a low bank of dark clouds to the north held the threat of rain later. As they stepped out of the church into the sunlight they exchanged smiles with one another. In spite of the Change, their lives seemed good that day; filled with promise. By focusing on the here and now they had everything they could wish for.

That morning the headline in *The Sycamore Seed* referred to a foreign country where a new type of tank had been developed that would soon roll onto undefended shores. Some glanced at the paper and looked away before meaning could invade their minds. Others absorbed every word, acquiring another layer of hopelessness.

---

Fred Mortenson desperately wanted to kill his wife. He refused to think of it as murder. Louise was always complaining about how miserable she was, and that's what you did, wasn't it? Put a suffering creature out of its misery?

Killing her should be simple enough. His dry cleaning plant employed a toxic solvent called perchloroethylene that would kill in a matter of minutes, but A: How to get her to drink the vile smelling stuff? and B: Could it be traced to him?

While watching himself in the shaving mirror Mortenson thought of half a dozen other methods using items from around his house, not to mention his collection of legally held firearms. But if he shot her with a gun registered to himself Sheriff Whittaker would be all over him like ugly on an ape.

Look how quickly he'd found Dwayne Nyeberger. And taken the man back to the hospital with another breakdown.

We're all suffering breakdowns, Mortenson thought. Innocent by reason of insanity.

He regarded himself in the mirror. Not bad; a little jowly perhaps, but not bad at all. Deserved a young, prettier woman, not someone who whined because he'd hung his shaving mirror too high for her to apply her lipstick.

Why wait? Spousal slaughter was happening all the time now. According to the *Seed,* murder rates were going through the roof. Okay. No time like the present. First he would get his .22 out of his rifle case and do a little target practice, just to be sure.

The locked rifle case was in the back hall. When he stepped into the hall the first thing he saw was Louise with a metal nail file in her hand and a grin on her face. Then he saw the rifle.

"Gotcha!" said Louise Mortenson.

Colin Bennett stood in the middle of his grandmother's living room with his fists planted on his hips. "I don't want to live in our old house again, Mom! Nothing works in it, everything's ruined. Besides, we'd still smell the smoke from the fire."

"You couldn't possibly," she asserted, "that's just your imagination. RobBenn was miles away from our house."

"I can smell it anyway. Why can't we stay here with Gramma?"

"We're too cramped here. Besides, it's a dreadful imposition on her."

"That's not the reason," the boy said. "You two fight all the time, that's why you want to leave."

"We don't fight all the time, Colin, you're exaggerating. We have differences of opinion, but that's inevitable when people live together in close quarters."

"So find some other place."

"There isn't another place available right now; don't you think I've looked?"

"How about Jack? Could we move in with him?"

"Jack Reece?"

"He takes you out in his car sometimes, doesn't he?"

"Yes, but we're just friends."

"He's got a super car and I'll bet he's got tons of money."

Nell could not remember how it felt to love Robert Bennett, but she loved his son; she did not want Colin to become the same kind of man with the same set of values. "I don't know if Jack has money and I don't care."

"When you go out with him you come back awful late. Me and Jess have been talking and we don't want you to marry some snot-clot who can't take care of you." The boy smiled then: not his father's self-centered smirk but an expression of concern that was purely Colin Bennett.

O. M. Staunton was not a sensitive man. But he could take a hint. Slowly and quietly in the beginning, not enough to cause a ripple on the surface, changes had been occurring in his body long before his daughter died. He had never paid much attention to his health, assuming it would serve him as obediently as did everything else in his life. Then he began experiencing bouts of nausea. A hollow pain at the base of his throat. A pounding heartbeat that awoke him in the middle of the night to find himself bathed in sweat.

Never one to panic, in his own good time he had gone to see his doctor. His doctor sent him to a specialist who sent him to another specialist

On Sunday afternoon Staunton appeared at Bea Fontaine's front door again.

"Miz Bea, I need to talk to you. Is anybody else here?"

"No, Jack's out for the day and I have no idea when or even if he'll return. You know how young men are."

"I can't even remember," Staunton said hoarsely. "Can I come in?"

When they were seated in the living room Staunton refused any offer of refreshment. "Let's make this quick; I have to. Since I was born the human life-span has lengthened dramatically; ninety is the new seventy and all that. But mine's done all the lengthening it's going to do."

Shock sent pins and needles through Bea's body. The Old Man had seemed immortal, like the Old Man of the Mountain in New Hampshire. "You can't mean . . ."

"I do mean. The medicos give me weeks, a couple of months at the most; I don't have enough heart muscle left to use as a shoelace. I'm not a candidate for a heart transplant, my lungs and kidneys are shot too. I've got to make arrangements pretty smartly and I need your help. I hate to keep asking you for favors, but . . ."

She found herself looking at his trousered knees as he sat in the armchair. Bony knees, thrusting sharply up like mountain peaks. When did he become so thin?

"Somebody's going to have to take over the bank while I'm still able to oversee the transition," he went on. "My son-in-law's off the rails. After Tricia's funeral I urged him to come back into the bank, hoping it would steady him, but . . . I want to appoint you as president of the Sycamore and Staunton. You know more about this bank than anyone else and I can trust you to do what I would. It's a poisoned chalice right now, but things are going to get better, they always do if you hang on long enough. What do you say, Miz Bea?"

Miz Bea did not say anything. To the dismay of them both, she began to cry.

She recalled that the stone face of the Old Man of the Mountain had crumbled away to nothing.

The bank of dark clouds that appeared in the morning sky had spread throughout the day, keeping the temperature unseasonably low, yet there was the faintest shimmer on the air, like heat waves rising from the earth.

Staunton stood beside Bea on her front porch, surveying the weather with a dubious eye. His familiar black car waited at the curb. "Is this supposed to be summer or winter?" he asked.

"Are you sure you're able to drive? What about your car?"

"I'm able to do anything I want to do, I just don't want to do much anymore. And that car'll go where I tell it to. You still haven't given me your answer, Miz Bea."

She drew a deep breath, like someone on a high diving board about to jump off for the first time. "If you really want me to . . ."

"I do."

"Well, then . . ."

"Well, then be in my office by seven in the morning, before anyone else gets there."

He did not say thank you. Or good-bye. He got in his car and drove away.

Dwayne Nyeberger was furious. "I'll go to the board of directors!" he shouted at Bea when she gave him the news on Tuesday morning. In his office, with the door closed, and him pounding his fist on the desk.

Bea was determined to remain calm. The Old Man expected her to be able to weather this storm, and she would. "Stauntons have chosen every member of the board since the bank was established," she reminded Dwayne, "and it's always rubber-stamped them. Don't worry, your job is secure. You'll continue on the same salary, he's insisting on that. But—"

"No buts! I'm going to take this to the banking commission and the board of trade; I'm going to have the whole rotten deal overturned! I'll have that old fool put away!"

"You'll be wasting time and money," Bea warned. "Don't you know him by now? He has every contingency covered." She lowered her voice to cushion the blow as she added, "He's already filed copies of your medical records to show that you are unstable; the authorities won't take your word over his. Be thankful for what you have, Dwayne."

Dwayne responded with the worst temper tantrum of his life. Bea insisted that he take the rest of the day off.

As she returned to her office—with its gallery of former bank presidents watching from the walls—she became aware that the parquet floor was sticky. She stopped. Bent down. Ran her fingertips across flooring made of imitation teak laminate that was just beginning to dissolve.

Bea straightened up. The eyes of Oliver Staunton's grandfather appeared to meet hers. The stern visage expressed mild disapproval.

Every portrait had been painted in the same style.

The Nyeberger boys were still recovering from their injuries at home; still cared for by Staunton's housekeeper and a rotating assortment of nurses when required. Haydon Leveritt, a stocky woman with frizzy hair and deep frown lines, was doing the best she could, but her temper had worn very thin. Years ago there reputedly had been a Mr. Leveritt, but according to town gossip, "He stepped outside one day for a quick smoke and just never came back."

Keeping house for the town's richest banker had been the height of her ambition. Being saddled with the young Nyebergers and their problems was a step too far. When their father rampaged into the house cursing and shouting, the boys were alarmed. Haydon was terrified.

Since the disaster at RobBenn, Flub, the elder—by eight minutes—of the Nyeberger twins, had not spoken. There was no physical reason, according to their doctors. As his father's uncontrollable outburst reached its peak Flub tugged on the housekeeper's arm. "Daddy's sick again. He's always sick. I wish he'd melt."

# 21

Martha Frobisher had never expected to be in a position to buy the florist's shop where she worked. As long as Gold's Court Florist was a going concern the owners were content to keep it in their portfolio of assets. One of the results of the Change was a decrease in the sale of luxury items such as commercially grown flowers. When the till receipts diminished enough to be worrying, the shop was put on the market while it still had some commercial value.

Martha's only connection with the S&S had been as a repository of her salary and widow's pension. She did not know how to go about applying for a mortgage; her home was the tiny cottage she had inherited from her late husband. It took several days to bring herself to the point of entering the bank.

She was surprised to discover that rough wooden planks had been laid across the floors of the lobby, like paths running in different directions. She was wary of stepping onto one until the receptionist got up from her desk and came toward her. "Can I help you?"

"I'd like to see an officer . . . a loan officer," Martha said timidly.

"That position's been amalgamated with the vice presidency; a reduction in staff, you understand. But the vice president is away right now. Would you like to see the president?"

The mere suggestion sent a shiver up Martha Frobisher's spine. Presidents were not on her radar. "I don't think Mr. Staunton would—"

"It's not Mr. Staunton anymore. Sit down a moment and I'll get her for you."

Martha perched on the edge of a chair, a bird about to take flight. The room with its marble surfaces echoed like a tomb. Her nerve broke. She was about to hurry away when Bea Fontaine appeared, carefully negotiating a path of planks.

When she saw who was waiting for her she smiled warmly. Over the years Bea had purchased a number of floral arrangements from Gold's Court Florist, a few for her own use but most to brighten up the bank. "Martha! What can I do for you?"

At Bea's request the receptionist brought coffee and cookies into the president's office—which also had planks on the floor—and left the room. For a quarter of an hour the two women discussed the weather and their mutual acquaintances. From time to time Martha glanced at the portraits on the wall. She couldn't help asking, "Do they ever make you nervous?"

"I'm starting to get used to them, but at first it was like having Mr. Staunton looking over my shoulder. Sometimes I wonder how he stood it all these years."

"Is he not coming back?"

"I'm afraid not. We're going to have his picture painted, though."

After checking Martha's financial situation, Bea assured her she could qualify for a business loan. "We'll give it to you in the form of credit. Not much actual money changes hands these days; people are trying to do all they can by barter. Barter depends on trust to a certain extent, but in a town the size of Sycamore River almost everyone knows everyone and you're unlikely to cheat a person you'll see again tomorrow. The situation's probably different in the cities, though."

"I used to wish I lived in a city with symphonies and theaters," the other woman said wistfully. "Now I'm glad I don't. Still, I don't understand how a bank can stay in business without using money."

Bea replied, "Money's just one way of representing value. The monetary quantity theory recognizes a distinction between nominal money and real money. 'Nominal' refers to a unit of currency, like dollars. 'Real' refers to the goods and services the dollars will buy." She did not realize she had fallen into Jack's lecturing mode, or that Martha was struggling to keep up. "We assume that what ultimately matters to purchasers is not the nominal but the real, so in the bank we've become brokers. We take a portion for our services."

"Oh my," said Martha Frobisher. "Does that mean I can pay off my loan in flowers?"

"Part of it, at least, as long as we need flowers or have a customer who does. It's different from the banking we used to do."

Martha was still nervous. "Are you sure everything's all right? I mean, is there anyone else who—"

Bea gave her a sad smile. "I'm it. There's no one left to ask."


Jack Reece was not the only person cursed with intuition. In Sycamore River as in communities around the world, anxiety was reaching a new level. Supplies of tranquilizers and sleeping pills had long since been exhausted. Patients suffering from hysteria and nervous exhaustion were sleeping on the floors in the hospital. The only questions were what, when and where catastrophe would strike. But it all came back to the Change.

The Wednesday Club discussed little else.

"As far as we know," Jack reminded them, "the Change still hasn't affected any *living* organism. Whatever damage is being done, we're doing to ourselves."

Gerry said, "If there's global war that'll be more than enough."

"Edgar Tilbury thinks humans have a biological need to cull themselves every few generations like lemmings," said Lila. "He says that may explain why we keep going to war: to kill off the breeding-age males."

"Why didn't he come with you tonight?" Bill Burdick asked as he set down a fresh pitcher of beer.

"He has a lot of things to get ready."

"Ready for what?"

"I wish I knew."

———————

Within the tunnels the smell of the earth was sweet and strong, the way he liked it. Better than coffee, even. Or at least as good as. Except for Jamaican Blue Mountain. Edgar Tilbury wondered if he should start weaning himself off from Jamaican Blue Mountain. Not only had it become nearly impossible to obtain, but luxury coffees were part of the world Up There.

Down Here was sanity.

He was carrying a heavy-duty flashlight as he made his way down the sloping tunnel, but he hardly needed its light; his feet knew every inch of the passage. Or so he thought until he tripped and fell to his knees. He made a mental note to smooth out the footing.

At the end of the passage a right turn gave way to another tunnel lined with wooden shelves holding several years' worth of dried legumes, rice and oatmeal in sturdy cotton sacks. An angle to the left led to the pasta stores—Tilbury was particularly fond of pasta—and tightly sealed cellophane bags of cookies and crackers. Beyond these were the fruits and vegetables. He loathed prunes only slightly less than he despised dried apricots, but healthy bowels and an adequate supply of vitamin C were necessities.

On other shelves hundreds of glass jars gleamed like jewels with the gold and red of canned peaches and strawberries and rhubarb, the dull green of runner beans and the fleshy hues of pickled mushrooms. Row upon row of cans held more soups and stews than a man could consume in a lifetime. Fruit cocktail and dill pickles, tomato paste and powdered milk, bottled lemon juice and packaged spices, salmon and mackerel and sardines and herring—it was all there, everything Edgar Tilbury liked to eat and a few things he was prepared to tolerate for the good of his health.

Deep in the ground below the barn, sound from Up There was muffled. Tilbury had taken the precaution of equipping his property with a highly sensitive alarm system that worked on sound vibrations and would warn him of any visitors. It was connected to the house, the barn and the cattle guard at the end of the lane. Whenever he entered the tunnels it was turned on.

The cattle guard was the first line of defense. Its warning was a shrill whistle that would galvanize Edgar Tilbury.

Finding himself confined to a hospital bed—and the suddenness with which the event took place—had unnerved O. M. Staunton. He issued the staff at the Hilda Staunton Memorial Hospital specific orders that he was to have no visitors. He did not want anyone to see him in his present condition.

Almost at once he rescinded the order and demanded to see Bea Fontaine.

The chief of the cardiac unit came in person to tell Staunton, "I'm sorry, sir, but we haven't been able to contact Miss Fontaine by AllCom. At this hour the bank is closed, of course. We dispatched an orderly to her house, but he reports no one home. Do you have another address for her?"

The once-sturdy frame beneath the bedcovers was hardly enough to lift the sheets. With a trembling hand Staunton shoved the oxygen mask aside. He regarded the doctor with baleful eyes. Every word was an effort. "Am I going to die? Or not?"

"We all die sometime, but—"

"Today!" Staunton rasped. "Am I dying today?"

The doctor was acutely aware of the money the Stauntons had pumped into the hospital over the years, and reluctant to do anything that might damage the relationship. The Old Man was going to die, and soon. Was it better to tell him the truth? Or to mollify him—at least until the next shift came on duty?

Buying time, the doctor picked up Staunton's chart and studied it intently, looking for the hope that wasn't there. His patient's labored breathing filled the room.

"Mr. Staunton, you're a strong man. We have every confidence that you will still be with us by the time Miss Fontaine is located and arrives here."

"I'd better be," Staunton growled.

Life gurgled in his throat.


Later—he had lost all sense of time—he heard her step in the hallway. Another moment and she was in the room, pushing aside the curtain that encircled his bed.

"You're here." His voice was unrecognizable.

"I came as soon as I could. I was in the—"

"Doesn't matter. You came."

"Of course I did." She pulled a chair over to the bed and sat down beside him.

Through failing eyes he tried to keep his vision fixed on her. "Miz Bea."

"Yes." She managed a tremulous smile. "Miz Bea."

"Bea," he said.

"Yes."

"Remember?"

"Remember what, Oliver?" She stood up and leaned over him, placing her warm hand on one of the cold, liver-spotted hands lying on the sheet.

"You remember what to do?" he asked again with the last of his strength.

"Everything."

"Good." The Old Man gave a satisfied sigh. And was gone.

When she returned to the bank she took the safe deposit box from his desk and opened it again.

The death of Oliver Morse Staunton was announced to a stunned town by *The Sycamore Seed*. Death had become shockingly routine, but his funeral would be the largest in local memory. The River Valley Transportation Service draped its newest vehicle in black crepe and conveyed the coffin to

Sunnyslope behind a team of black horses purchased from a breeder in Nolan's Falls.

Shay Mulligan handled the reins himself, with his son, Evan, sitting beside him. Both wore black.

So did Lila Ragland, who walked alone just behind the hearse.

Dwayne Nyeberger was furious once again. "That's crazy; my wife was his daughter, I should have been the principal mourner!"

In a signed and legally witnessed codicil added to Staunton's will a few weeks before his death every detail of the funeral had been specified, including the horse-drawn hearse "to be followed by my granddaughter Lila."

Everything was done as the Old Man wanted.

Bea Fontaine had authorized the loan with which the transport service had bought their latest carriage and horses. The church where the funeral was held, as well as the hearse and grave, were spectacularly heaped with flowers from Gold's Court Florist.

Jack escorted Bea to the services. He noticed that her eyes were red, but she was not crying. "You were fond of the old tyrant, weren't you?"

"He wasn't a tyrant. He hated sentimentality, but you always knew where you stood with him. Oliver was a rock; the last of the bedrock this town was built on. There's hardly a family here today that didn't have reason to be grateful to the Stauntons at one time or another." She shook her head. "There's been an awful lot of changes, Jack; I'm afraid this might be one too many."

"I doubt it, Aunt Bea. You're a rock yourself, that's why he left you in charge."

"No, he left me in charge because I could keep a secret."

"Lila Ragland?"

"Her mother was Oliver's illegitimate daughter. He'd lost track of her—maybe he'd wanted to, he wasn't what you'd call tolerant. But when we opened her safety deposit box it contained papers identifying her, together with Lila's birth certificate. No father's name on it, of course. I almost thought the shock would kill Oliver then, but it didn't."

Once Staunton was in his grave, Dwayne Nyeberger set out to wage war. He had been robbed. Robbed! Under the terms of Staunton's will, half of his estate would go to his granddaughter. His five grandsons would share the rest, as well as the family home or proceeds from it. Nothing had been allotted to his son-in-law.

Obviously the will must be set aside.

Bea tried to reason with him. "Oliver provided for his blood kin, he was that kind of man. He wanted you to stand on your own feet, Dwayne, the way a man should. You're a bank executive with a good salary; what more do you want?"

"Recognition! That old snake recognized his bastard granddaughter, and I demand what's rightfully mine!"

Bea and Staunton had discussed this. His wishes had been specific and she remembered them to the smallest detail. She presented Dwayne with a large cardboard carton containing all of his clothes, toiletries and golf clubs. The label read "Rightfully Yours."

Frank Auerbach put a black border—or as near black as his ink substitute would allow—around the front page of *The Sycamore Seed.*

"The funeral of Oliver Morse Staunton was a tragic milestone in the history of Sycamore River. His death followed a tragic anniversary; it has now been over a year since the onset of the Change. O. M. Staunton represented all that was solid and constructive about our town. The Change, which has damaged modern technology and mechanization around the globe, is a force for destruction. In this badly crippled world the Change goes on, but O. M. Staunton is no longer with us.

"May he rest in peace."

At the next gathering of the Wednesday Club Jack asked, "Anything around here dissolved lately?"

"Nothing I can name offhand," said Bill, "but not a day goes by that my customers aren't bellyaching about something."

"Out of curiosity, when was the last complaint?"

"I dunno; yesterday maybe. Folks love complaining to a bartender. They pound my ear about everything under the sun—except the Change. Not so much about that anymore."

"Maybe it's become the new normal," Gerry suggested.

Jack raised an eyebrow. "The Change the new normal? Not likely."

"You think things will get better?"

"I don't go in for wishful thinking."

Nell turned toward him. "If you did, what would you wish for?"

Jack smiled. "I plead the fifth amendment."

She smiled too. "One of my wishes has been granted: my children have agreed to move back into our old house. It won't be easy, not for any of us, but it's for the best. Since your car's still running I was hoping you'd lend a hand. We have a lot to move over; I hadn't realized the kids had so much stuff."

When he took her back to her mother's apartment later Jack could feel a change in the atmosphere. Instead of getting out of the car immediately Nell sat still. They both leaned in at the same time, resulting in a tender collision.

When the kiss finally ended he said, "Tomorrow?"

"Tomorrow," she said.

And that was that.


Before the Bennett family could return to their former home Nell hired a contractor to replace every damaged article in it, from the light switches to the chandeliers. "I can't give you a guarantee on any of these," he warned. "If the Change destroys them you'll have to buy more."

She also purchased new appliances and had the rooms repainted. "This will cost you a fortune, dear," her mother fretted. "And it's so unnecessary."

"Exorcism can be expensive, Mom. But in this case it's very necessary."

When the work was finished Jack drove her to the gated community west of town to inspect the results. The mock-Normandy château stood like a silent sentinel in the midst of a vast, freshly mowed lawn. Larger, more lavish, more conspicuously expensive than any of its neighbors.

Nell sat in the car gazing at it, recalling how impressed she was the first time she saw it. How proud of himself Rob had been.

"Do you want me to go in with you?"

"Thanks, but no, Jack. I have to do this myself."

He leaned against the scarlet Mustang and watched her approach the double front doors. Because of the problem with AllComs they were now locked with old-fashioned keys. Framed by the antique copper carriage lamps she had chosen in what seemed the distant past, Nell took a key from her handbag, squared her shoulders and inserted it in the lock.

One small step for womankind.

She opened the door and went in.

# 22

Bud Moriarty was disappointed that Jack had not suggested he invest in the River Valley Transportation Service. The business obviously was expanding. Lacey Strawbridge was even more disappointed. "I thought you and Jack were partners! How could he cut you out like that?"

"He didn't cut me out of anything, it's a separate business entirely. Besides, it doesn't belong to him."

"Are you sure? I'll bet he has a finger in it, a silent partnership maybe. Jack's always had an eye for the main chance and those two are friends of his."

"That doesn't mean they're joined at the hip. Don't worry about it, Lace, we're doing all right, aren't we?"

"We'd do a lot better if you had more gumption. The tire business isn't nearly as good as it was at first because there are so few cars on the road—so the garage is failing too."

"It isn't failing," he assured her. "I still have my tools and I'm doing more repair work than I ever did. Most anything that comes apart gets brought to me."

"Mending the handles of pots and pans. What sort of work is that?"

"Damned good work, Lace, and I'm glad to have it. People

aren't throwing things away anymore, and it's not just pots and pans. Frank Auerbach was mighty happy I could repair his typewriters, that's where I got the advertising posters I put up in Friendly Foods. They've brought in a lot of business. We could have had more if you'd taken some posters to Goettinger's."

She was appalled. "I used to model for Goettinger's!"

"There's nothing to be ashamed of about putting up posters."

"I'm not ashamed of anything—except that I was fool enough to give up a modeling career for this."

Your modeling career gave you up, Bud thought, but did not say.

Jack took Nell home after every meeting of the Wednesday Club, and always allowed enough time at the end of the evening to enjoy a brief tussle with Sheila and Rocky. The setters adored him. His scarlet Mustang continued to provide reliable transportation; he subjected it to an exhaustive examination morning and evening. He even broke up the cement floor in Bea's garage and dug a mechanic's pit so he could get at the undercarriage. Bud Moriarty had long since replaced the few vulnerable items in the classic car with substitutions of his own devising. "If I could just get my hands on an old Model T . . ." he said.

But no one was selling antique cars.

Nell enjoyed riding in the convertible with the top down; it reminded her of the brief, carefree time before her marriage.

She brought a silk scarf to keep in the car's glove compartment and wound it around her head and throat to keep her hair from blowing.

"You look like Grace Kelly," Jack told her.

"Who was she?"

"A movie star years ago. She married a prince."

No matter how late the hour Nell's children were always waiting up for her—a development Jack had not anticipated. They would not go to bed until they knew she was in the house. Colin still suffered from terrible nightmares. Jessamyn sucked her thumb in her sleep.

"It breaks my heart to see her do that," Nell confided to Jack.

"She'll outgrow it, give her time."

"What if there are psychological problems that haven't surfaced yet? After all they've been through there could be serious damage. How do I protect my children?"

You can't, he thought privately. Nell, so gentle otherwise, became a tigress where her children were involved. She refused to accept any advice from a man who had no children of his own.

There were other elements of Jack's relationship with Nell that he tiptoed around. Sex was one. Or the lack of sex, to be accurate. Under the circumstances it did not happen very often.

On the few occasions when they did manage to be intimate he discovered to his delight the playful sensuality hidden beneath her reserved exterior. When he made the mistake of comparing her to a kid in a candy store she was embarrassed. "How could you say that? Oh, Jack, am I—"

He laid a restraining finger across her lips. "Absolutely perfect for me? Yes, you are."

Gerry Delmonico prepared rigorously for the next meeting of the Wednesday Club, even searching through college textbooks that had survived the problems with ink. He explained to Gloria, "I keep hoping to find a clue to the Change, one that's been overlooked."

"Do you think there is one? Surely by now the other scientists have—"

"Scientists are only human, Muffin; they find what they expect to see. Jack Reece once said something that's stuck in my mind ever since. He said, 'The man in the street might be better than a panel of experts.' So I'm trying to look at the problem like that man, with no presuppositions. Random violence is increasing because of the stress we're all under and I want to offer our friends a ray of hope. If not hope of a solution to the Change, at least hope of understanding it. I've even jotted down some notes and tucked them in my shirt pocket, just in case. Jack's bound to have questions."

"Doesn't he always?"

That evening Gerry waited until the others arrived and drinks had been ordered before he asked, "What do any of you know about quantum physics?"

That got their attention.

"I have a layman's acquaintance with theoretical physics," Jack offered. "E equals mc squared?"

"Einstein's famous equation, that's right. But what does it *mean*?"

"Energy is equivalent to mass?"

"Basically, yes, but there's more to it than that," said Gerry. "Mass is congealed energy. Energy has inertia, which is the defining feature of mass. When something like plastic dissolves there can be a mass-to-energy conversion. That's what happens in nuclear fission. Less than one gram of mass was converted to energy in the explosion at Hiroshima, which will give you an idea of what powerful forces we're dealing with here. For over a year we've been seeing the Change release the energy from apparently solid objects. Why? Where in hell is all that energy going?"

Gerry swept the room with his eyes. He had a rapt audience. "Take a step back. That equation is E equals mc squared. Energy equals mass plus the square of the speed of light. That's the c squared part, which is a constant of proportionality linking energy and mass. Every time energy is released there is some decrease in mass. Conversely, every time energy is gained there is some increase in mass, though I don't see how that could apply here."

Lila Ragland leaned forward. "Is the Change some huge *experiment*?"

"I'm not saying that, but the possibilities are—"

"Frightening," Gloria interrupted.

"Not necessarily. It could indicate that a very powerful mind is at work here, which means the Change is not uncontrollable but being controlled. If so that's the good news. Maybe." Gerry waited for a response.

"You referred to quantum physics," said Jack. "That's a lot more complicated than what you just outlined."

"It is, but it begins with the tiniest known particles, because they're the building blocks of the universe."

"Particles! Like the highly charged particles in solar flares."

"That's right, Jack. All the interactions in our universe involve the creation and annihilation of particles. The Change is a perfect example."

"So is the Change good, or evil?"

"Neither or both, Nell. I suspect it's like power; it all depends on how it's used."

"And who's using it," Tilbury said darkly. "You have any theories about that?"

"Not yet, but if I'm right about what's happening we may be able to find out. To track the Change to its lair," Gerry added hopefully.

Another round of drinks was ordered.

An hour later Nell recalled, "When I was a girl I used to hear my grandparents complaining because everything was changing, and I didn't know what they meant. To me it seemed that nothing changed. Every day was like the one before. I thought I'd give anything for a change."

Gloria said fervently, "I'd give anything for the Change to

stop." She glanced at the baby lying beside her on the seat, snugly wrapped in blankets and sound asleep. "I want Danielle to grow up in a stable environment."

"When were we able to guarantee that?" Jack asked. "Consider the whole span of history. There have been some quiet periods, sure, but inevitably a disaster shook everything up: revolutions, world wars, the atom bomb . . ."

"'Scuse me, too much beer." Gerry got up and headed for the rest room.

"Humans were responsible for those things," Edgar Tilbury pointed out, "but the Change is different."

"No, we only think it's different because we don't know who's behind it."

Bill said, "So you'll grant that someone *is* behind it. What happened to your other theories, Jack?"

"None of them helped."

"Nothing's gonna help either," predicted Hooper Watson. "The fuckin' Change is gonna go on and on until we fall into a giant sinkhole like the ones on the asphalt roads."

Morris Saddlethwaite said, "You're a li'l ray of sunshine, arncha?"

"Well, it's true."

"We don't know what's true and what isn't," Lila argued. "There are times when it seems like a huge magic show, with the Wizard of Oz behind the curtain, pulling the strings. Any minute I expect him to pop out wearing a clown mask."

"Make it stop," Gloria whispered. She could feel everything

piling up: all the familiar items that had disintegrated, the growing worry and uncertainty, the gradual failures of the society she depended on, the unfocused anger and onrushing fear. There was no end to it. Just growing and growing and . . . "Make it stop! Oh please, God, make it stop, I can't take any more!"

Her sudden collapse stunned the others.

Evan Mulligan jumped to his feet and scooped her into his arms. "Go get her husband and somebody take the baby," he said over his shoulder. "Hurry!" He bent his head over the sobbing woman. "It's okay, it'll be okay, just take deep breaths."

The frozen tableau came to life. Jack ran to the restroom to bring Gerry back, while Nell produced a handkerchief and Bill Burdick poured a glass of brandy.

It was Edgar Tilbury who comforted the baby.


The Change continued, as inevitable as the changes that marked the passage of a day, a month, a year. On an unstable planet revolving in a finite solar system nothing remained the same. True stability, if such a thing were possible, would have broken the law of gravity and torn the space/time continuum.

Yet even the Change must change. How could it be otherwise?


Before he went to sleep Edgar Tilbury sat on the edge of his bed and looked at the photograph in its plain gold frame.

A beautiful woman with finely cut features, her full lips slightly parted as if she were about to speak to him.

Hers was the only photograph in the house. He kept it in his bedside drawer, next to the old AllCom that still worked occasionally.

"We've got children at last, Veronica," he told her. "Never thought it would happen. That Lila—she's a hard case, isn't she? Needs a lot and won't admit it. Maybe that freckle-faced veterinarian can give it to her, if she wants him. He's a decent guy and there aren't many of those around. There's room for them both here . . . and more."

He raised his eyes from the face in the picture and stared into space, thinking. Lovingly tucked the photograph back in the drawer. Scratched his chest and turned out the light.

Dwayne Nyeberger knew who to blame, and it wasn't the Change either. It was the woman he thought he killed, the woman who had stolen everything that should have been his. He could not sleep at night for thinking about her and planning ways to get even.

He needed to get her alone, and to do that he needed to find out where she lived. Where she went, what she did.

The obsession grew like a dark cloud over his head.

———

Evan Mulligan's AllCom emitted a series of random clicks, then a pulsating tone muffled by the fact that it was in his jacket pocket. The jacket was hung on a hook outside Rocket's stall.

The boy was kneeling on the straw beside a long-legged colt, trying to persuade the little creature to accept a leather halter on his head. Evan would have preferred to use a halter of woven nylon, which was softer, but most of those had disintegrated.

Rocket stood close by, nudging her little son with her muzzle to reassure him. His black baby coat would give way to gray as he grew older; he was finely bred. Evan had saved his own money to breed the mare to an Arabian stallion in Nolan's Falls. He had been hoping for a filly, though he was delighted with the colt. Next year he would take Rocket back to Nolan's Falls and try again.

When he recognized the ringtone of his AllCom he got to his feet carefully, so as not to startle the colt, and retrieved the device. He was surprised to see Lila Ragland's face appear on the screen. "Evan? Is your father home?" She sounded as if she were whispering.

"He's still in the clinic, I think. Want me to go get him?"

"That's all right, when he comes in give him a message for me, will you? Ask him if he can come over here tomorrow and get me."

"Tomorrow's not Wednesday."

"I know that, Evan. Just tell him, please. I think somebody's stalking me."

# 23

Shay Mulligan was surprised. "I didn't know Edgar had an AllCom that still worked. Lila never mentioned it."

"Maybe she didn't know about it until now. She was sort of whispering, like she'd just found it or something and didn't want him to know. I was afraid the connection would fail while we were talking, but it didn't."

"Do you think she's ill? Or injured?"

Evan shrugged. "She looked okay, but I could only see her face."

"Maybe I should head over there now."

"She seemed to think tomorrow would be okay. The horses have been working all day and they're tired, Dad."

"Of course they are; what was I thinking?" It would be foolish to rush off to rescue a damsel in distress when he didn't know if Lila was in distress. But the whole thing was decidedly odd. During the past year so many strange events had taken place that Shay's imagination operated at fever pitch. Tilbury was an eccentric; such a person might do anything. He might even . . .

After he went to bed Shay tossed and turned. Karma, who shared his bed, moved onto each warm spot he vacated until at last she lost patience and went to Evan's room to sleep with him.

———————

When Nell Bennett was sure her children were asleep she took a flashlight and went through the house, scrutinizing every item she thought might be vulnerable to the Change. This had been her habit since they moved back in. She was alert for the slightest droop or sag—as she had once checked her mirror for the slightest sign of aging in her face.

There were more important things to worry about now. She felt like the guardian at the gates. Beyond those gates the forces of chaos waited. That's melodramatic, she told herself, but we're living in melodramatic times.

After a sleepless night Shay was up at dawn. He wrote out detailed instructions for Paige when she arrived at the clinic, took Jupiter from his stall behind the Delmonico house, saddled him and headed toward Tilbury's. He kept the horse at a spanking trot the entire way. By the time they reached Tilbury's mailbox the gelding's hide was creamy with sweat. Shay dismounted and led Jupiter over the cattle guard and up the lane to the house.

Lila met him at the door, with Edgar Tilbury behind her. At one glance she took in the lathered horse. "You didn't need to rush, Shay."

"Your call sounded urgent."

Tilbury cleared his throat. "What call?"

She turned to face him. "I used your AllCom."

"But it was in my—"

"I know; I went looking for it. I knew you must have one, you're so careful about being prepared."

"All you had to do was ask."

"I guess I'm a born snoop."

"But you're not in any trouble?"

"I don't know, Shay. Yesterday afternoon when I walked down to the Simpsons' place to buy eggs for our breakfast I thought someone was following me. They live in the valley," she explained, "and there are a lot of trees. It seemed like a man was hiding among them."

"Did you get a good look at him?"

"Every time I tried he ducked out of sight."

Tilbury said angrily, "Why didn't you tell me when you came home?"

"It might have been my imagination and I didn't want to bother you for nothing. But after supper, when you were down in the tunnel, someone looked in my window."

"You're sure now?"

"That's when I got up and went for your phone, Edgar."

He clenched his fists. "You should have let me take care of the bastard!"

Shay was white beneath his freckles. "The two of you out here alone, and you not a young man—"

"I'm able to take care of any damned intruder!"

"I'm sure you are," the vet said hastily.

Bill Burdick looked up when Shay and Lila entered the bar and grill. "I didn't expect to see you two today. Are you here for a drink, or a meal?"

"A couple of drinks," Shay told him, "and a little information. Do you know anyone in town who might have a room to rent? Someplace on the south side, maybe."

"Scarce commodity these days. Who's it for?"

"Me," said Lila.

"Unh-hunh. You're not staying with Edgar anymore?"

"I was, but now I'm here."

"Did you and he have a falling out?"

"It wasn't like that."

"Unh-hunh. Well. I can ask around . . . but I suggest you go to Frank over at *The Sycamore Seed*. He runs a few classified ads in the paper, he might know of something."

Shay waited while Lila went to the newspaper office alone. "She makes her own decisions," he said to Burdick.

"Why don't you put her up at your place?"

"The mood she's in, I'm afraid she'd slap me down."

"Unh-hunh. It gets complicated, doesn't it?"

"You can say that again. Give me a refill, will you?"

Lila returned to Bill's within the hour. One look at her glowing face told the story. "There's a nice room with a private bath over on Cleveland Street, available right now. It's in the home of a friend of Bea's. And better than that . . . I have a job!"

"I didn't know you were looking for a job."

"Of course I was, Shay; I have to be able to pay my rent, don't I? Frank Auerbach said my arrival was providential, he's been looking for a typist to transcribe the news. I didn't train on the typewriter, but it's not that different from a computer keyboard. And I can certainly write a simple declarative sentence."

Another hour was spent getting Lila settled in her new room: a large bedroom and bath on the second floor of a private home overlooking Cutler Park, one block over from Elm Street. There was a Colonial-style double bed, a matching chest of drawers, a mirrored dressing table in an alcove. Clean sheets were on the bed and clean towels in the bathroom. The striped dimity curtains on the windows looked new.

"Everything's within walking distance," Lila pointed out to Shay.

"I guess you won't need me, then."

"Of course I will. Aren't you taking me to the next Wednesday Club meeting?"

He was tempted to point out that now she could walk the short distance, but he didn't.

Before he left her Shay went around the corner to Gold's Court Florist to buy a flower arrangement to brighten the room. "Is this for someone special?" Martha Frobisher asked coquettishly.

"Yeah."

"Then you'll want real flowers and not artificial ones. The

artificial ones last longer, but we used to have trouble with them dissolving."

"Used to?"

"It's not happening anymore. I sold a lovely arrangement of artificial peonies just last week."

As Shay returned home he felt a little guilty about Edgar Tilbury. The man had been kind to Lila; she had revealed enough of the story for Shay to understand what had been done on her behalf. Tilbury was probably lonely and his intentions were good.

He wondered how much the old man knew about Lila.

He wondered how much he really knew about her himself.

When Jack arrived on Wednesday evening to take Nell to the bar and grill, she got into the car with a spiral notebook in her hand. "I've discovered something fascinating!"

"Fasten your seat belt first. I just had them installed; they didn't come standard with the car."

"Wait a minute." She twisted in her seat. "There. Now can I tell you about this?"

"Aren't you going to put on your scarf? The top's down."

"Jack, you're becoming a regular fussbudget. Please, listen to me. Since we moved back into the house I've been writing down every item that dissolves so my contractor can replace it. I've been recording them all by date, and it's been a month yesterday since I found anything wrong. Here, look at my notebook."

"I'm driving," he said patiently.

"A month yesterday! Doesn't that tell you anything?"

"Only that your contractor's using better quality materials than the last one did."

"Oh, you. Do you think it's possible the Change is stopping?"

"How could it stop without us knowing?"

"It started without us knowing. Just a bit at a time, remember? It took a while for the news to get around, so we don't know exactly when or where it actually began, but I doubt if it was in Sycamore River. We certainly aren't the center of the universe."

"It's a nice idea, Nell, and I'd like to believe you're right. But the Change isn't the catastrophe it used to be, not with actual war looming. We have something worse to worry about now."

She closed the notebook and put it into the glove compartment. For the rest of the drive into town she watched the scenery go by.

They were almost the first members of the Wednesday Club to arrive. Some of the other tables were occupied and there was a lineup at the bar, including Hooper Watson. He waved but did not get off his stool. That honor was reserved for the arrival of Shay Mulligan, who could be expected to buy the former sheriff a drink before joining the others.

"While we wait for them," Jack said to Nell, "how about taking a poll to see if anyone else has noticed a lessening in the Change?"

Bill's customers agreed to participate, but the results were inconclusive. Like Jack, most had stopped paying attention to what had become a commonplace event. Art Hannisch, the jeweler, told a different story. "A few months ago I bought a porcelain tea set to display in my front window. Quality merchandise; you could almost read a newspaper through one of the saucers. Several customers came into the shop to inquire about it, but I'd marked it at the price the sales rep recommended, which was pretty stiff. Sooner or later someone would buy it, though, and I'd make a good profit. I was sort of counting on the mayor's wife, in fact.

"Then one day that damned tea set . . . slumped. Not exactly melted, you understand; it sort of collapsed. Stuck fast to the expensive silver tray it was on. I had to scrape the stuff off, which ruined the tray too. If I ever get my hands on that sales rep again I'll break his damned neck."

"How long ago was this?"

"Three weeks, Jack, give or take a day or two."

"And nothing like that's happened since?"

"No. Wasn't that bad enough?"

When Shay and Evan arrived they had Edgar Tilbury with them. He glanced around the room. "Is Lila here?"

"Lila Ragland?" Bill called from behind the bar. "I imagine she'll be along as soon as she gets off work."

Tilbury's shaggy eyebrows rose in surprise. "Lila has a job?"

"Didn't she tell you? She's working for *The Sycamore Seed*."

"That girl's just one surprise after another," Edgar remarked.

The first topic of the evening was Nell's theory. Laying her spiral notebook on the table, she invited the others to have a look. "You'll notice that the meltings—dissolutions, whatever you want to call them—appear to be tapering off."

"Martha Frobisher in the florist shop told me their artificial flowers used to melt," Shay said, "but they don't anymore."

"You sure this isn't wishful thinking?"

"I'm not sure of anything, but can't it be a possibility?"

"Anything can be a possibility," said Gerry, "*if* you have the science to back it up."

"I'm not a scientist, but you are. Could the Change be reversed?"

"Well . . ." Gerry considered while the others watched him eagerly. "Look at it this way. Plastics are organic compounds that're held together by the polarization of the electronic charge cloud on each molecule. If they're being destroyed on a molecular level, as I believe they are, then when the molecular destruction stops the destruction of plastic stops. Would the Change be reversed? No, but it could be over. And we would have dodged a *very* large bullet."

Jack said, "You're leaving out the most important part: what caused it in the first place. You talked about tracking the cause of the Change 'to its lair,' but are we any closer than we were?"

"Maybe we don't have to be . . . not if it's stopping on its own, the way it started."

Jack shook his head. "Nothing in the universe starts or stops spontaneously."

"Now, wait a minute here!" Morris Saddlethwaite interjected. "What about that Big Bang you talked about? Wasn't that spontaneous?"

"They're still trying to determine—"

"Aha! So you don't know!"

Edgar Tilbury gave a snort. "We don't know anything, Morris, until we admit how much we don't know."

"You're one of those folks who talk in riddles, you are. I don't like that; I like black or white, yes or no."

"In this world there are no absolutes," Jack stated emphatically.

Nell's shoulders drooped. "And there may be no end to the Change."

"Don't take it like that," Jack said to her. "People everywhere will be working to find substitutes for what they've lost, same as we are. The world is going to go on. Different, maybe, but it will go on, and who's to say it won't be better?"

Something was being born, something so fragile they dare not expose it to the light. A nascent hope.

When Lila entered Bill's Bar and Grill she was carrying the latest edition of *The Sycamore Seed*. The headlines were enough to crush hope.

## SINO-RUSSIAN CONFLICT ESCALATES
## BOTH SIDES THREATEN CONVENTIONAL WARFARE

She laid the newspaper on top of Nell's notebook. "I'm sorry to be the bearer of bad news, but Frank Auerbach was monitoring the shortwave this morning and it's pretty certain. We've got more hard copy, we'll use it in the next edition." Lila gave a self-conscious smile. "He's letting me try my hand at writing."

Nell was puzzled. "What do they mean by 'conventional' warfare?"

"It means no nukes," said Jack. "Looks like neither side has any computers left."

"That's good, isn't it?"

"Depends on your point of view, I guess. Dead is dead, whether it's ten people killed or a hundred thousand. No matter what weapons they use, there's no way America can stay out of it. Because of our international treaty commitments we'll have to support one side or the other. Hobson's choice."

"In spite of all we can do," Gloria mourned.

Tilbury's response was acerbic. "Just exactly what did we do? Like lambs to the slaughter we've allowed a few power-mad individuals to gain control of the world. We've been led to the edge of a cliff and—"

"And we have to turn around and run like hell in the opposite direction!" Jack slammed his fist onto the table so hard he knocked off the newspaper and notebook.

"What else can we do?" said Gerry. "Stage a coup in every belligerent country? Convert all the soldiers into farmers? Even if it were possible, and it damned sure isn't, we don't have enough time. And World War One didn't use nukes."

Tilbury exchanged glances with Lila Ragland. She was standing straight with her shoulders back and her chin lifted. Life had pummeled her until she was no longer afraid of anything. There was an admantine quality in the woman.

He could almost feel the levers shift inside himself.

If the bombs came he would not go into the tunnels either.

Nell bent down to retrieve the papers from the floor. She gazed at the *Seed* for a moment, then held it up. "Look, everyone. The newsprint isn't blurred!"

# 24

Although it was very late, Bea was waiting for Jack when he came home that night. "How did the meeting go?" she asked as she always did.

"I keep saying you should join us."

She pursed her lips. "You young people don't want me."

"Hooper Watson and Morris Saddlethwaite aren't young, Aunt Bea. And Edgar Tilbury certainly isn't."

"Edgar Tilbury? What does he have to do with it?"

"He's the newest member of the Wednesday Club; didn't I mention that?"

"I would have remembered," said Bea. "I've known him all my life; we went out together before he met Veronica. Nothing serious, at least on my part; he was too intense for me. Then he met her and that was a perfect match. It doesn't always happen."

"You liked him."

For a moment she had a faraway look in her eyes. "Edgar was smart and clever and we had a lot of fun. But I knew other men who were smart and clever and fun."

"You were looking for more than that?"

"It was a long time ago, Jack. I don't remember what I was looking for."

"Aunt Bea, I don't often lay down the law to you, but you're going to come to the next meeting of the Wednesday Club if I have to sling you over my shoulder and throw you into my car."

Tyler Whittaker resented the Change as a personal affront to him. It made his job as sheriff of Sycamore River infinitely more difficult than he had anticipated. Since he took over the office once occupied by Hooper Watson a kind of craziness had set in. In what had been a pleasant, easygoing town, the citizens had become edgy and suspicious. People who had been honest were now devious. And the devious had begun deliberately breaking the law.

Violent crime was up fifty percent by Whittaker's calculations.

The Change was making everyone meaner, that was for sure. Every little thing that went wrong, some irate taxpayer came running to him wanting him to fix it. They didn't seem to have any idea what "keeping the peace" meant.

The sheriff's office consisted of two rooms plus a lockup in a squat brick building at the end of Miller's Lane. Because the town had never been a major crime area, the facilities were modest. On the rare occasions when secure incarceration was required the police came down from the state capital to take custody of the guilty party.

Today Whittaker wished he had a reason to send the man

confronting him to prison. He was a colossal pain in the ass. "Do you know who I am?" he demanded.

The sheriff sighed. By now he knew who almost everyone in town was. "Of course I do, sir, you're the manager of Friendly Foods. I assume you have another complaint. Sir." Whittaker added the second "sir" as a precaution.

"That's right, and I insist you take out a warrant against those Gypsies who're running the horse-and-buggy service. Their animals keep dropping manure on the street in front of my store. It's against all the sanitation codes and it's filthy. Just look here . . ." He lifted one foot and waggled it in the air. "I even got shit on my shoe!"

Whittaker regarded the soiled shoe impassively. "They're not Gypsies, they're local businessmen providing a legal and badly needed service to this community. All I can do is ask them to be more conscientious about cleaning up behind their horses."

"That's not good enough!"

"It's the best I can do. Sir."

After the supermarket manager stormed out of his office, Whittaker took his cap from the peg and went to see Shay Mulligan.

"I'm sorry to bother you about this, Doc, but we've had another complaint about horse manure."

"From the same source as before?"

"'Fraid so."

"Sheriff, I can't hire people to run behind every carriage with a burlap sack."

"What about attaching sacks to the backsides of your horses?"

"Diapers on horses? Are you serious?"

Shay enlivened the next meeting of the Wednesday Club by recounting his conversation with the sheriff. The society also welcomed a new member; Bea Fontaine arrived with Jack and Nell.

Edgar Tilbury was seated in the booth when they entered. He smiled and raised his glass in a salute. "I'm mighty glad to see you here, Bea. Can I buy you a drink?"

"Jamesons?"

"Bill can't get any more, I'm afraid; but I've got a half bottle of my own stashed behind the bar and it's all yours." He patted the seat beside him.

Bea slid into the booth next to Tilbury. "This has become a different world in such a short time," she remarked. "None of us can keep up with it."

"Nell Bennett thinks the Change may be slowing down."

"Does she really?"

He scratched his neck. "Yep."

"What do you think, Edgar?"

"I'll admit there've been some signs, but it's too soon to tell. If we start getting the news from abroad maybe we'll have a better idea."

"The news from abroad," Shay echoed. "I never thought that would sound exotic."

When Morris Saddlethwaite offered a pithy suggestion about what the supermarket manager might do with horse manure, Evan Mulligan laughed so hard he sprayed cola across the table.

Without quite knowing how it happened, the meeting morphed into a party. Bill's other patrons joined in. When someone suggested a singalong Gerry Delmonico revealed an exceptional baritone voice.

Closing time came and went.

When his sister-in-law came out of the kitchen and announced she was going home—"If you lot want any more food you can fix it yourselves"—Bill Burdick guiltily consulted the railroad clock on the wall behind the bar. He called out, "Closing time!" No one heard him.

With difficulty—Bill had consumed his share of the liquor—he clambered onto the bar and stood up, swaying and waving his arms. "Closing time *now!*" he shouted.

Jack Reece caught him before he hit the floor.

There was no question of Tilbury trying to drive his "hybrid" the long distance home after drinking so much. Shay and Evan took him to their place in the trap, behind Jupiter. Edgar would awake in the morning to the smell of someone else cooking breakfast for a change.

Jack and Bea accompanied Nell to her house. He drove very carefully because there was horsepower under the hood and not in the shafts.

On the following day the British Ministry of Defense announced that its entire fleet of warships had been called into port.

Looking back on the evening at Burdick's, it was hard to reconcile it with the onrushing apocalypse.

"We were whistling past the graveyard," Bea said as she and Jack sat on the front porch, drinking tomato juice liberally laced with Tabasco.

"Aunt Bea, do you think there's a chance Nell could be right?"

"About what?"

"The Change slowing down. The light at the end of the tunnel. If so, maybe there won't be a war either."

"What does your intuition tell you?"

"Nothing, it's stopped cold. I want to believe Nell's right, but I don't know."

Bea gazed at her small front lawn. A teenager could mow that in ten minutes. "Nell's a lovely woman, Jack, but she comes with a ready-made family."

"I know. Hostages to fortune."

"I fell in love with a man once," she said slowly. It was the most intimate statement he had ever heard her make. "It wasn't right; I knew it and I think he knew it, but we went ahead anyway."

"And?"

"There wasn't any *and*. I told you, it wasn't right. Just when I thought things couldn't get any worse, they did. Shay

Mulligan has a cat named Karma. Do you know what that word means?"

"You're changing the subject, but yes, I know what karma means. A person's destiny; their fate."

Bea nodded. "I've seen it at work too many times not to believe in it."

Jack waited for her to continue.

She set her half-empty glass on the floor of the porch and went into the house.


Following the recall of the British fleet other military forces were gathering themselves. *The Sycamore Seed* dutifully reported every available scrap of information.

Auerbach was allowing Lila to write articles herself. He did not give her a byline, but one morning she came to work to find a neat black-and-white sign propped on her desk: "L. E. Ragland Staff Reporter."

Dwayne Nyeberger knew where she was now. He made it his business to always know where she was, at any given time.


Spurred by an imminent global war, the manufacturing of armaments went into overdrive. Assembly plants and full-on production facilities sprang up almost overnight, operating not in bold new ways, but in the reliable old ones.

Before the town of Sycamore River knew what was happening

trucks full of building material and construction workers began arriving at the site of the former RobBenn complex. The chain-link perimeter fence was reinforced with corrugated panels surmounted by razor wire, making it impossible for anyone to see what was happening inside.

Rumors sprouted like the weeds along the bank of the river.

Finbar O'Mahony, recently returned from his lakeside idyll, told Nell Bennett she was a lucky woman. "I came out of retirement to get you the best possible deal for the property," the lawyer boasted. "It's all here." He gestured at the stack of documents on the large marble coffee table in the great hall of her house. "Survey reports, condemnation orders, site clearances, engineers' findings; it's a big project. Mayor Dilworth personally went to Washington to campaign for this; it was his idea in the beginning and he was the man to promote it; the chairman of the Ways and Means committee's an old friend of his. It's quite a coup; it'll put Sycamore River on the map. Think of the jobs this will mean, Nell."

"I don't understand, Finbar. I thought the Nyebergers' lawsuit had everything tied up."

"Not where the federal government's concerned. What the fed wants they can get, and they want that land to put a new munitions plant on. It's centrally located, you see; there's even proximity to the railway."

"What about the financial records in the Cloud? They're still somewhere, aren't they? Proving ownership?"

He smiled knowingly. "Uncle Sam doesn't care about that,

Nell. This is wartime, or going to be wartime, and the rules are changed."

"You said it would mean a lot of jobs for the town, but there aren't many construction workers in Sycamore River and probably no factory workers at all since RobBenn closed down. Who's going to benefit?"

"The necessary people will be brought in from outside," O'Mahony assured her.

"So our local unemployed will remain unemployed?"

"Think about the service industries," he said. "There's going to be a whole influx of new people with money in their pockets. They'll need food, accommodation, everything; there'll be plenty of money made from them. Take your real estate business, for example; you can sell houses to the upper echelon and arrange rentals for the rest."

The skin tightened around her eyes. "Isn't that what they used to call profiteering?"

The lawyer was offended. "My dear woman! It's called turning a profit—or have you forgotten what that means? Your late husband certainly understood it. Consider the house we're sitting in right now. The profits made by Robert Bennett bought every square inch of this place. Which reminds me . . . I think the papers are here somewhere . . ." He leafed through the stack of documents. "Yes, here we are. I've requested that you receive the deed for this house and grounds 'free and clear of all encumbrances' as part of your financial package." He looked at her proudly, anticipating gratitude.

"But the Nyeberger boys—"

"Nell, you're not listening to me. You're making an issue out of a couple of tiny scratches on a bar of solid gold bullion. This is the federal government we're dealing with; such an arrangement is an everyday matter for them." The lawyer's good cheer was evaporating. "If you want to give the Nyebergers a charitable donation out of your share of the proceeds that's up to you, of course, but I wouldn't recommend it. You'd be creating a bad precedent, opening the door to endless demands."

"Let me get this straight." Nell's voice was cold. "First we take advantage of the Change to deny those children compensation, then we use the federal government to do it?"

"I wouldn't say that."

"I would, Finbar, and it's an outrage to my moral compass. If there's anything the last couple of years have taught me it's the true value of money. Which is zero."

"Are you telling me you don't want to do this? I'm afraid you don't understand. For the last time, the government is *going* to do it whether you agree or not. The only question is what it will mean for you."

Not many restaurants were still open in Sycamore River, but several enterprising men and women had turned their dining rooms into informal eateries and were doing a brisk trade in home cooking.

When Jack came to take Nell out to dinner she told him about the situation.

"You don't sound very happy about it, Nell. Most people would be thrilled to have the government take a white elephant off their hands for a fair price."

"The price is fair enough, but it wasn't really on my hands. The Nyebergers have a legitimate claim on it, at least on part of the money from the sale. Now Finbar says their entitlement will be obliterated as if it doesn't matter."

"Did you actually make that remark about your moral compass?"

"I did."

Jack was amused. "It must have come as a bit of a jolt to him. I doubt if moral compasses are discussed in law schools these days."

"Then they should be. And another thing, Jack. The trees."

"I don't follow you."

"Surely the munitions plant, no matter how large it is, won't take up all of Daggett's Woods. What about the nature conservancy? Shouldn't some of that be protected? It was given to the people of this town and they have a right to it."

He drove on for a little way before pulling over to the curb and stopping the car. He switched off the engine, took a hand-kerchief out of his jacket pocket and wiped his face. Twice. Then he turned toward her.

"Eleanor Richmond, will you marry me?"

She sat up very straight. "What?"

"I asked you to marry me."

She stared at him. "Were you serious?"

"I've never asked a woman to marry me before, so I must be serious. Do you want me to get down on my knees? I'd have to be a contortionist to kneel in this car, but if you insist I'll try."

Nell put her hand against his chest. "Please don't. Why did you call me Eleanor Richmond?"

"Because if you say yes you won't be Eleanor Bennett anymore."


At the next meeting of the Wednesday Club they were the last to arrive. When they entered Bill's Bar and Grill Jack took hold of Nell's right hand and did not let go.

Nell was glowing.

Engaged, Jack was thinking. Me, Jack Reece. Engaged to be married. To be *married*.

He had not planned it; had not even thought, consciously, about proposing to her. The words had poured out as if his brain and mouth were not connected.

"We're going to get married," he said aloud.

After a startled silence Gerry began to applaud. The others joined in.

"Way to go, buddy!" Bill called from behind the bar. "When did it happen?"

"Just now. I mean, an hour ago."

"Have you set a date yet?" Gloria asked as she hurried over to them.

Nell said, "It's far too soon, I haven't even thought about dates."

"Well, what about the ring? Did you give her a ring, Jack?" Gloria reached for Nell's left hand, then frowned in disappointment. "No ring yet. Jack, you've got to get your act together. First the ring, then the proposal."

"I've never done this before."

"Then tomorrow morning you take this girl down to Art Hannisch and make the engagement official."

Nell was embarrassed. "All this fuss . . ."

"It's important."

From his place at one end of the booth Evan Mulligan declared, "Nobody gets married anymore. And nobody buys engagement rings either."

Shay told his son, "That's not true."

The boy saw his opportunity. "So are you going to marry Lila?"

"Wait a minute!" Lila protested.

Conversation swirled around Nell as if she were in the eye of a storm. Which was how she felt. Questions, suggestions, recollections of other weddings . . . the Wednesday Club was delighted with the unexpected turn of events: a happy topic to replace all the gloom and doom.

The threat of war was so close now. The air almost smelled of death and destruction.

But two people were in love.

Champagne was ordered. She and Jack were given seats in the middle of the booth. "So you can put your arm around her," he was told.

She was almost painfully aware of his physical presence. He seemed to radiate heat.

I've been married before and it was nothing like I expected. Will this be any different?

I love him. And I'm in love with him, at least I think I am. They're not the same thing, but I know the difference.

"About the date . . ." Nell said tentatively.

Jack looked down at her. "Don't worry about that; like you said, it's too early."

Is she trying to back out? Suddenly he realized how very much he wanted this.

"About the date," she reiterated. "And making all the arrangements . . . it won't be easy, the way things are. But . . . it's going to get better."

They were all looking at her now.

I have to believe in something, and here it is.

"The Change is slowing down," she said, "I'm convinced of it. As soon as it's over we'll get married."

"That's what I'd call a giant leap of faith," said Edgar Tilbury.

Little things. Knobs on kitchen cabinets. Buttons on clothes. Covers on checkbooks thrust into the backs of desk drawers.

Did not melt.

Cessation was not instantaneous. The Change had taken months to build to its full fury; it would not abate for months more.

But the end was coming.

The members of the Wednesday Club devoted themselves to sniffing out every instance of returning normalcy.

Lila wrote an article about it for the *Seed*. She did not mention Jack and Nell, but she reported that people were making plans for the end of the Change. She encouraged her readers to watch for examples and report them to the paper.

Within a week the letters began to come in.

Bit by bit, a sense of excitement pervaded Sycamore River. It was like a giant treasure hunt. At the end everyone would win.

Beyond the Sycamore River Valley, across America and around the globe, others also were aware of the improving situation. The puzzle that could not be solved was starting to go away. Soon it would be possible to concentrate on other matters.

In the meantime the race to provide acceptable substitutes for plastic continued. The Change had disrupted too much for the modern lifestyle to be restored completely, but some of the discoveries and innovations forced on the human race had proved themselves better than the originals.

Bamboo surgical stents, being organic, were more readily

accepted by the human body and did not need to be replaced as often.

Some though not all of the people who had substituted real horses for automotive horse power found the slower pace of their lives too pleasant to relinquish. For them, returning to the combustion engine was viewed as a retrograde step.

But.

The international armaments industry continued to move ahead. The old-style weapons they had begun producing could be manufactured more cheaply and required less training to use than their modern counterparts. Battle would become the preserve of the infantry again, rather than a technological game played out by opponents who never saw each other. The nuclear option was shelved. For the time being.

However, the genii had been let out of the bottle and might find a way to escape again in the future.

After an absence from toy store shelves, startlingly realistic guns and other weapons—with no plastic parts—became available again, and were heavily promoted.

War had never gone out of fashion.

# 25

"I'm sorry, Nell, but there's nothing I can do about your trees."

"They aren't my trees, Finbar, they belong to my grandchildren and their grandchildren. Did you explain that to the people you were talking to?"

"In the federal government? I didn't even try. They're too busy with everything else that's going on to—"

"What about at state level? Surely—"

"They reminded me quite firmly that we have a perfectly good state park in this area, at Nolan's Falls. To fund another so close by would be—"

"But they don't need to fund it," she argued, "it's already there. We just have to keep the authorities from destroying the trees."

He tried to placate her. "You don't know they're going to do that."

"Yes, I do. My friend Lila Ragland works for *The Sycamore Seed* and they've learned the entire forest is going to be cut down. To make room for a military airport!"

"I'm sorry," O'Mahony said again. "My hands are tied. At a time like this—"

"Blast you and the 'time like this'!" Nell was almost screaming.

―――――

When Jack arrived to take her to the Wednesday Club she was still tense with anger. "Don't take it so hard," he counseled. "Sometimes you have to walk away."

"I don't think I can."

"Why not? You lived close to that forest for years and never got involved with the conservancy, so why's it upsetting you now?"

She had no answer for him. She did not know the reason herself, but the feeling was very strong in her. If he loved her, really loved her, he should take it on blind faith.

Bill's Bar and Grill had become more than a meeting place; for each member of the club it was, in one way or another, a haven. Among themselves they talked more freely than they would anywhere else. Trusting their friends to understand.

A haphazard mix of disparate personalities had turned into something greater than the sum of its parts.

Shay Mulligan understood when Nell bemoaned the projected fate of the forest. "It's going to break Paige's heart," he told her.

"Paige?"

"Paige Prentiss, in my clinic. She's the girl who took your Rottweiler; he goes everywhere with her now. And she's one of the most dedicated members of the conservancy."

"Do you suppose she could draw up a petition of protest and get lots of signatures?"

"I'm sure she could, Nell—but would it do any good?"

"Not with the federal government," Edgar Tilbury interjected. "We're like ants at a picnic to them. What you need is an appeal to a higher authority. And there is no higher authority."

Tilbury felt sympathy for Nell. She was an intelligent, sensitive woman—perhaps too sensitive. She had never acquired the armor plating Lila Ragland possessed.

On his own he wrote some letters, made some inquiries—and had to admit that Finbar O'Mahony was right. In a matter of months Daggett's Woods would cease to exist.

Scorched earth, he thought. Some folks just can't resist pushing the destruct button.

As the Change loosened its grip the sun seemed to shine more brightly over Sycamore River. Spirits began to lift. People greeted each other on the street again instead of lowering their eyes and hurrying past.

The five Nyeberger boys had returned to normal—or what was normal for them. They were living in their parents' home as temporary wards of the court, being cared for by Haydon Leveritt because their father was rarely home. Even when he was, Dwayne Nyeberger was not an acceptable parent figure.

Flub was usually speechless, but he could talk if he wanted to. When someone mentioned the approaching war he said, "The best thing about dying young is you'll never get old."

Kirby, once the handsome pick of the litter, bore scars he would carry all his life. But they were all alive, that was the main thing.

When Nell saw them in town she thought of Rob.

It was becoming easier to remember the good things, harder to recall the bad.

Jessamyn and Colin were delighted when she told them she was going to marry Jack Reece. Colin enthused about having a car like the Mustang. "When you get all that money from the government you could buy one easy," he told his mother.

"It's not going to be a fortune, and I don't think we should waste it on sports cars. That money will take both of you to university and give you a start afterwards."

Colin went straight to Jack. "Talk to her, will you?"

"I warned you about taking on a ready-made family," Bea told her nephew when he related the conversation. "You're likely to get caught in the middle."

"I have to be careful, Aunt Bea. They're not my children, not even my stepchildren yet. Not children at all, actually. When the war starts Colin will be old enough to fight."

"You said 'when,' not 'if.' I hope the wedding will happen first."

"It will, Nell's finally agreed. April sixth. There are so few incidents of the Change now, she's not going to make me wait any longer."

Bea ducked her chin and peered at him over the rims of her glasses. "I was under the impression she's not making you wait now."

Jack smiled.

Nell wanted a traditional wedding. An afternoon ceremony in a chapel, with flowers and music. Beeswax candles and flowers from Gold's Court Florist. Gerry Delmonico would sing a medley of her favorite songs. Jessamyn would be her bridesmaid, Colin would give his mother away. She would wear a fitted silk suit in a pale golden shade that complemented her hair, a tiny matching hat with a wisp of veil across her face . . . and the ring.

Arthur Hannisch had outdone himself with the ring. She did not want diamonds—Rob had given her diamonds. The ring Jack would put on her finger was a square-cut emerald that glowed like green fire.

Jack assured her the date she had chosen would be fine. "We might be cutting it close, but I doubt it. You can be sure there's a lot of diplomatic maneuvering going on behind the scenes, and as long as they're talking, they're not fighting."

Yet Nell felt an irrational anxiety building in herself, like her experience on the morning she took the children for a hike to Daggett's Woods. Nothing awful had happened then—so why should she worry now?

Pre-wedding jitters, that's it.

The Change was becoming a memory, the wedding would be beautiful and maybe there would be no war after all.

Please. Please!

Lila Ragland had become Nell's confederate, writing up the engagement announcement for the paper and surreptitiously informing her of the latest developments gleaned from abroad. "I don't want Jack to know I'm worried," Nell confided.

"We're all worried, but put it out of your mind and enjoy the day. At least we won't be watching a three-dimensional war on a wallscreen."

"Guns, tanks, missiles . . . they're gathering now, Lila. Can't you feel it? I can."

Lila said sharply, "Stop obsessing over it, you're going to make me nervous."

Dwayne Nyeberger read the engagement announcement with interest, particularly about the members of the wedding party.

Arguably the most beautiful building in Sycamore River was a little chapel on Cornelius Place, in the peaceful heart of the south side. Built at the end of the nineteenth century, the small building was constructed of golden sandstone and contained a much-admired stained glass window depicting the Good

Shepherd with his flock. Generations of townspeople had been christened and married there—though not the Bennetts. On the occasions when he felt obligated to attend church Robert Bennett went to the much larger one on Pine Grove, where his presence would be observed and noted.

Once in a great while, when she felt overwhelmed, Nell Bennett had visited the chapel just to sit in a pew at the back and absorb the atmosphere of serenity. The silence within the golden walls was not dead; it was alive with the inaudible prayers of ages past.

Nell booked the chapel for April 6th.

The morning of the wedding presented a mixed weather picture. The sky overhead was clear, but silvery clouds along the horizon were wearing black skirts, pregnant with rain.

There had been no rowdy bachelor's party the night before, but the reception after the wedding would be held in Bill's Bar and Grill, which would introduce a slightly raffish touch. The idea, to Jack's delight, had been Nell's.

To prevent him from seeing his bride before she walked down the aisle—a tradition the women insisted on—the male members of the wedding party would also gather in Bill's before the wedding. The bar and grill would otherwise be closed for the day.

Nell would be getting ready at her house, accompanied by the female members of the Wednesday Club and Katharine Richmond, the matron of honor.

The celebration began early at Bill's. By common consent

there was no discussion of the looming war, and Bill kept a close eye on the amount of alcohol being consumed. "Nobody's going to that wedding drunk! You guys can do your heavy drinking after. Except for Jack," he added with a wink at the soon-to-be bridegroom. "Nell might thank me for keeping you sober."

"The idea of getting married is enough to make any man sober," Edgar Tilbury commented.

Shay said, "You've never considered remarriage?"

"I thought I was finished with all that."

"You thought? Past tense? You old dog, have you met somebody?"

Instead of answering Tilbury went back to the bar for a refill.

Bill Burdick was keeping a close eye on the time. A bachelor himself, he was enjoying the celebratory atmosphere. It had been a long time since his customers had been so merry. Mentally Bill considered three or four Sycamore River women whom he might consider marrying. A man who owned a bar had an opportunity to meet almost every attractive girl in Sycamore River.

The end of the Change would mark a passage in the life of the town. On one level it could start to be normal again. There was the war, of course; if war came it would change life in a different way. The threat of personal extinction was enough to make a man grab what happiness he could while there was still time.

Tyler Whittaker had not been invited to the wedding, nor did he expect to be. The fading of the Change—like many people, he was unable to accept it without reservation—meant the sheriff needed to be as watchful as ever. "No more Change *is* a change," he remarked to Hooper Watson on the morning of the wedding, "and any change seems to upset people one way or another."

Watson had dropped in at the sheriff's office on his way to the bar and grill. A daily stop by the office and a cup of coffee with its current incumbent was part of his way of keeping "plugged in," as he called it.

"You still carrying your gun?" he asked Whittaker.

"'Course I am, Hoop. You know a gun comes with the job."

"I don't mean a pistol; I'm talking about your revolver. Now, *that's* a gun."

"Straight out of the Old West," Whittaker boasted. "Not actually, of course, but it's part of the image. Like a Stetson and cowboy boots."

"If you wore those in Sycamore River you'd be laughed out of office."

"I know that. But I always carry my revolver; there's something about the sight of it that quiets people right down. Even that nutjob who killed the Nyeberger woman gave in as soon as I shoved it in his face."

"I still carry a gun too," said Watson. "Guns work when nothing else will and I don't feel like me without it. 'Course I won't take mine to the wedding."

"'Course not." Whittaker glanced at his wristwatch, wondering if AllComs would be back on the market anytime soon. "You better get on over to Bill's, Hoop. Look here." He extended his arm. "It's later than you think."

Dwayne Nyeberger was waiting down the street from the chapel. After a diligent search he had found the perfect vantage point, a large residential lot landscaped with specimen trees surrounded by rhododendrons. The homeowners were away. Their luxuriant shrubbery provided excellent cover, and when he stood behind the largest tree he was confident no one could observe him from the street.

Him and his shotgun. He carried a pistol in his pocket.

He had been in place since early morning. Not thinking of anything much, that was the trick of it. If you didn't think about what you were going to do it was easier to do it. All he thought about was what should have been his. All the good things of life, the rewards of the heroes.

When he got tired he sat down, in slow motion, careful not to disturb a leaf. When he had rested he stood up again. In slow motion.

As the first car pulled up in front of the chapel he froze. Vestry staff. They were inside for a long time before anyone else came. This time it was a florist's van with boxes full of flowers. While they were being arranged the clergy arrived. Then the first trickle of guests, carrying the invitations Jessamyn Bennett had written out in a careful hand. Soon the little chapel would be packed.

Dwayne waited. He had waited for a long time; he could wait a little longer.

When the wedding party began to appear he almost laughed out loud. This was what the town's leading lights had been reduced to! Served them right. Horse-drawn carts and carriages and an absurd vehicle that was half pickup truck. A couple of automobiles.

Then Jack Reece and his aunt in his Mustang, with Nell's children in the back.

Getting close now. Almost here.

Inside the chapel Evan Mulligan watched Jessamyn Bennett enter with her brother. For a moment she paused below the stained glass window, gazing up at the shepherd and his flock. A ray of light streamed through the glass and illuminated her hair, giving her an angel's halo.

In that moment she was the most beautiful creature Evan had ever seen.

By the time Hooper Watson reached the bar and grill the "Closed" sign was on the door.

Watson began to run, pumping his arms as hard as he could and turning very red in the face.

Wearing a pale green silk dress with a matching jacket, Lila Ragland drove Nell's car. The bride sat beside her. Nell felt as if she were caught inside a bubble. "I wish today was over," she said.

"You don't mean that; this should be the happiest day of your life."

"It is, it will be. But I don't think I'll really appreciate it until I look back on it. Jack says we see more clearly from outside than inside."

"Well, *I* see that fool Hooper Watson running like an idiot! What does he think he's doing?" Lila braked in front of the chapel and called out the window, "You're not going to miss anything, the bride just got here!"

Watson turned and trotted toward the car just as Lila started to get out.

The blast of a shotgun shattered the day.

# 26

The next edition of *The Sycamore Seed* carried, under the byline of Lila Ragland, the following article:

"Sycamore River has endured more than its share of violence over recent years, but the tragic deaths on the sixth of April shocked us all. Hooper Watson was a lifelong resident of the town and an asset to the community. We unite in sympathy for his wife, Nadine, their daughter, Angela, their extended family and many friends.

"Tyler Whittaker had only been with us for a few years, but he was well liked as a man and respected as a law enforcement officer. His courage in apprehending the murderer of Patricia Nyeberger is a testimony to his character. He displayed that same courage in pursuing the alleged killer of Mr. Watson, who only briefly escaped. Both men died in an exchange of gunfire several blocks away.

"It is hoped these two will be the last victims of the Change, for that is the way Dr. Gloria Delmonico, staff psychologist at Staunton Memorial Hospital, describes them. In an interview yesterday she told this reporter that since the inception of the Change the number of people suffering severe neurological disorders has multiplied tenfold, not only in Sycamore

River but probably throughout the world. The stress of living under constantly increasing uncertainty with no end in sight can permanently damage the human psyche, according to Dr. Delmonico."

Three funerals on three successive days, as if the earth of Sunnyslope could not receive so much all at one time. Every service was well attended, including a large turnout for Tyler Whittaker, who was buried last to allow time for his relatives to come from Ohio.

"The sheriff certainly was a hero," Bea Fontaine said to her nephew as they finished lunch the following day. Neither had much appetite, but Jack had perked up at the sight of Bea's layer cake waiting on the kitchen table. "It was heroic of Nell to go to the funerals too," she added. "Nell and Lila saw what the rest of us didn't."

"Nell's stronger than she realizes," said Jack. "It wasn't easy to mourn for Dwayne Nyeberger."

"We all did it for the sake of his boys, so they wouldn't remember their father as such a pariah."

Jack's fork attacked a large wedge of cake. "Y'know, this is a pretty good town."

"Haven't I always told you that? And while I'm handing out plaudits, Lila did a fantastic job with the article in the *Seed*. A lot of reporters would have sensationalized it."

"Not if they'd been eyewitnesses, Aunt Bea; no one who was

there would want the gory details. The damned bastard used a double-barreled shotgun."

"Thank God the children and I were already in the chapel," said Bea. "Who was Dwayne after, does anyone know? Surely not poor Hooper Watson."

"Guess we'll never find out. It's like Gloria said, his mind broke under stress."

"I'd known Dwayne Nyeberger for years, Jack; that wasn't a sound mind in the first place. It didn't take much for the Change to tip it over."

Jack helped himself to a second cup of coffee. "Maybe what happened can't be blamed entirely on the Change. But there's no way to quantify how much damage it *has* done."

"Do you think it really is over?"

"Looks like it. 'No end in sight' seems to be an error."

"But how could it start and then stop again?"

Before Jack could answer, Gerry Delmonico ran up the steps and onto the porch. "Jack!" he called at the door. "Are you ready to go?"

"Come on in and have a cup of coffee with us first. And while you're at it, tell my aunt how the Change could start and then stop. I'd be interested to hear that explanation too."

They went into the kitchen. When Gerry rolled an eye at the cake, Bea cut a large slice for him. "Where are you two going?"

"The bar and grill."

"But this isn't Wednesday."

"I know. But since, well . . ."

"Some of you feel a need to be together," Bea finished. "Human nature. Is Gloria going with you?"

"She's keeping the baby at home; she's had all she can take for now."

"You want to come with us, Aunt Bea? I'm driving."

"No thanks, Jack. My cats are tribe enough for me; when I'm troubled there's no comfort like stroking a purring cat."

While Gerry enjoyed his coffee and cake he explained about mass being congealed energy. "Every time energy is released there is some decrease in mass," he elaborated, "even if it's very slight. It's called a decay event. A fundamental probability is at work in quantum physics, Bea. In decay processes it's revealed in the seeming randomness of individual events, which is what we saw with the Change. But the universe also has laws of conservation, which means that the *total* energy it contains, including that held in mass, doesn't change. So there really *wasn't* a Change, just a redistribution. The force behind it was making adjustments. Starting and stopping."

Bea turned to her nephew. "You agree with all this?"

"I'll accept it's scientifically sound, but I'm still not convinced. I've always had a hunch that the sun—"

"You two are maddening!" Bea exclaimed. "You haven't answered my question at all; I wanted to know about the force itself! Who or what is it?"

"That," said Jack, "is still the sixty-four-thousand-dollar question."

When he and Gerry entered the bar the Mulligans and Edgar Tilbury were already there. So was Lila Ragland. Jack thought she looked smaller, diminished. Mass and energy, he mused. Sitting down beside her, he said, "Your story in the paper struck just the right note, Lila: dignified."

"After what we saw in the street a lot of dignity was required."

"That was your jacket over—"

"Hooper's head and face, yes. I wanted to hide them from Nell and the people coming out of the chapel."

"That was fast thinking."

"No it wasn't, Jack. It felt like time had frozen."

"Time's relative; I learned that when I was a kid. I climbed too high in a tree and fell and broke my leg. It took an hour to hit the ground, and a lifetime before my aunt stopped scolding me about it."

"Where's Nell?" Tilbury asked Jack. "I thought she'd be here."

"When I took her home after the sheriff's funeral she said she wanted to be alone with her kids for a few days. Quality time. She'll be trying to help them come to terms with what's happened." He hesitated. "Under the circumstances she, I mean we, have decided to postpone the wedding. You don't need to say anything about that in the paper, Lila."

"I wouldn't anyway. Later in the year, maybe?"

"I don't know," he said tightly. "Up to her, I guess."

Jack was uncomfortable. The marriage seemed cursed. Would Nell look at it that way? Could the violence on her wedding day have caused an irrevocable change in the woman he loved?

To change the subject he said, "Isn't Morris coming?"

"He took Hooper's death hard," Shay replied, "but I imagine he'll be along. Strange, isn't it? So much tragedy on one hand and the Change fading away on the other. Like scales balancing."

Jack shook his head. "That's not an equal balance."

Bill Burdick passed around drinks. "On the house," he announced. "Like a wake."

"I have a better idea," said Evan Mulligan. He raised his glass. "Let's toast the future. It's gotta be better than the last year or two."

Shay rumpled his son's hair. "Good boy. The future it is!"

# 27

When Morris Saddlethwaite burst through the door of Bill's Bar and Grill his face was ashen. "You're not gonna believe this! I mean, you're not gonna *believe* this!"

"You're repeating yourself," said Bill. "Sit down and have a drink, you look like you need one. Or have you had too many already?"

"Is that your red car parked outside the door?" Saddlethwaite asked Jack.

"You know it's my car, there's not another one like it in the state. If it's in your way I'll move it, though."

The other man lifted his right arm and waved it in the air. The sleeve was covered with a flaky substance that resembled dried blood and crumbled from the fabric. "I don't know if you can move it, Jack. I just brushed against your fender and this stuff came off on my clothes. Now the goddamned *metal's* rotting!"